K.J. DUFF

HALCYON SUICIDE

A NOVEL

First edition

ISBN: 979-8-9923656-0-3

This book was professionally typeset on Reedsy.
Find out more at reedsy.com

For everyone whose hands have helped mold my mind
and shape my reality,
thank you for your love and guidance.

"We are all trapped in this swirling cesspool. No matter how far or how long we stray, we wind up back in its grasp, heaped on top of one another like a barrel full of trapped rats. We tread water, fighting to keep our heads from going under, clinging to silent desperation. Ultimately, however, we succumb to the thought of the inevitability of being swallowed into its vortex and dragged undertow. At that moment, we accept our reality and allow our bodies to go limp."

THE VOICE

Contents

HALCYON
SUICIDE

A NOVEL

K.J. DUFF

Praefatio

I have no godly idea what I'm doing. I should stress this right now so the point is absolutely clear. I am not a writer, an author, novelist - whatever term you prefer - I am not that, nor do I aspire to be. Any literary notions I could ever have would not be romantic musings, but blatant delusions.

Only now, enveloped in the silence of this room, at this desk, with this notebook open before me, and this pen held firmly in my hand, do I realize the overwhelming weight of this monumental task I've decided to undertake. Yet, this story needs to be told; not because this particular story is fascinating, mind you (I doubt reading my words will have any type of an impact on your life), but simply because this notebook and this pen beg for it. No, *beg* is not the correct word. Let me try that again - simply because this notebook and this pen *demand* it. Yeah, that's better. Any benefit or enlightenment you attain from this poorly constructed prose is, I assure you, unintentional.

I didn't *just* decide I could write. I've been *disturbed*, unable to escape this feeling of unease. I can only equate the feeling to what I imagine it must be like to live in skin that doesn't quite fit. Yeah, that's exactly it. I've been wandering aimlessly this way, uncomfortable in this person's skin. For how long? Too long to bear.

Still, here I am, writing. It was as if the culmination of all my choices, all the twists and turns I've taken in this life, the few bright

1

paths, through many dark narrow corridors, were for the sole purpose of being *right here*, in this exact spot, at this exact time, in this exact moment, to receive this revelation. It was not necessarily a "eureka" moment of clarity or getting struck by a bolt of lightning that was crafted specifically for me by the Kyklopes. It was the most infinitesimal voice whispering in my ear as I stood over the sink mindlessly rinsing the soap off my dinner plate. That is when it hit me, where I finally understood: *this notebook's sole purpose for existence is to be written in, just as this pen's raison d'être is to spill its ink between the empty lines of these pages until it is completely spent. Anything short of this goal, and their purpose for existing goes unfulfilled. I am but a mere instrument, an empty vessel through which these objects dictate.*

Once I understood this, my skin fit better. If only slightly.

The scalding summer sun is setting, sinking behind the tall loblolly pines far off in the distance, wobbling like a large egg yolk being lowered slowly into boiling water. In an effort to stay cool, I'm dressed in pin striped boxers and a loose-fitting gray tank top. The air conditioning unit hanging from the window is running on full blast, condensation forming around the vent, struggling to compensate for the humidity outside, so much so that I've had to put a towel underneath to absorb the condensation and stop it from seeping into the walls and giving birth to mold. My desk is simple, made of cheap particle board wood (the type of wood that falls apart when it comes in contact with water or any type of moisture), it has sturdy legs, but it wobbles wildly when I write. Populating the desktop: this notebook, a clean crystal ashtray, a worn copy of *Kafka on the Shore* by Haruki Murakami, a tall glass of ice water (with a coaster underneath to avoid damaging the cheap desk with water-rings), and a stack of index cards to jot down random notes and asides. Deep breaths...

I doubt you will ever read this. However, in order to write this - in order to be *vulnerable* enough to write this - I need to believe that you will. That you are. And I do. Believe, that is. Before you read any further, there are two things I need you to keep in mind. First, the tale I'm about to attempt to weave for you is true. If you are not able to accept that when you reach the end, then... I want to say that's your problem, but in all honesty, standing in your place, I doubt I'd believe it myself. However, I assure you, it's all true. Secondly...

... This is *not* a love story

Chapter One

I woke up shrouded in darkness, my lungs seized by rapid breathing and the sound of my heart drumming between my ears. I sat up quickly; everything from my white tank top, my boxers, and my pale beige bed sheets were soaked in my cold sweat. I didn't recognize where I was. I understood I was in my apartment, but for a brief moment, that moment wedged in the space between dreaming and reality, it certainly didn't *feel* like I was in my apartment.

An abnormal storm raged outside. The raindrops sounded like large pebbles pelting the window. The panes creaked and strained against the frantic force of the bewitching wind. A flash from the wrathful bolt of lightning crept through the thin seams between my blinds and heavy curtain. What made the storm *abnormal*? For all the lightning that crackled across the black night like a spider's web, no thunder ever followed.

I found myself in the throes of quiet desperation, trying to cling to, and make sense of, the dream from which I had just been yanked from. All I could manage to retain were images: an infinite black void, blood-stained fingers clawing into an exposed chest, burnt black twisting tree bark. However, it wasn't my dream nor was it the storm that suddenly had me awake in the dark. *Something* woke me.

What was it? I couldn't ascertain. A thunderous boom? A reverberant crash? Whatever it was, it was *loud*. Loud and *powerful*.

Powerful enough to stir the gods and their Heaven. What I knew for certain was that it wasn't the storm. Like I said, there was no thunder, and even if there were, I've never had issues falling and staying asleep during a storm. As long as the room in which I am sleeping is devoid of light, I can pretty much sleep through a category five hurricane, which, being born and raised in Loblolly Pines, a small nothing town in the middle of nowhere South Florida, I have done on more than one occasion. My apartment only had one window, at the head of my bed, so plunging the room into total obscurity was as easy as shutting the micro-blinds and tightly sealing my thick black curtain. Absolute darkness, *that* is the only way I can sleep. *Sleep*, not *rest*. I am well aware of the distinction.

Yet, that night, I was awakened, and quite violently at that. It took me a moment to shake the cobwebs off my brain and clear the fog from my mind. It wasn't until the mist lifted from my eyes that I noticed several streaks of a soft orange light cutting through the darkness, violating my air space. Dust particles and pieces of drywall swirled and cascaded down through the intrusive beams like a pathetic snowfall.

Even with a - somewhat - clear head, I couldn't make sense of where exactly these lights originated from. I lifted my right hand, reached out to the light, and observed it as it crashed against my palm. My eyes traced the light back to its source. It was coming from the left side of my wall, the wall I share with my neighbor.

In one swift motion, I rolled onto my knees, braced myself against the wall with both hands, and peeked into the hole, hoping to catch a glimpse of my neighbor's apartment, but all I could make out was an orange blur. I put my ear to the wall carefully, half expecting the wall to explode on contact, but the silence revealed just as little.

All I wanted was to go back to sleep, back to my abyss, but with those lights invading my bubble, bouncing off my walls, sleep would now prove an impossibility. I crawled out of bed, ripped the soaked sheets from the mattress, stripped my clothes off and threw them in the full laundry basket. I put on some dry pajama bottoms and a fresh white t-shirt and headed for my door.

I peered into the hallway, expecting to find other tenants of the building inquiring in hushed tones about a loud sound they'd heard, or at least the odd weather, but found it with nary a soul. The hall was narrow and windowless, and the pastel gray walls and the chestnut brown carpet were softly lit by the faint red glow of the two exit signs on either end of the corridor. The red light was like a thin layer of film that gave the hallway an eerie presence akin to that of a haunted house or an abandoned building where junkies chased the dragon. The air in the hall felt artificial and damp, with a faint smell of mold circulating through the vents. There was nothing unique about the apartment doors that hinted at their occupier's personality. If it were not for the rusted silver-plated numbers on each door, no one would be able to find their residence.

The coast clear, I stepped into the hall barefoot, quietly closing the door. In three generous strides, I was at my neighbor's apartment, 6G. I lightly tapped the door with the tip of my middle finger, listened for an answer, but was met with more silence. The thick toxic moisture that hung in the air strangled my tongue. I rapped at the door once more, this time much firmer, and waited. Still nothing. I sighed through my nose, ready to retreat to my apartment when I gave birth to a thought. Before I could debate the ethical implications of my actions, my hand reached for the door handle, turned it, and cracked the door open with all the courtesy of a drunken husband coming home late from an alcoholic binge. After confirming that no one was around to be the voice of reason, I let myself in and closed the door as quietly as the sound of cotton falling on a bed of soapy foam.

I was immediately accosted by the scent of bleach. Too much bleach. The way a hospital uses bleach to mask the smell of death. My neighbor's apartment was the mirror image of my own. On the right was the spotless kitchenette, fully equipped with the same linoleum counter tops and generic appliances. Past the kitchenette was a small area designated as the "living room," but too small for any real furniture. A fifty-five-inch flat-screen television hung perfectly leveled on the left side of the wall, an exact three and a half feet off the ground. A white faux leather futon was across from the TV on the right side of the apartment, and a small black coffee table held its place between them both. Past the living room was the back and final area of this box. The right- back corner was the bathroom, big enough for a shower, a toilet, and a porcelain sink. On the left back corner was the nook where the bed was situated. My eyes followed the flow of the apartment and froze when they landed on the bed.

Lightning flashed, and there, dressed in a nice blue suit, a clean white shirt, tied together neatly with a silk red necktie, sitting in bed with a shotgun still smoking at the barrel, under the same disruptive pale orange light, was my headless neighbor. Chunks of flesh, bone fragments, brain matter, and thick blood stuck to the wall behind his corpse, slowly oozing downward, pooling onto his broad shoulders, soaking the fine suit. His face was obliterated; the only thing that remained of it began from the chin down. The window behind the head of the bed had no curtain or blinds, and even though it was storming outside, the night was pitch black, like the apartment was traveling through a black hole. The body gurgled from what used to be its mouth, the last bit of air escaping from its body. *The death rattle.*

I glanced at the apartment once more. It was clean, immaculate even. There was not a dirty dish or the tiniest crumb in sight. The futon was second or third hand, but the faux leather shinned like it was authentic. The coffee table was clear of clutter and water rings; only the remote control for the TV and a little black notebook with a metallic silver pen resting on the cover. There were no greasy fingerprints on the TV

7

screen or layers of dust on the backside. There was no mold growing on the corners of the bathroom, no mildew on the tiles, no residual plaque tainting the rim of the sink. The carpet retained its original luster, absent of poorly cleaned stains, and not the slightest hint of matted or frayed fibers from years of heavy foot traffic. Even the bed was made with the covers and comforters tucked in with five-star hotel quality precision. There was absolutely *nothing* in this room that definitively indicated there was any sign of a mental struggle.

My blank eyes came back to my neighbor's body. I stood in silence, my head empty. The body suddenly slumped off the wall and toppled over to the floor with all the heaviness of a sack of dry cement. More blood came spilling out from the gaping hole where his head used to be and onto the beige carpet, like a full can of paint with a loose lid was tipped on its side. That is when I noticed the tiny holes in the wall, coated in my neighbor's matter.

I stepped deeper into the apartment, stopped at the coffee table, and peeked over at my neighbor, half expecting his body to get up and put on a kettle for a cup of green tea. It didn't.

I looked down at the notebook that was on the coffee table. Thinking my neighbor may have written a suicide note, I picked it up and leafed through it, but found all of the pages were empty. The notebook reeked of fresh paper, and the pen still had a full stem of ink. I scratched the top of my scalp with my fingertips and stood akimbo. I just wanted to go back to my world next door, back to sleep, catch up on the time that was stripped away from me by this unwelcome interruption.

Besides, I thought, *someone else will happen by. Let that person go through the hassle of doing what needs to be done. I'm too tired.*

A yawn developed in my chest and gave birth in my mouth. My eyelids twitched manically with exhaustion. I rubbed them roughly, shrugged my shoulders slightly, turned on my heel, and, with notebook and pen in hand, left the apartment, turning the lights off before closing the door behind me.

* * *

The light from my neighbor's apartment no longer spilling into my own, I lay in bed, thumbing through the empty leather-bound book and examining the sleek heavy pen like it was the mighty Excalibur. I rubbed my dry beard, lost in a thicket of thought.

Did my neighbor decide to buy a notebook before eating a shotgun? Did he already have it and just never wrote anything? Maybe it was a gift? Maybe he wanted to write but didn't know how to start, and the inability to do so drove him mad?

I conceded to all notions. I'd never know either way. I simply decided all possibilities were true, closed the book, and tucked it and the pen underneath my pillow.

The storm continued to thrash against my window. I turned my attention to the tiny holes in my wall and grimaced. *What a pain.* Now I was going to have to go out of my way, make an extra stop after work, and spend money on the plaster and the sandpaper to properly cover them up. I wished I could've just left it as is, but I couldn't.

Sleep once more took hold of me. As I fell under its spell, I pictured a miniature version of myself scaling up the wall and climbing into one of the holes. In the bowels of this particularly bleak hole was a large study with bookshelves filled with a fantastic blend of both classic and contemporary novels, neatly stacked floor-to-ceiling and wall-to-wall. In the center of this study was a grand desk made of rich mahogany and a white leather chair more suited to a King's throne. A golden lamp cast a spotlight on the black notebook. The notebook opened up to the last page of the book on its own like a gust of wind took spectral form to perform this task. I stepped toward the desk, examined the pages, and discovered that the book was written in completely, all the lines jammed with tiny words. I sat at the throne, took the silver pen, and put the tip to the very last punctuation on the paper. The pen began to move with fervor as if it had become self-aware that my hand was the vessel for its soul. However, instead of writing, the pen inhaled the ink from the paper and proceeded to leave the notebook blank. My first reaction was to remove my hand from the pen, but my hand would not let it go. No matter what I did, I couldn't pry my hand free. It was determined to see this through to the end, yet I had a feeling I didn't want to get there. Unfortunately, I no longer had control of my body. I couldn't move.

Panic gripped me. I could feel someone, some shadowy figure lurking behind me, getting closer, hovering over my shoulder. I fought with all the power left in my body to turn my head, however before I could see anything, I finally submerged into the shallow end of slumber and drifted away from the shore.

Chapter Two

It was dawning when my eyes opened again, and I was struck with immediate weariness. The bags under my eyes were swollen and heavy, and my mouth was dry, like heaping scoops of sand from the Namib Desert was poured into my mouth while I slept and absorbed all the moisture in my tongue. The airways in my sinuses were clogged, and my body was as stiff as a corpse. This was typical of every morning, it just got progressively worse with each passing day.

While my mouth worked to generate saliva, my right arm instinctively craned up and back for my phone resting on the cheap Carrara marble windowsill. I brought the phone to my face and rudely poked at the screen. The screen burst to life, and, as if in protest, its light cut through the darkness, temporarily blinding me. I rubbed my eyes and sifted through starburst vision for the time: 5:27 a.m. I woke up before my alarm again.

I rested the phone on my chest and lay supine. The storm had long gone, replaced by the faint hum of engines and tires roaring over the cool concrete of the not-so-distant highway. Birds were squawking from all angles, either communicating to other birds that the day was soon to start, or where they should look for their early worm. Possibly both, I imagined.

Unsurprisingly, my first thought was of Evelyn. Evelyn curled up next to me, her beauteous face mere inches from mine; Evelyn's small delicate hands tucked under the side of her blushed cheek like a sleeping angel; Evelyn's naked, near-flawless snow-white body glowing in the pre-morning sheen; Evelyn's long, kinked and crinkled chestnut hair falling over her face, her emerald green eyes peering up at me through the curls like a beam of light cutting through a dense fog; a smile parted Evelyn's full pink lips.

"Good Morning," she silently mouthed.

After so much time apart, Evelyn continued to be my first thought in the morning. I no longer questioned why, nor did I mind. In fact, I'd go as far as admitting that it was the part of the day I looked forward to most. I never allowed myself to stay in that place with her for too long. I boxed the thought up and stored it away in one of the many dark recesses of my mind. As had become the custom of every morning, I accepted the plain truth: I was alone.

I took up my phone and looked at the screen again, this time in search of any sign that perhaps I too was Evelyn's first thought in the morning.

I wasn't.

Resigned, I tossed the phone at the foot of my bed, half in disappointment, half in disgust for allowing myself to hope.

It took all of my strength just to roll over from my back onto my stomach, and even more to push myself up onto my knees. I grabbed the bottom hem of the curtain, slid it fully to one side, and twisted the blinds open, allowing the light to spill into the room. The sun was not up yet, but the tip of its rays gripped onto the horizon hidden behind the towering loblolly pine trees. The sky was in the process of shifting from a dark purple to a royal blue. Not a wisp of a cloud or a residual twinkle of a far-off star was anywhere to be seen. The pines swayed to the rhythm of the late spring morning air as Pine Warblers jumped from one tree branch to the next, trilling merrily.

I looked down at the poorly lit parking lot of my apartment building.

Cars were already pulling out of their respective parking spots, slowly weaving through the lot like mice in a maze roaming for a chunk of cheddar.

From this vantage point, I could see everything and nothing. Tall pines, birds, a highway, a parking lot, and a vast sky (that was now going from royal blue to a deep auburn). I thought of Evelyn again, then looked down at the parking lot and frowned.

Usually, after a furiously raucous downpour, the parking lot would be flooded in uneven parts where the drainage was blocked by dead leaves and debris, but there was nothing, not even a puddle. Apart from the moisture that came with the morning dew, there was no attestation that a thunder-less storm ravaged the previous night. I licked my dry chapped lips and pursed them together, my brow ridged. *Was I dreaming?* I wondered, staring out into the dry morning. No. I was sure there was a storm. *Then why is everything dry?* The questions continued to roll around in my head until my alarm screamed to life. 5:45 am. I put all lingering thoughts aside; it was time to get ready for work.

If there is anything that passes as "interesting" about me, it's that I'm a slave to habit. My morning routine always followed the same sequence: empty bladder and/or bowels, shower, apply lotion to visibly ashy areas lotion, and dress. If I was going to work, I wore my uniform. The mandatory attire was a combination of a white, gray, or black dri-fit polo shirt, relaxed fit blue or black jeans, moisture absorbent socks, and comfortable non-slip boots. I was not the type to stay hip to what constituted "fashion" (As evident by my use of the word "hip"). My casual wardrobe was pretty simple: several different colors of the same comfortable short-sleeved hooded shirts, cotton shorts, and off-brand running shoes. This is how I dressed on my days off.

Once I'm dressed, I eat breakfast. If I don't have much time or much of an appetite, I eat two pieces of buttered toast and wash it down with a short glass of orange juice. I only had a big breakfast on my off days, and - even then - I kept it relatively simple: eggs, buttered toast with one slice of Swiss cheese, two strips of bacon, a short glass of orange juice, and a tall glass of iced water. After I was dressed and fed, I would end the ritual by brushing my teeth.

That morning was no different. I emptied my bladder, showered, slathered on lotion, got dressed for work (opting for the gray polo), ate two pieces of buttered toast, drank juice, and brushed my teeth.

I rinsed my mouth out and put my toothbrush away. I took a deep breath, braced myself, lifted my head and peered into the mirror. There I was, overweight, balding, sunken, glossy eyes, dark dry skin full of deep pores, nose riddled with whiteheads, and a patchy, wiry beard. Staring into my dark eyes, I could hear *The Voice* whispering to me in a tone that was simultaneously soft and stentorian:

You are a piece of shit. You are a fat fuck! You are garbage. No, garbage is the carcass of something that was once useful. You are nothing. Insignificant. A worthless spec of aimless dust. You disgust-

The Voice stopped as I turned my gaze from the mirror, reached for a hand towel and

thoroughly dried my face. Once I was sure I had everything I needed for the day, I grabbed my belongings and left my apartment.

The gloom of the windowless corridor wasted no time in enveloping me as I stepped into the dank hallway. I locked my door and shoved my keys in my pocket. Before I headed for the staircase, I looked at my neighbor's apartment. Slowly, the memory of the night gained steam in my mind like a boulder rolling down a steep hill. Suddenly, the hairs on my arms stood on end as the images from the thunder-less stormy night flooded into my head and along with it, the questions I had set aside. *If there was no storm last night, does that mean I didn't find my neighbor's dead body? Was I in fact dreaming?* No. I don't have dreams *that* vivid. I could smell the mold in the hall and the bleach in the apartment. The only way to put all doubt to bed was to open the door and confirm for myself.

I looked up and down the corridor to make sure no one was around, stepped toward the door, knocked, and waited. No answer. I put my hand on the door handle and just as I went to turn the knob, the apartment door adjacent to me began to click and rattle. I jumped back to my door, pulled my keys from my pocket, and shoved it in the door, pretending to be locking it as that rattling door opened and an old woman came out into the hall. She closed the door and locked it in one swift impatient motion. Her face bore a miserable expression, stress etched into her jowls and every wrinkle in her tired face. She swung her large purse around her shoulder and marched past me, disappearing down the stairway.

I pulled my key out of the lock and turned my attention back to my neighbors door. There is no rush, I conceded, shrugging my shoulders. If by chance, I wasn't dreaming, and there is a dead body in there, it would be there when I got back.

With a pin in that, I placed my keys back in my pocket and followed the old woman's path down the staircase.

The parking lot was nearly deserted. A few cars were scattered about, no doubt belonging to people who just came home from a night shift or had a rare weekday off. My car was in the middle of the lot, a '92 Chevy Monte Carlo coup. The once-proud champagne gold color was stripped away by the suffocating Florida sun. The plastic parts were severely faded, and the metal areas around the wheels and the trunk were all but rusted, courtesy of the saltwater moisture in the air.

The interior was just as worn. The seats were blemished with cigarette burns and holes in the decades old fabric. The plastic dashboard suffered from desiccation cracks, and the passenger side back window was secured with a piece of a wooden block wedged at the base. The car leaked oil constantly, which baffled the mechanics, who could never discern its origins. The alternator was temperamental, causing the car to seize and start when it chose, and the evaporator drain was so clogged that any time I made a dramatic left turn, all of the excess water from the evaporator drain would flow into the cabin and onto the passenger side floor, soaking the carpet and forming a pool of water. I used all the cleaning products available to clean the mold from the passenger side carpet floor. However, the smell still lingered, assaulting my senses every time I opened the door. Despite its cosmetic flaws, the components - the AM/FM stereo, cassette player, A/C, even the cigarette burner - all still worked. I bought the car with my own money when I was a senior in high school, and it was reliable. That was all that mattered to me.

I got in my car, put on my seatbelt, and turned the key in the ignition. It clicked twice but stalled. The alternator again.

I didn't stress it; it was a familiar position. It could take a handful of seconds or a couple of hours for the car to choose to start. It all hinged on the alternator's mood. My only option was to wait. I took the key out of the ignition and sat back. I manually rolled the window down so I wouldn't suffocate on the moldy malodor. I didn't want to be late, but I tended not to concern myself with things beyond my control. If my wages were to be docked, so be it. Only a fool resists fate. I leaned my head back on the headrest and closed my eyes just as a cool breeze swept through and broke away like a rolling tide.

After a few minutes, I gave it another shot. I turned the key in the ignition. Still nothing. Again, I waited.

I looked at my apartment building. Perdition Towers, it was named. From a distance, it was a beautifully mundane building. Nothing Gothic or Rustic in its rudimentary architecture. It was a solid brick wall smoothed over with commercial white plaster, unimpressive windows, and two entrances. Some green bushes surrounded the property populated with dianthuses, marigolds, and Angelonia flowers to give the place a modicum of color. If there was no sign at the front of the building, people might have mistaken Perdition Towers for an office building. All the units in this building were designed to be the size of a rectangular prism. Just one palatial room. No illusions about apartment living. It stood tall at five stories high, six total floors, and two elevators. Upon closer inspection, one would find that the elevators did not work (at least as long as I'd lived there), and the apartments were barely big enough for one person, let alone a couple or a small family. However, the rent was the lowest in town, so people sacrificed comfort for the hopes of financial relief.

We are all trapped in this swirling cesspool. No matter how far or how long we stray, we wind up back in its grasp, heaped on top of one another like a barrel full of trapped rats. We tread water, fighting to keep our heads from going under, clinging to silent desperation. Ultimately, however, we succumb to the thought of the inevitability of being swallowed into its vortex and dragged undertow. At that moment, we accept our reality and allow our bodies to go limp.

I shook The Voice from my head, jammed the key into the ignition, and turned the engine over. The car came alive as if brand new. I pulled the gear into drive and drove out of the parking lot and into the rat race.

* * *

I worked for The Company. Not *A* company. *The* Company. The Company is a conglomerate, with its fingers in every conceivable industry: Food and beverage, education, restaurants, clothes, banking, real estate, pharmaceuticals, engineering, and even cinema. Perdition Towers, my apartment complex, is managed by Alister Mortgage Group, an LLC owned by Magenta Properties, a subsidiary of The Company.

I worked in the production division. My official title was Clean Room Assembly Technician or CRA Tech. As the title implies, I did - in fact - work in a clean room; I had to gown up from head to toe in a hazmat suit, wear a mask, goggles, latex gloves, and disposable shoe covers.

Now *what* we assembled in the cleanroom, I couldn't tell you. It could be anything from alarm clocks to nuclear bombs, for all I knew. The parts we were given came in "Assembler Kits," so no one ever really knew what exactly we were constructing on any given day. Either way, it mattered extraordinarily little to me. The pay was shit, but The Company provided great benefits: medical insurance, dental insurance, paid time off (PTO), and sick leave. The Company also allowed employees to work and accrue as much overtime as desired, and lunch was provided free of charge.

The Company's main headquarters was in the heart of town, a stone's throw away from my apartment; however, the production facility was on the outskirts of town, surrounded by uncultivated agricultural land. It was out of the way of the Target-centric shopping centers, Hyundai dealerships, Dunkin's, bowling alleys, and 7 Elevens. I didn't mind the drive; I knew the fastest routes to get there and which roads to take to avoid getting caught in police speed traps. It also allowed me extra time to listen to talk radio or peep what was passing for music these days. It was my calm before the soul numbing storm.

From a distance, the production facility looked like a university campus designed by Georges Braque, a floating fortress from the future formed from puzzle pieces shaped like cubes from parallel dimensions.

I arrived at the facility fifteen minutes early, scanned my ID badge to get into the building, and made my way to the auditorium where, at exactly seven a.m., all the present employees - Assemblers, Boxers, Production Coordinators (PC's), and Machine Operators (MO's) - gathered for the mandatory morning calisthenics Nothing extraneous, just light yoga and stretching to loosen up stiff joints and muscles.

After the morning exercise, everyone listened to the Senior PC give the morning announcements that were really just new rules set by headquarters for that week. That week, all bathroom breaks were to be documented, and the lunch period had been reduced from thirty-five minutes to just half an hour. After morning announcements were through, I made my way to the gown room, found my locker, put on my protective gear, and followed my co-workers into the clean room.

There was nothing spectacular about the clean room. It was a posh overgrown warehouse complete with twenty-foot-high ceilings adorned with rows of bright white LED lights and commercial grade epoxy resin floors. There were fourteen lines, industrial tables connected to conveyor belts. Of the fourteen lines, thirteen were for the most common kits. The assemblers worked in groups of three. Each line worked on separate kits, whatever they were assigned for that particular day. Once the groups pieced together their kits, they put the finished product on the conveyor belt. The conveyor belt sent the product to the PCs, who did quality control. Once they deemed it worthy, they handed it off to the MOs, who put the items through the sealing machine, labeled them, and sent them to the boxing division. This is what all thirteen lines dedicated 120 hours a week to. Line fourteen, however, worked on orders that were more complex and required a lone worker with finesse and unlimited patience. This was my line.

I preferred to work alone. Not that I disliked any of my fellow employees, I just refused to waste any energy pretending to. To them, I was mysteriously reserved. Sometimes they'd sit down next to me during lunch and strike a conversation. Once they gleaned that I was not a misanthropic sociopath, they left me in peace, their fears assuaged.

That morning went just like all the others. We got our assigned kits and immediately went to work. The engines of the sealing machines were at full throttle, and the assemblers gossiped about their personal lives, their hands working independently from their brain and their mouths. The PCs roamed the lines like slave overseers on horseback riding through the cotton fields, quick to crack the whip at the slightest sign of unproductive loafing about and idle chatter.

I wasted no time on my assignment. I reviewed the kit sheet, studied the assembly instructions, and took my time intricately putting together the first kit. When I finished, I doubled and triple- checked that the final product matched the diagram. Once I felt confident in my abilities, I emptied my mind, found a comfortable rhythm, and sped up my production.

There were no windows in the clean room, so once I entered the zone, I lost all sense of sound and time. It wasn't until a PC came over and tapped my shoulder that the world came rushing back to my ears, and I realized it was almost time for the first break of the morning. I'd been working for nearly three hours.

Everyone used their first break to talk and gossip, make phone calls and doomscroll through whatever social media platform they frequented. I stood outside by a small pond beyond the parking area. Sometimes I saw turtles poke their head up for air and sink back into the safety of the water. Other times I observed a scattering of herons splashing about on the surface of the pond while others were just at the shore, wings spread, sunbathing. That day I saw minnows feeding on mosquitoes that got stuck to the surface of the water and heard dragonflies buzzing somewhere in the distance. I took a deep breath and exhaled slowly.

Suddenly I got the feeling I wasn't alone. I looked over my shoulder to find Grant, one of my elderly co-workers, standing off to the side, his steele-blue eyes absorbing the scene playing before us. In his late sixties, Grant was the oldest person in the clean room. He stood at a whopping five foot two inches, with most of the height coming from his hunched back. His flesh was dried and wrinkled worse than a dehydrated prune. His white eyebrows were so thick and bushy they hid his eyes like an old English shepherd dog. He stood with the assistance of a cane, like a wise martial arts master, one arm nestled behind him.

Grant looked over at me and smiled, then his eyes drifted back to the far-off trees.

"What do you think is waiting behind those pines?" he asked, lifting a shaky finger to point to the loblolly pines beyond the pond.

I looked in that direction and tried to see past the tall pines but could only imagine, given where we were, that it was more trees and farm land. I gave up and shook my head.

"Life," I replied, half-jokingly.

"If you're afraid enough," he said, smiling warmly.

"Don't you mean brave enough?" I asked, my forehead furrowed in confusion.

Either he didn't hear me, or he felt the question didn't warrant a response; either way, Grant remained silent, his eyes transfixed on the pines, or perhaps peering past it, as if he could see clearly what was behind them.

"This town is surrounded by these trees. We are confined within their towering lumber," he strained to crane his head upward, "but they aren't."

I looked up and saw two herons riding the thermals high in the morning sky. We watched them disappear behind the trees.

"I've lived here all of my life," Grant continued. I got the feeling he just needed to speak, it didn't matter who was listening. I just happened to be there. "I've been reliving the gilded age of my youth. Reveling in them. But to remain in those halcyon days is to become a prisoner of them. When you're a prisoner of them, you start to think there is

21

nothing worth seeing beyond those loblolly pines. That's the illusion. The only way to break free, is to commit halcyon suicide."

The bell rang, signaling the end of our morning break. Grant winked and smiled at me, turning, and hobbling back toward the building. I looked at the trees, Grant's words echoing in my head. There was no time to fully absorb them. I took one last look at the pines and made my way back to the building.

* * *

The employees all corralled into the clean room like cattle, full of newfound energy and vigor. I reclaimed my spot on the fourteenth line and picked up where I had left off. My eyes wandered around the room. Such an assortment of people; men and women, young to old, every spectrum of color. My eyes landed on Grant.

As everyone got back into their work, Grant just sat on his stool, looking up at the ceiling. He slowly lowered his head, and, for the first time, I saw his eyes glow vibrantly. From across the room, the metallic blue eyes pierced and locked with mine, I couldn't peel them away. Grant struggled to smile, but the wrinkles on his cheeks held his lips in place. My heart thumped in my ears, in unison with the engines of the sealing machines. Grant put both hands on the table. He took a deep breath and exhaled. His head swung into his chest like his neck could no longer support its weight, his shoulders went limp, and he fell off his stool, his body hitting the floor, headfirst, the stool spinning around until finally toppling after him. And then… silence.

It took a moment for everyone to understand what just happened, but I knew immediately. Grant was dead. He was dead before he hit the floor. Assemblers rushed to his body, but the PCs ordered them back on the line. The lead PC then asked a few of the male employees for help to remove Grant's body from the room. Three men came and heaved the body up off the floor and followed the lead PC out of the room. No one spoke. The sealing machines continued to churn. After a couple of minutes, the assemblers all got back to work, murmuring softly among themselves.

I turned back to my kit and looked at the pieces. For a moment, they looked like foreign objects, alien things not of this world. I fiddled with them until the instructions slowly came back to me. I found my stride again and worked full throttle, in a fog, until lunchtime.

The cafeteria was large, the walls were white, and the ceiling was one big skylight, which, on extremely hot days, made the room feel like an oven. The lunchroom was electric with the news of Grant's death. I sat in my usual spot, a secluded cream colored fiberglass table, and though I could hear some of the conversations, I didn't really listen. I was picking at my cold, soggy ham and cheese sandwich when two fellow employees, Martin and Yoel, placed their plastic lunch trays on the table and took a seat near me.

Martin was short and stocky. His wild black cotton hair was stuffed poorly into a hairnet, and his beard was so thick, one couldn't tell if he had a neck or not. He had dark skin, typical of most Dominicans, he'd say, and would almost be intimidating if it weren't for his high-pitched voice. Yoel was tall, with the girth of an English soccer ball goalie. He had blue eyes and slightly curly blond hair. People often confused him as being of German descent, but he was Cuban and had the accent to prove it. He was overly friendly and always wore a genuine smile.

Martin and Yoel were in mid conversation as they sat down. They sent a salutatory gesture my way but didn't miss a beat.

"Did you see the way they carried him out of here?" Martin said, taking his plastic utensils from its wrapping.

"Como si fuera basura," Yoel responded, shaking his head sadly.

My appetite was waning; I added mustard to the tasteless sandwich, but it somehow made it less appetizing.

"Exactly! I'm surprised they didn't just take a broom and sweep him out the door!" Martin said, stabbing his cold piece of dry pork and shoving it in his mouth.

"Es porque en sus ojos solo somos números. Nos matamos y ellos ganan todo el dinero," Yoel scoffed, trying, and failing to spread hard butter over a stale bread roll.

The main cafeteria doors opened, and a group of people walked in. Unlike the production facility employees, these people were all in business attire. The men wore traditional suits and skinny black ties, and the women donned power suits and dresses. All of them had folders and notebooks. It looked like they were on a walking tour of the facility or there for PR purposes, game planning on how to spin a workplace death.

"Bro! If it weren't for the benefits, I'd be doing something else," Martin said. "There're plenty of jobs out there that pay better. Grant, he worked here I think almost fifteen years and look what he got."

The group broke off on their own, each one talking to employees. The blood flushed from my face. Among the group was Evelyn.

"Diablo! ¡¿Quince años?! ¡Él estaba ganando ese dinero!" Martin and Yoel carried on, oblivious to the new commotion.

"Not even, bro, but I'm sure he was banking on those bonuses!"

"¿Que bonuses?"

"You didn't know? Yeah, I think if you're here five years they give you a twenty-five hundred dollar bonus. If you're here ten years they give you five thousand dollars and a paid month vacation."

My eyes stalked her; every motion, the slightest movement done with grace and intent. Her once curly hair was now straightened and tightened into a bun held together with the help of a generous amount of gel. Still, little strands of hair curled around her earlobe and her cheek. No matter what she did, she could not conceal her Afro-Latino heritage. Elegant gold-rimmed glasses framed her face perfectly. She

24

was the only person from the group without a suit coat which allowed her silk-white blouse and black pencil skirt to show off her natural curves.

"Wow! ¿Y si llegas a los quince años?" Yoel continued to inquire.

I was caught in Evelyn's aura, like a floating object in outer space caught in a planet's gravitational pull. Martin and Yoel's conversation no longer interested me, not that it did in the first place. I didn't even know who was talking anymore.

"I think it's something like five thousand dollars, the paid vacation, and they also pay for you to go on a trip."

"¿En serio? ¿Como adonde? ¿Canadá?"

"Yeah."

"¿Tokyo?"

"Yeah."

"¿Hawaii?"

"Anywhere, bro."

Evelyn smiled as she made her way from table to table initiating small talk. I instinctively felt myself smile like I was walking alongside her.

Someone whistled.

"That's good, man. I like that! But me? I'm only doing this for a year or two until I have enough money to open my restaurant."

"Oh yeah?"

"¡Claro! Que crées, ¿que vine aquí para ser una chacha limpiando l'el culo de estos blanquitos? No mi hermano."

My heartbeat quickened as I realized she was nearing my table.

"Yeah, I've been here seven years. Three more and I get that bonus."

"That's right there, around the corner, como dicen."

"That's right. But once I get that bonus, that's it!"

"¿That's it?"

"That's it. I'm outta here."

25

"This place really does have good benefits."

One of the male suits came up behind Evelyn, grabbed her gently by the waist, and pulled her aside. He appeared to be a man of high culture. The type to get a two hundred dollar haircut from a personal barber who always ended the session with a hot towel and a close shave. He wore a gray tailored suit and had sharp black shoes that shinned in the fluorescent cafeteria light. He reeked of wealth and wore a smile that could charm a wolf.

"Yeah... poor Grant. He was almost at that fifteenth."

"Si... pobresito."

The man in the gray suit was mouthing something. Whatever it was, it made Evelyn laugh. When she laughed, she laughed with her entire body, and even though she was on the opposite side of the cafeteria, I could hear her as if she were standing right by my ear. She put her hand on the gray suit man's chest and let it linger as she spoke in response.

"Makes you wonder: what's the point?"

"¿El punto de que?"

"To work so hard at something that is really meaningless. What's the point?"

"Eso pasa cuando uno no le asigna un verdadero propósito a la vida, termina significando absolutamente nada."

The male suit grinned, his eyes swooning, took his finger to the loose strand of hair around her ear, and brushed it back. My heart sunk into the pit of my stomach. I looked down at my food; it did not look appetizing before, but now it made me want to puke.

Martin looked over at me as if I had just sat down at the table.

"What do *you* think?" He asked me.

I shrugged my shoulders and stood up from the table quickly, careful not to draw attention to myself.

"I think," I began, picking up my tray and tossing the contents in the trash, "it's time to get back to work."

I shelved the empty tray and left the cafeteria before Evelyn could see me.

* * *

The end of the workday had finally come. All of the employees spilled out into the parking area like students on the last day of school. I emerged from the building and navigated my way to the parking lot, wading through the groups of people talking excitedly among each other on the sidewalk. The late afternoon sun warmed my body quickly.

I was mulling over dinner, debating whether I should have baked chicken or if I should save myself the effort and heat up a packet of beef ramen noodle soup, when I looked up at my car and my heart pounced into my throat: Evelyn was there, waiting for me. She stood between me and my car, pacing back and forth like Ladon, talking on her cellphone animatedly. My heart returned to its spot in my chest but could not cease skipping several beats. I took in a significant amount of air in my lungs and let it out behind an agonizing groan.

Evelyn was so enthralled by her phone call that she didn't see me coming until I was a few steps away from my driver-side door. She told whomever she was talking to that she'd call them back, hung up her phone, and held it in her hand along with a ring of several keys. I forced the best smile I could.

"Hi, stranger!" she exclaimed.

She opened her arms and wrapped me in an embrace I was not ready for. I twitched awkwardly, like I was averse to touch, but quickly adjusted and settled into her hug. I was a good foot taller than Evelyn; she was about 5'2" - 5'4" in heels - even so, she had to get on her tippy toes to fully bring her arm around the back of my neck. Her embrace was tight and warm; I couldn't help but sink in. My nose, mere inches from the nape of her bare neck, was invaded by the sweetness of her signature perfume, Victoria Secret's Heavenly. It sent my mind sifting through the extensive video library in my memory, and inserted a scene from our time together: us in the throes of lovemaking, sweat beading off our naked bodies, her wild hair fanned perfectly on the pillow like a Japanese ōgi, eyes closed, biting her bottom lip as I gently traced her neck from the jugular groove up to the tip of her round chin with my lips.

Evelyn released her embrace, and the scene cut to black abruptly.

"You look good," I acknowledged, hating the fact that she did.

"Please! I'm disgusting. This monkey suit makes me sweat every-where," she said, showing off the coin-sized sweat stains forming under her pits and the line under her large breasts. My eyes glided over them, but I quickly turned away, blushing. They were big for a girl of her small frame. Bigger than I remembered, actually.

"Nah, you're good. It suits you. The outfit, I mean. Not the sweat," I stammered, quickly correcting myself. No matter how much time passed, her presence still made me nervous, like a schoolboy trying to plant a kiss on his first crush. I could feel my hands getting cold and clammy.

She smiled. Her eyes were large behind the frames of her elegant glasses; I could see every detail of her iris, down to the flecks of gold in the field of green.

"I've been looking for you," she said, "If I hadn't seen your car, I'd've thought you weren't here."

I shook my head and looked down at my feet. I could only bring myself to look at her for a split second before I was overcome by the familiar feeling of unworthiness.

"Nah, I'm here. Same schedule," I said, shrugging my shoulders.

"Yeah, I see that," she said, the smile still plastered on her face. She sounded sincere, but I couldn't help but detect a hint of judgment.

"How've you been?"

I shoved my sweaty hands in my pockets.

"Good. You? How's life in Babylon?" I asked, quickly turning the spotlight away from myself.

Evelyn's eyes lit up.

"Oh my God! It's going great!" she exclaimed. "The work is as tedious as ever, but the benefits are amazing! They've renovated the building. Now each floor has a gym. There is a movie theater on the top floor, and a bar on the roof. Oh, and the pay is so much better, I was able to get rid of my Isuzu, finally! Do you remember my Isuzu?"

"Of course. I loved that car."

"Really? I couldn't stand it. It was so *old*. The brakes always crapped out on me. I thought I was going to have to resort to using my feet to stop and go like Fred Flintstone," she laughed. "I'm so glad I was able to get into Babylon," she quickly got back on topic. "The people, they're incredible. I wish I could pry open their skulls and study how their brain works. There's a guy there who can calculate - *actually* calculate - how many windows are on a building, without having to do the math on paper!"

"Wow, really? That's cool. I'm happy for you. Really," I did my best to feign sincerity.

"Yeah, sure as hell beats being out here on the Plantation," she quipped.

I knew she was trying to cut me with that remark, but when I didn't react to her comment, she paused. I could feel the tone was about to shift.

"Actually, there are going to be a few spots opening up in headquarters in a few months. Some people got promoted to a different position, others retired, etcetera, and you know that The Company prefers to promote and hire from within, right."

"Yeah?" I knew where she was going but proceeded with caution anyway.

"They asked us for suggestions, employees who could be assets in the Babylon office, and, well... I... suggested you."

"Why?" I said, more annoyed than I wanted to sound.

"Why?" she echoed, genuinely surprised by the reaction. "I don't know. Could it be because you're qualified? Because you're intelligent? Because you've been with The Company for nearly ten years? You have seniority? You want me to keep going? I mean, *geezus*, if anyone deserves a shot at a better position it's you, don't you think?"

The question was rhetorical for her. Her admonishment made me want to retreat, I nervously fidgeted with the keys in my pocket.

"Yeah, you know Evie, I wish you wouldn't have done that."

"Why not?" she demanded to know.

I felt Evelyn's increasing agitation; she placed her hands on her hips and tapped her foot. She was looking for a good explanation. I didn't have one.

"What would I be doing?" I asked.

"Data Entry. Moving numbers from one column to another and making sure they balance. That's it! You'd be making much more than you are now and think about how much you'll save on the commute!" she was selling hard.

I shook my head and looked everywhere except at her. "Yeah... I don't kn-."

"Plus," she interjected, "We'd be working together again. I mean we'd be in different departments, but we could have lunch together, like we used to. I miss us talking. Don't you?"

"Yeah, of course, but-"

"So, what's the problem?"

I conceded. I knew I couldn't win. Not with her. Her phone vibrated in her hand. She looked at it quickly and pressed something. She turned her attention back to me and sighed slightly. Her giant eyes found mine.

"Corazón," she began. That's what she used to call me when we were together. She knew that would cripple me instantly. "With your record, the job is basically yours if you want it, but I know you. You're quick to reject anything that makes you uncomfortable, and I feel you miss out on the good things life has to offer you when you do. But before you turn down *this* opportunity, will you at least consider it? You have a week or so before any real decision is made. Mull it over for a few days, and if you still decide it isn't for you, then I'll take your name out of the running."

I looked down at a spot on the ground. The image of my headless neighbor's body falling over flashed before my eyes. My shoulders slumped in defeat.

"Okay," I sighed. "Fine."

Evelyn smiled. "You'll do it?"

"I will *think* about it," I corrected her.

Evelyn let out a squeal of excitement and hugged me tight, trapping my arms at my sides. Her phone vibrated in her hand again.

"Alright, I have to go," she said after peering at her phone. "Thank you! Thank you for

thinking about it!" She let go of me and backed away smiling.

"I should be thanking you... for thinking of me." I managed to pull the words from the

depths of my stomach.

"Always," she retorted.

I couldn't help but smile. I took the keys I was fidgeting with out of my pocket and unlocked my car door, preparing to get in.

"Oh, by the way, Happy Birthday," Evelyn said.

I looked at her blankly. "What?"

"It's your birthday, right? Happy Birthday," she said, as if she were talking to a patient who had just emerged from a long coma.

I thought it over. I didn't really know what day it was. It very well *could* be my birthday.

"Thank you," I said, deciding to accept it as fact.

"How old are you now?" she asked.

I had to think this over as well before I could find the number.

"Thirty?" The number tumbled out of me, unsure. "Yeah. Thirty," I confirmed. "I'm thirty," The realization began to settle in.

"Wow. You're still a baby," Evelyn chortled.

"That would make you what then, a cradle robbing cougar?"

"Asshole. I'm only four years older than you," she replied, laughing.

The sound of her laughter warmed my soul. It wasn't a chorus line of angels singing in harmonic sotto voce, but it was to me.

"You know, thirty is scary. At thirty, you should already know who you are and what you want to do if you're not already doing it. You don't want to die here like Gary did, you know, rest in peace and everything."

"Grant."

"What?"

"His name is Grant."

"It was," she corrected me.

A sleek luxurious Lincoln Navigator with all the bells and whistles pulled up in the lane behind us. The windows were tinted with the darkest black, so I couldn't see who was behind the wheel, but I had a good idea. Whoever was behind the wheel honked the horn. Evelyn looked back and waved.

"I have to go," she said, backing up quickly. "Do me a favor?"

"Name it."

"It's your Birthday. Do something else besides go to the movies," she said, bounding closer to the Lincoln.

"But I love the movies," I responded in all seriousness.

"In that case, do what you love! Bye!" Her smile beamed across two rows of parked cars. She sent me a final waive. We stood on separate mountain tops. I sent her back another forced smile and half-hearted waive across the chasm as I watched her climb into the passenger side of the Lincoln and drive off.

I got into my car and closed the door. I rolled down the window (that mold smell was especially strong in the afternoon) and stuck the key in the ignition. Before I turned the engine over, I was struck with another memory of Evelyn.

We sat in the middle of a dark movie theater surrounded by nothing but empty fold-up seats. Evelyn wore one of my white sweaters that was so big, it made her look like she was wrapped in a giant blanket. Her skinny jeans hugged her legs perfectly, and her hair was down and extra wavy. I was in my usual black short-sleeved hoodie shirt and gray cotton shorts. Light from the film projector beamed over our heads and onto the screen. A big tub of popcorn rested between us, both of us dipping our hands into the bucket, robotically stuffing our mouths. Our eyes were transfixed on the silver screen, our pupils drinking up the action. Evelyn hugged my arm tight, resting her head on my shoulder. I smiled and kissed her on the forehead. *What movie were we watching that night?*

The parking lot was empty, and the afternoon sun was beginning its descent, slowly making room for the upcoming moon. I turned the key in the ignition, but the car did not start.

* * *

I went to the Parthenon Pavilion Movie Theater. Most moviegoers preferred Studio 20 because they had recently done renovations and now had reclining seats that vibrated, blew air, and sprayed water; it was basically a carnival ride. Regardless, I remained loyal.

The Parthenon was between an ice cream store and a gym. Though it had not had any renovations done since the Cold War, when I was inside the Parthenon, and the doors closed, the outside world melted away. I felt true freedom, floating alone in a void outside of time and space.

I'd been coming to the Parthenon Pavilion since I was a kid. Every year, when my birthday came around, all I wanted to do was spend the day at the movies. It didn't matter what movie, as long as I got to sit in the dark with some buttered popcorn and an ice-cold bubbly beverage. From the trivia games before the previews to the end credits, I was happy. Truly happy. There was a certain synergy between the moving pictures and my eyes; it caused the hair on my neck to rise. Any time something exciting happened on screen, or when my emotion was evoked just right, a warmth spread through my body like hot cocoa on a snowy winter night.

There were other movie theaters in town: Silver-Screen Mercado, Town Square 6, Studio 20, but when The Company settled in town, they purchased those theaters, made extensive renovations, and began to only play big-budget franchise blockbusters, reboots, and remakes. Parthenon Pavilion was the only theatre still not owned by The Company. This allowed them the freedom to play virtually any film they desired. Though they played big studio flicks, they also dedicated several screens to independent films, both foreign and domestic, that focused more on illuminating the human condition, rather than dressing it up in sugary spectacle.

When I arrived, the Parthenon had a screening of Andrei Tarkovsky's *Solaris*. I bought my ticket at the kiosk, got a small bag of popcorn and a small Sprite, found my seat in the tiny theatre, sat down, and waited for the show to begin. From the middle seat of the middle row, I could see the entire screen. I thought I was going to have the entire theatre to myself, however, right as the movie was about to start, the door to the theatre opened, and a young couple entered. The guy looked like he was either nineteen or twenty, and the girl looked like she was a fresh seventeen. They came in laughing and giggling but quickly shushed each other when they noticed me in the room. They took a seat in the last row and settled in.

I shut them out and turned my attention back to the screen. The moment the first scene began to play, I heard what sounded like kissing coming from behind me. I looked over my shoulder to find the young couple in a fierce lip lock, their tongues engaged in a brutal tug of war. I rolled my eyes and shook my head in disgust, not in the act itself but in the sheer display of disrespect for the film. I turned back to the screen and tried to concentrate. Every so often, though, I could hear their heavy panting and moans of pleasure. After minutes of this, I was forced to turn around and ask them to keep it down. When I looked back, all I saw was the girl's legs spread and hanging over the empty chairs in front of her, a hand (not hers) massaging her breasts over her shirt, her head back in pleasure. The man's head was bobbing up and down between her legs, the sound of sucking and licking overpowering the movie's audio. I turned back to the movie and sank in my chair, heaving an audible sigh.

By the time I emerged from the theater, night had descended over the town. I stopped at the grocery store on my way home and got some things to restock my fridge. Fruits, veggies, orange juice, eggs, crackers, nothing too extravagant. I also remembered to get the Spackle to cover up the holes in my wall.

I pulled into the parking lot of Perdition Towers and found a spot to park on the far corner. The lot was overfull; it seemed like everyone was back from the battle of the day, licking their wounds. I climbed four flights of stairs to my floor, walked down the dark, damp corridor, reached my door, put the grocery bags down on the floor, and fiddled with my keys. I unlocked the door and pushed it open. I bent over to pick up the shopping bags and looked at my neighbor's door. From the bottom crease, I could see the light was on. Everything came rushing back to me.

I looked around the forsaken hall, took a few steps over to the door, and wrapped my hand around the handle.

Don't do it. You do not want to open this door.

I turned the handle and opened the door.

There were moving boxes everywhere and piles of books stacked on top of one another, a TV blaring music, clothes scattered all over the place, and fast food bags and containers littered the kitchen counter.

A tall, ample, dark-bronze skinned young woman with honey-colored frizzy hair stood in the middle of the living room, her athletically thick body dripping wet, fresh out of the shower. Her back was to the door, and she was in the middle of humming a tune, drying the front of her body, when she spun around quickly. There was a tattoo of a word written in a fancy font right below her left collar bone, but before I could read what it said, she lifted her towel up to cover her exposed breasts.

"What the fu-!" she began to shout.

I closed the door before she could finish. I quickly unlocked and opened my door. I grabbed my grocery bags off the floor, but because I did it with so much force, the bags ripped. Oranges, onions, and apples fell out and rolled in different directions on the floor. I tried to pick them up, but in my panic, they kept slipping out of my grasp and thudding to the ground. Finally, I decided to just kick them into the apartment. I shut the door and stood in the landing area, my back against the door. Beads of sweat formed around my forehead, and my heart was racing a mile a minute. I tried to calm down but I could hear the young woman on the other side of the wall thumping around. I followed the thunderous footsteps as they crossed the length of the apartment to the front door, into the hallway, and finally arrived at my door. She pounded on my door so hard the cabinets in the kitchen trembled.

I sighed through my nose and opened the door, ready to accept my well deserved tongue lashing. The young woman was in an oversized black graphic tee shirt of a logo I didn't recognize that came down to just above her knees. The shirt sopped up all the water dripping from her wet frizzled hair. The way her hair stuck to her square face made it look like she got caught in an unsuspected rainstorm. Her bare legs weren't completely dry, and her feet were small and dainty, her perfectly trimmed toenails painted a light purple.

I looked at her apologetically. She was huffing and puffing angrily. She rose a finger, prepared to unload a seething tirade upon me, but her plump dark lips didn't open. She pursed her lips and squinted her almond-shaped eyes, scanning my face. She exhaled through her nose, dropped her finger to the side, and slowly walked back to her apartment, her squinting eyes never breaking from mine until she was well out of sight.

I closed the door slowly and stood motionless in the entryway, green apples, navel oranges, and white onions scattered about my feet. I turned around and stepped over the fallen items toward my bed nook. I examined the wall. There were no holes. I ran my hand over the spot where the holes had been to see if by chance maintenance came in and fixed the wall while I was gone, but there was no sign that the spot on the wall was new or painted over.

Maybe I was dreaming, I thought.

I went back to the kitchen and picked up the groceries, a myriad of thoughts swimming around my head. I put the groceries away, put on a small pot of water, brought it to a boil over the stove, and cooked some quick ramen noodles. I stirred it with a fork until the noodles softened, drained the water, and seasoned the noodles with the flavor packet. I poured myself some sweet tea, sat on my futon, and watched some sports highlights while I ate.

37

When my hunger was satiated, and the dishes were done, dried, and stored away, I got undressed. I could smell Evelyn's perfume on my shirt as I pulled it off. I bunched it up in my hand and took another whiff, allowing myself to float on the memories the smell evoked.

The clothes all went into the hamper, I put on some clean PJs, and flopped on my bed, staring up at the ceiling. The moonlight spilled into the room from the window. I tilted my head backward and gazed upon it hypnotically, the moon hanging in the night sky like a picture frame. I got on my knees, shut the blinds and the curtain, laid back down and placed my head on the pillow. My head hit something hard.

I stuffed my hand under the pillow and retrieved the black leather notebook. I looked at it and at the wall where the holes were. My face contorted in confusion. I stuffed the notebook back under my pillow, careful, like it was a vial of nitroglycerin in Henry Clouzot's *The Wages of Fear*, and gently laid my head on the pillow.

I closed my eyes and recalled the events of the day, the young woman next door, the couple in the movie theater, Evelyn, Grant, and my headless neighbor. My headless neighbor in the blood-stained blue suit and red tie. I stared into the darkness of my room. Heavier and heavier my eyelids became like a slab of osmium hung on both lids. I was losing the fight with slumber. Just as I was ready to surrender, I thought I felt something heavy settle at the foot of my bed. I pried my eyes open a crack and swore I saw the corpse of my headless neighbor sitting at the end of the divan. Its left leg was crossed over the right, left arm planted on the bed for support, and right-hand nursing a steaming cup of tea.

It appeared to be "watching" over me, but, before my brain could grasp the logic, I fell into a deep sleep.

Chapter Three

It wasn't a dreamless sleep. The moment I woke up and exposed my eyes to light, the images burned away like an exposed roll of film, unsalvageable. I turned on my back and stared up at the popcorn textured ceiling waiting for my eyes to adjust to reality, my pupils dilating like a camera aperture focusing on different shapes and forms.

Evelyn's head rested on my chest. She was curled up next to me, my soft penis in her hand. She massaged it between her palm and slender fingers, rubbing the tip with her thumb. I gulped. Evelyn looked up at me and flashed a lascivious smile. She returned her attention to my stiffening member. Her hands were magic; it didn't take long for my penis to become stone. Evelyn moistened her lips and hungrily took my penis into her warm mouth, sweeping me away on a wave of ecstasy. My breathing grew shallow as her expert tongue worked wonders.

She was on top of me. My hands gripped her bare thighs and squeezed them as she shifted her hips in the perfect position to successfully fuse our bodies. She grabbed my penis and guided it toward the doors of her glistening vagina. I could feel the goosebumps forming on the surface of her skin as she teased her moist hole with the tip of my sensitive penis. A moan escaped my throat. A smile crept onto her lips as she slowly inserted me into her with absolutely no friction or resistance. Her body shuddered with pleasure. We were one.

Evelyn tore off her oversized shirt and tossed it aside into another dimension. Her wild hair fell over one side of her face. I sat up and cradled her full breasts in my hands and took her pink, swollen nipples into my mouth. She wrapped her arms around my neck, digging her fingernails into the back of my head. With each stroke and grind, she heaved air in and out of her chest, cursing quietly into my ear. I could feel the walls of her vagina contracting around my penis. She was ready to climax, and knowing so brought me to the zenith of release. We maintained our rhythm. I wrapped one arm around her waist and pulled her in closer to my body, going deeper into hers. I twisted her hair around my other hand and gently pulled it back, forcing her to reveal her neck. I dove at it like Bram Stoker's *Dracula*. Her body went into sharp convulsions as she was hit with several orgasmic waves.

I couldn't hold on anymore. A few more moments and I too would succumb to this passion, and this primal ritual would come to its inevitable end. I leaned back to take her image in but my eyes didn't find Evelyn straddling me anymore. It was the young woman - my neighbor - gyrating in my lap, naked, her body covered in sweet perspiration. Her nipples looked like frozen dark chocolate kisses. She ran her hands along her body and cupped her breasts. I reached out, held her hips in place, and proceeded to move my torso with the precision and power of a jackhammer. I felt my neighbor orgasm multiple times, her eyes rolled into the back of her head, her mouth agape with pleasure, and her fingernails dug into my chest.

She bent down and whispered in my ear, "Cum in me."

I exploded, draining my semen deep into her body. The sudden burst of warmth inside her made her tremble. She looked down at me and smiled as her vagina thirstily absorbed every drop. My head fell onto the pillow, and I closed my eyes, listening to my heart pumping madly in my chest.

When I caught my breath, I opened my eyes. Both Evelyn and my young neighbor were gone. I was alone, and my hand was wet, covered in cold semen; I'd ruined another pair of boxers. I took off my tank top and cleaned the ejaculate off of my hand and from the head of my penis before it receded back into its foreskin. I tossed the sullied tank top to the ground, sighed, and shook my head.

You are thirty.

I pursed my lips and nodded my head in agreement.

"I am thirty," I confirmed. The moment of pleasure was gone, replaced by the all-too-familiar feeling of guilt and shame.

While taking a blistering hot shower (not because I particularly enjoyed it, but because it was the only way to get truly clean. Like the only way to expel my body of compunction was to wash it away with a bar of soap and scalding water), I sat on the shower floor, hugged my knees, and buried my head in my arms, allowing the water to fall over me as I dove deep into thought.

I thought of Evelyn's offer to join her in The Company's headquarters (Babylon as we used to call it), under a "new title," with "better pay," and "amazing benefits." None of those terms interested me. The only thing I found enticing was the fact that I'd be closer to her. But she appeared spoken for now. Another man. A *better* man. What good would it do to be near someone I could only touch in memory?

By now, you should know who you are and be on your way to attaining what you want. Her voice echoed in my head.

I know who I am. Of that I had no allusions. What do I want? I wanted Evelyn. I had Evelyn. I lost Evelyn. After her, there was nothing else *to* want. Yet, I was tortured by the desire to appease her. I was indifferent to my current position and changing it all now would make little difference to me. That much I certainly knew. That's not what she meant, though, I knew that as well. So, the questions remained open. Questions I never considered giving any real thought. If I once did, I had long forgotten.

The water started to turn cold, prompting me to get up, turn off the water and step out of the shower without an answer.

The rest of the morning went as usual: I put on lotion and got dressed in my work clothes (black polo shirt), made some toast, and spread some butter. I took a quick bite and frowned. The toast tasted awful, like a muddy leather boot. I checked the expiration date on both the butter and the bread; both were still good. I took another bite to be sure, maybe I just got the moldy end of something, but the taste was worse than the previous bite. I spit it out and tossed the toast in the trash along with the bread and the butter. I downed a glass of water, brushed my teeth, and grabbed my things. I clutched the door handle and stopped.

I held my breath and tried to listen for my young neighbor, but it didn't sound like she was awake next door. I quietly opened the door and exited my apartment. I locked the door quickly, keeping my peripheral vision on her door. Once the door was secure, I bounded down the corridor toward the exit and down the stairs.

I maneuvered through the parking lot to my car, the only champagne-colored Chevy Monte Carlo in the lot, sifting through my thoughts.

"Hey, Perv!" A voice called out.

I looked around and saw my young neighbor waving me over. She was standing by a white Jeep Grand Cherokee. It was an older model, maybe an '02, but it looked significantly better than my car. The white paint looked practically new, and the chrome rims shined even with the most minimal light. Her driver's side door was open, and the hood of the car was up. She appeared to be having some issues.

She was dressed in casual clothes, nice tight-fitting high-waisted acid wash jeans, white sneakers, and a white polo shirt tucked into her jeans. Her honey-colored hair was tied back into a ponytail, and if she had any make-up on, I couldn't tell. Her skin was imperfectly perfect and natural. She looked like an Amazonian far removed from her element.

My heart leapt into my throat. I pretended not to see or hear her and quickened my pace toward my car.

"Hey! Don't pretend you can't hear me!" she yelled.

I conceded and turned toward her. I looked around and behind me as if maybe she was talking to someone else, pointing at myself, looking for one last confirmation that she was indeed talking to me.

"Yes. You, Perv. You're the only one in this parking lot besides me. Come here!" she said, every word spoken soaked in annoyance.

I dropped my shoulders in defeat and walked over to her. She urged me to hurry, aggressively waving her hand like a third-base coach telling a runner to hustle to home plate. I finally made it and looked at her. The word *guilt* felt like it was etched onto my forehead with the tip of a rusted nail.

"Do you know anything about cars?" she asked.

"The basics," I replied, shrugging my shoulders.

"That is substantially more than me," she said, climbing into her driver's seat. "Listen to this." She turned the key in the ignition and the car clicked several times. She looked to me for an acknowledgment. I actively averted her light brown eyes and focused on the sound.

"You see," she said after several seconds of trying. "Nothing. It won't start."

"Do you happen to know how old your battery is?" I asked.

"Christ, I don't know. Fairly new, I guess. I can't remember the last time it was replaced but then again, I barely remember what happened yesterday so…" she trailed off.

I walked around to the left side of the hood of the car and examined the battery. It wasn't new but it wasn't old. The casing was dirty, but I didn't find any signs of corrosion around the terminals or wires. I came back to her.

"Well, your battery looks fine," I confirmed for her. "If I had to guess, and this would be a poor guess at best, I'd say it's your starter that's probably gone bad."

"Would jumping the battery help?" she asked.

"If it doesn't work, the only thing you would've lost is time," I said, shrugging my shoulders.

The young woman looked at her phone, shook her head, and sucked her teeth.

"Forget it. Time, I do not have. Like the White Rabbit in *Alice in Wonderland*, Oh dear! Oh dear! I shall be late," she started. She looked at me. "Can *you* take me to work?" she asked.

"Oh, I don't... know. I work kind of... out of the way." I stammered.

"Yeah, I know, for The Company, right?" she said, as she got out of the car and made her way to the hood.

"Yes. In the Clean Room," I answered, surprised.

"Boxing," she said, pointing to her ID badge hanging on the rearview mirror. "I've used up all my PTO, and I can't be late again. It'll be my third PCN, and you know what that means."

She tried to close the jeep's hood but couldn't undo the hood lift stand. "Do you mind?" She asked me, as I blankly stared at her, questions cascading down my mind. I'd never seen her before. Not at work or the apartment building for that matter. Not that I was ever looking. I snapped out of it and helped her close her hood.

"Thanks. So, how about it? Will you be my Don Quixote and give me a ride?" she demanded.

I couldn't think of a reason not to.

"I can't think of a reason not to."

The young woman closed her driver's side door, turned, and looked at me slightly amused. "I'm sorry, do you want to see my breasts again?" she sassed.

The image of her wet breasts flashed before me. I closed my eyes

44

and put my hands together, praying for forgiveness.

"No. No. Of course not. I can give you a ride. Absolutely. No problem," I was sweating

profusely now. "My car is this way."

"Okay. Thank you," she said, sarcastically. "I just need one second. I'm going to have to call someone to come pick up my chariot."

"No problem. I'll wait," I said.

"Yeah, you will."

I rushed to my car, unlocked the door, and got in. I wiped the cold sweat from my forehead. I watched her in the rearview mirror as she spoke on the phone. She left her keys on the wheel and made her way to me.

I put my key in the ignition and turned it, praying that today it doesn't give me any issues. When the car came to life with no struggle, I felt relieved. She reached my car, climbed into the passenger seat, closed the door, and put on her seat belt. I followed suit, put my car in gear, and drove out of the parking lot.

She finished her conversation and ended the call. She shoved the phone in her pocket and turned to me.

"We're not going to fuck," she said suddenly.

I nearly veered off the road.

"I'm sorry?" I said, gaining control of the vehicle.

"Yeah, I bet you are, you libertine!" she punctuated. She lowered the sun visor and looked at herself in the mirror.

"No, I don't mean 'I'm sorry' as in I'm sorry we're not- I mean... 'I'm sorry' as in I wasn't expecting you to say-," all I could manage were fragmented sentences.

The young woman put the sun visor back up and burst into laughter.

"Good grief!" she exclaimed through chortling. "I'm just messing with you. Relax man."

I could feel her eyes piercing the side of my head. I kept my eyes on the road. Beads of sweat started forming around my forehead again.

"Well," I began. "I *am* sorry about... you know."

"Bursting into my apartment and seeing me naked?" She finished the sentence for me.

I pursed my lips and nodded my head, my face warm with shame and embarrassment. She smiled, sat back in her seat, and looked out the window.

"Ah, no big deal. I have a nice body. But I do, however, subscribe to Hammurabi's code. An eye for an eye, and a tooth for a tooth. Or in our case, tit for tat," She pointed at my crotch, a grin painted on her lips.

I gulped audibly, causing the young woman to burst into another fit of laughter.

"Wow. You are wound way too tight," she said as she began to dig into her small bag but, unable to find what she was looking for, she groaned.

"Damn it! I left my book in my car! Finally, I have a chance to read and I forget it! My dad would be so pissed at me. I can hear him now saying 'always carry some literature to read and a notebook for thoughts and notes on what you read'," she mocked.

"I can go back," I said. I couldn't, but the words came out before I could stop myself.

"No, we're too far, and I really can't be late. It's fine. It's fine. You'll just have to enthrall me with riveting conversation," she shifted her body so her entire being was facing me.

"Conversation?"

"*Riveting* conversation," she corrected me. "Note the modifier. In the 17th and 18th century, before TV and social media warped everyone's minds, the French would hold gatherings they called Salon's where people would gather to discuss a wide array of topics from politics and philosophy to poetry, music and literature," she smiled. "No pressure."

Uh oh. She's going to find out just how truly dull and hollow you are the second you open your mouth.

"How long have you been working for The Company?"

The young woman's eyes filled with instant disappointment, yet a smirk crawled on her lips.

"You can do better than that," she encouraged.

No, you can't.

I gripped the steering wheel tight, my lips trembled slightly. The silence felt like an eternity. I asked the next question that came to mind.

"What does *Fernweh* mean?"

Thaleia squinted at me. It was the tattoo on her shoulder I managed to glimpse when I accidentally walked in on her.

"It's German," she said with a smile. "Plainly translated, it means *Far-sickness*. The desire, the aching for distant places, a yearning for travel."

"You travel often?"

"I try. I love to think of myself as one of those people who can up and go whenever adventure beckons," she said.

We shared a silence.

"That's all you got?" She teased.

That's all you're capable of.

"What's your name?"

She smiled and sat back in her seat, looking out into the distant road.

"That's too intimate," she said.

"Intimate?"

"Tell you what," she began turning to me with a mischievous grin, "I'm going to ask *you* a series of questions. Depending on how you answer, and if you answer all of my answers *truthfully* - imagine the word truthfully is italicized - then I will tell you my name. What do you say? You in?"

"Okay," I responded. By this point, the situation was beyond my control, if it ever was.

"Promise me you will only answer everything truthfully, I cannot stress that detail enough," she forewarned.

"What if I lie?" I asked.

"I'll know," her tone was serious. "Something you should know about me is I *despise*, I *loathe*, I *detest*, I *abhor* liars. If you lie to me, this is where our conversation ends. Do you agree to these terms?"

I thought it over for only a few seconds.

"Yes. I agree," I didn't really have a choice.

The young woman stuck out her hand, waiting for me to shake it. "Your word means nothing unless you look me in my eye and shake my hand."

"I'm driving," I reminded her.

"Then do it quickly."

I obliged, looked into her large light brown eyes, and shook her soft hand firmly. She smiled and sat up straight in the chair excitedly. "Are you ready?" She asked.

"Yeah," I said with a nervous smile.

"Great," she exclaimed, rubbing her hands together. "Let's see, let's start you off with something soft." She bit the nail on her thumb pondering the question. "Are you a Republican or a Democrat?"

"Neither," I said. "I'm not even registered to vote."

"Proud of that are you? Voting is the only power we have in this country as citizens. Not just on the federal level but in local and state elections, too. People are pulling the strings of your daily life and you're okay with that? Ignorance isn't bliss; it's a hotbed for Fascism. We can't afford to be cynical," she chastised.

"I don't think I'm cynical. Just lazy," I half-joked.

"Are you religious?" she moved on, unamused.

"I *was* raised Catholic," I responded, hoping to avoid another verbal reprimand.

"That just means your mother made you go to church. Do you believe in God?"

"Do I have to decide right now?" I asked.

"It's not what you answer, but how you answer remember?" She reminded me.

I grappled with the question as best as I could so early in the morning.

"I've always taken for granted that there is one because of the way I was raised but truth be told I've never thought about it deeply. I don't have the unwavering faith to believe one way or the other," I said.

She pursed her lips slightly and nodded her head, absorbing my answer.

"What was the last book you read?" she asked. "And if you say *Harry Potter*, this conversation is over."

I also had to think this over.

"*The Stranger? The Count of Monte Cristo? Crime and Punishment? The Jungle? The Old Man and the Sea?* 1Q84. Give me something!" she pleaded, rattling off titles to books I'd never even heard of.

I couldn't believe it but as I thought about it, I realized it was true: I hadn't read a book for leisure since college. Then I remembered a book my mom got for me for my twenty-fourth birthday.

"I started to read *Awake in the Dark* by Roger Ebert, but I didn't get far. I don't even know where I put the book." This admission actually made me feel embarrassed and guilty. Like I was standing in front of her naked during a blizzard.

"Oh, Roger Ebert, huh? Are you a cinephile?" she asked.

"Not really. I love film but I'm no cinephile. I don't even like that word. It makes me think of some short chubby guy with a thin creep mustache and a sweaty upper lip getting off to rolls of exposed celluloid," I said.

She laughed. A good laugh. The tension in my body softened a bit.

"What's your favorite movie?" she continued with her line of questioning.

That question didn't require any effort.

"*Le Samouraï* by Jean-Pierre Melville," I said without hesitation.

"Ooh, a French film. What's it about?" she pressed.

"It's no *Seventh Seal*. On the surface it's a neo-noir crime thriller about a hitman who botches a job and spends the next few days trying to elude the police as well as evade the people who hired him, as they send other assassins to kill him. But the main character, Jef Costello, he lives such a stoic existence. He has a code, and he adheres to the code. He barely speaks, only when it's necessary...," I was about to keep going but I could see her smiling from ear to ear.

"Yeah, you're definitely a film head," she teased.

I didn't push back against her. I just smiled; my cheeks flushed hot.

"Okay," she began, "one last question."

"I'm ready," I said, confidently.

Her lips curled mischievously, and she moistened her lips with the tip of her tongue. Her eyes flashed.

"Did you masturbate this morning?"

My eyes widened slightly, and my heart skipped several beats. I opened my mouth to speak, but she cut me off before I could form the beginning of an answer. Her eyes didn't leave mine, waiting to catch the slightest hint of deception.

"And remember, *don't lie*. You gave me your word," she quickly reminded me.

I needed a way out of answering this question. I could stay quiet for the rest of the drive. There was no rule against *that*, right? Or I could unbuckle my seatbelt, speed up to over a hundred miles an hour, and plow full force into a cement light post. I'd fly out of the window and smash into the cement post. That would instantly kill me, but at least I wouldn't have to answer that question.

50

"Yes," I finally caved. My face was hot with embarrassment. She studied my face and nodded her head.

"Did you come?" she asked.

"Yes," I answered. There was no use turning back now.

"A lot?" she asked.

"I don't really measure the quantity," I answered.

"When you came, did you think about me?"

I squeezed sweat from my eyes and pursed my dry lips until they looked so thin, they were practically nonexistent. My throat was suddenly dry. Sweat was running down my cheek. I tried to wipe it away subtly and gripped the steering wheel so tight my knuckles turned white. All I could manage to do was nod my head slowly while I desperately looked for my voice.

"Yes," I finally managed to croak.

Satisfied with my response, the young woman smiled from ear to ear and relaxed in the passenger seat.

"Give me your phone," she demanded.

"What?"

"Your phone. You do have a phone don't you?" she asked.

"Yes."

"Give it to me," she held her hand out, waiting for me to surrender my device.

I dug my phone out of my pocket and handed it to her. She entered my phone and took a picture of herself making a funny face. I watched as she texted away, like a helpless prepubescent boy who's afraid his mother is going to go through his internet search history.

"How did you know I masturbated this morning?" I asked. That was the only question swirling around in my mind.

"The walls are paper thin. Why? Are you embarrassed?"

"Obviously," I said in a sour tone.

"How Catholic," she said with a chuckle.

"No. It's just that, it was a private moment," I stammered again.

"Did it feel good?" She asked.

"Yes, but-"

"Did your pleasure cause someone else extreme pain?" she continued.

"Well, no but-"

"Then shut up. People masturbate. Nothing to feel ashamed of."

I opened my mouth to respond but didn't know what to say. I was left profoundly speechless.

The Production facility was coming into view from the road. She took out some perfume and sprayed a fine mist around her body. The smell was faint but sweet, not overbearing on the nostrils. She put the perfume back in her purse and leaned back in the seat, closed her eyes, and sighed slightly with a smile floating on her lips.

I couldn't help but stare at her.

Who is this woman?

We arrived at the plantation and found a parking spot by the pond. The young woman handed me back my phone, took off her seat belt, and opened the car door.

"I'd say thanks for the ride, but, you know... you saw my breasts," she reminded me.

"Tit for tat, right?" I asked.

"Not even close, you knave!" she laughed, tears forming in her eyes, punching me in the arm. She had tiny fists, but her knuckles felt like Roman concrete. She finally found a pocket of breath and got out of the car.

"Thank you," she said, turning back to me.

She prepared to close the door.

"I'm assuming you've decided against telling me your name?" I asked.

She bent down and looked at me.

"Well, you don't have any thoughts on politics, I'm assuming social or economic, you don't have any real thoughts on the concept of religion, and your knowledge of classic literature is abysmal at best….," she began.

You are garbage.

Her lips curled into a smile.

"Check your phone," she said.

She closed the car door, waved goodbye, and walked toward the building. I watched in the rearview mirror as she blended in with the arriving crowd and vanished. I scrolled through my contacts in my phone and found her picture, the picture she took in my car with her tongue sticking out. Underneath it was her information: her phone number, and her name. A small smile found its way to my mouth as I quietly recited it aloud...

... *Thaleia.*

Chapter Four

The rest of the workday went on as usual. I clocked in and headed straight to the auditorium for morning exercises. I found an open spot in the back of the room and, as I twisted my torso from left to right as instructed, gave the auditorium a thorough scan twice. I'd hoped to put my eyes on Thaleia, but either I didn't see her, or she just wasn't there.

Once the exercise was over, all present employees took a seat and listened to the morning announcements. The lead PC, a short, chubby middle-aged man with a Napoleon complex and thick hairy forearms, covered new directives passed down from Babylon. He wiped the flop sweat from both sides of his widow's peak, held a print out in his hand, cleared his throat and read them aloud.

Three new directives: production times need to ramp up to meet the increase in demand and avoid missing deadlines (everyone groaned), new kits will be distributed today, we were to take our time to assemble them right so there are no errors (a contradiction of the first directive), and finally no more idle periods before the end of shifts. Everyone was to work until it was time to de-gown and clock out.

A collective grumble washed over the auditorium, but since no one was upset enough to voice their objections, everyone just dispersed and trudged over to their respective departments.

When I arrived at my line, as expected, the new kits were already lined up, awaiting my expert hands. Like I always did with new kits, I studied the instruction manual, examined the pieces, and took my time assembling the parts. As always, I had no clue what I was putting together; it wasn't my job to be curious. After the third kit was done, I felt confident enough to pick up the pace.

Before I dove in, I looked around the room. Everyone was busy at work, chatting away about who-knows-what. They were all smiling and laughing behind their face masks. No one seemed to remember that less than 24 hours before, Grant keeled over in the very spot where they were now talking about whose fries were better: Checkers or McDonald's. It was as if, along with his passing, so went any memory of his existence. I turned my attention toward the task at hand, took a deep breath, shut off my thinking mind and let my hands go to work.

The first break snuck up on me. I had no idea how much time passed or how many kits I put together. I shuffled out to the pond and stood at my usual spot, watching the small circle of life play out over the shimmering surface of the murky water. I found myself looking over my shoulder, hoping to see Grant standing in his spot looking past the loblolly pine trees. No one was there.

A small flock of Grasshopper Sparrows chased each other playfully over the pond and then took off into the clear mid-morning sky, disappearing behind the swaying pine trees. I waited for them to return, but after a few moments, I gave up and went back inside just as the end-of-break signal rang.

Lunchtime came around. On the menu: a roast beef sandwich on soggy toasted wheat bread with a slice of American cheddar cheese and limp lettuce. I slathered mayonnaise and yellow mustard, but it did nothing to help the bland taste; I lost my appetite after two large bites. I drank a bottle of water to wash the bad taste out of my mouth, got up from the lunch table, and tossed the half-eaten sandwich in the trash.

As I gowned back up, preparing to finish out the day, I received a text message from Evelyn. One word: *Hi.*

I stared at the word for several minutes, considering if "hi" had a deeper meaning than its simplicity implied. I concluded that it was her not-so-subtle way of reminding me of her proposition.

Honestly, I had no intention in taking the job, but I did promise her to really consider it before giving her an answer. I had regretted not being able to be the man she deserved in our relationship. If I could do anything for her, even something as effortless as considering, no matter how pointless the gesture, I would do it.

I chose not to respond to her text, put the phone away in my locker and finished gearing up.

The end of the workday came quickly. Everyone crowded around the punch clock, desperate to get out of the building and on the open road, back to their lives. I was in no rush. Thursday was technically my Friday; the moment I punched the clock, I would have five days off. Laundry needed to be done, my apartment needed a heavy cleaning, the fridge needed to be properly restocked, and I usually reserved those tasks for my long off days. After all of that was done, I'd treat myself to a movie at the Parthenon. Perhaps I'd even make it a double feature.

The parking lot was congested. I navigated around the mess of outgoing and incoming cars, careful not to get lost in my odyssey. At last, when I arrived at my car, I breathed a sigh of relief. Last time, Evelyn was waiting for me. This time, there was no one hovering around it. I'd be lying if I said I wasn't a little disappointed, but truthfully, I was relieved she wasn't. I dug into my pocket and retrieved my car keys.

"Yo! Perv!"

My spine snapped straight, like ice water dropped down my back. I turned and saw Thaleia several yards away by the curb waiving to me above the crowd. She squeezed her way through everyone and made her way toward me, nearly getting struck by cars she neither saw nor acknowledged were even there. She walked like a person wired on Coca-Cola. When she finally reached me, she was out of breath as if she completed a 5k marathon. She was folded over, inhaling oxygen, her hands on her knees. I politely waited for her to regain her breath.

"Urm... hello?" I said, concerned.

She attempted to straighten up, clutching the side of her stomach, panting.

"Hi!" she exclaimed in a high-pitched tone. She was still finding her breath somewhat, but she sounded genuinely happy to see me.

"You good?" I asked.

She waved me off. "Sure. Sure," she assured, still fighting for breath. "Jesus! I'm out of shape!"

I gave her an extra moment to regain her composure which she happily accepted. Finally, her breathing found a steady rhythm.

"Hi, Perv," she smiled.

"Hi," I said, in a tone meant to convey my displeasure with that nickname.

"You going home?" she asked.

"Yeah," I responded with trepidation. I wanted to go home, make dinner, watch the Miami Heat game with a beer and go to bed, however, I could sense a favor coming. I prepared for it the moment she hollered for me across the parking lot. Still, I hoped to be wrong.

"Awesome! Would you mind giving me a ride, seeing as we're neighbors and I'm sans vehicle?"

There it was. I fought to keep my face expressionless, but I got the feeling she could see the struggle in my eyes. Worse, she seemed to revel in my silent despair.

"Sure. No problem," I agreed, through gritted teeth.

"My hero," she said, already knowing what my answer would be. "If you can take me home, then you can take me to the mall," she said, making her way to the passenger door. She opened it and smiled. "You know, since it is... *no problem.*" She got in the car and closed the door.

I opened the door to my car and looked at her. My face told her all she needed to hear.

"I need to go to the mall, but since my chariot is temporarily out of commission, you, my knight with the bleeding heart, will be taking me, your distressed damsel. Unless... you think I'm imposing," she feigned a gasp, "am I imposing?"

Again, she flashed a playful smile, waiting for me to answer. I scratched my earlobe and nearly ground my teeth into a powder. I loathe the mall. I can't stand the overpriced clothes, the clashing, nauseating scents of the food court, and the unintelligible humming of the hundreds of patrons aimlessly trekking from store to store pretending to accomplish something. Most importantly, the mall is the setting of the demise of Evelyn and mine's relationship. I can still see her sitting across from me. Her bulbous watery eyes...

...I shook the memory away before it fully formed.

"Ok," I said, resigned.

"You sure? It's not an imposition?" she said, her humility soaked in artifice.

"Absolutely not an imposition," I lied, getting in the car, closing the door, and strapping on the seat belt. "Can this be my penance for intruding on you last night?" I asked.

"Nope."

"You're going to continue to guilt me, aren't you?"

"Yep!"

* * *

There was no need to specify which mall. There was only one in Loblolly Pines: Coastal Mall. Loblolly Pines was home to retirees from all over the globe. There were no real night clubs or outdoor concerts. Nor any theme parks. There used to be an arcade - Merlin's - complete with laser tag, batting cages, and Go-Karts. However, the owners sold the property, and Merlin's was torn down and replaced with a Mercedes dealership... which was right next to a Toyota dealership... which was adjacent to a Chevy dealership.

There were recreational county parks scattered around Loblolly Pines, but they hadn't been renovated for decades. Basketball courts were cracking and crumbling; most rims were bent and twisted at odd angles. The nets were either always worn, torn, or missing altogether. The soccer pitches were nothing but fields of dirt surrounded by chain-linked fences. The baseball fields were mere mounds of red clay dirt with parched patches of brown grass grasping to dear life. There was a small waterpark off of Huffington Road, but it had been under construction for the past eight years. The playgrounds all looked abandoned. The swings were rusty, the mulch discolored and stiff, the slides moldy. While the retirees enjoyed a plethora of Golf Clubs, fine dining, and valet parking, their grandchildren were relegated to going bowling, going to the movies, or going to the mall. Since window shopping costs nothing, the mall is where most people gathered.

I parked in a spot near the food court. Thaleia looked up from her phone as if she had just come out of a hypnotic state.

"We're here already?" she noted, genuinely surprised.

She jumped out of the car and stretched her legs. I cut the engine off, undid my seatbelt, rolled my window down, and began to reach for my phone. Thaleia bent over and stared at me, confused.

"What are you doing?" she demanded to know.

"I'll wait for you here," I said as if we had discussed the plan earlier and she had already forgotten.

"No. You're coming with me," again, she demanded.

I shook my head frantically, as if trying to shut out a terrifying image.

"That's okay. I don't mind waiting," I said.

"But I do," she replied. "If you wait here then I'll feel like I'm being rushed, and I really hate shopping against a clock. Besides, it is *sweltering* out here. You'll be beef jerky before I get back. I mean, Jesus, look you're already sweating."

She wasn't wrong, sweat began to bead around my forehead, and I could feel it trickling down my back and into my fat folds. However, I was determined to stay put.

Thaleia threw her hands up in defeat and scoffed.

"Fine. If you are hellbent on being infantile, so be it. I'm not going to twist your arm," she conceded. She grabbed her small purse and closed the door. She walked away slowly, purposely, like fresh boiled molasses.

"I'm walking away now!" she dramatized aloud for my benefit. "O, how I long for the company of a noble man! A *gentle* man!"

She turned her head slowly over her shoulder to see if I was stirred enough to join her. I hadn't even twitched.

"Woe! Woe! Woe is me I say!" she continued. Still no reaction. She dropped the charade and slammed her palm on the trunk of the car.

"Are you seriously not coming?" she yelled out, dropping her act.

I sighed heavily, pursed, and bit my bottom lip, and rolled up my window. I got out of my car and closed the door. I looked at her and forced a wry smile. Her demeanor softened as I finally reached her.

"Alas. The noble man emerges. Mine eyes drink and swallow thy countenance til mine cheeks blush and lips part with inebriated smile," she recited.

"That from a book?" I asked.

"No. It's my poor attempt at Shakespearean prose," she grinned wickedly, like an anime character, making her eyes squint like she was staring at the sun, yet I could still, somehow, see them sparkle behind the dark cloak of her heavy lashes.

She clutched my arm and we crossed the parking lot to the main entrance of the mall side by side.

I pulled the glass door open, and Thaleia walked in ahead of me, curtsying as she passed. As expected, the mall was full of high school-aged teens fresh out of school, buzzing around the mall like overactive bees in a hive. The smell of food slapped me across the face mercilessly. So much so, my stomach began to churn, and I immediately felt nauseous.

Thaleia power walked around people with incredible speed and grace while I, on the other hand, struggled to keep up with her.

"Do you already know what you need?" I asked. I didn't really care; I was trying to keep my mind off of being queasy. The words *puke* and *vomit* scrolled from side to side in my mind.

"Not really," she replied. "I need to get my friend something for her birthday, but I have no clue what. I'll know it when I see it, though. It'll just jump out at me. Come on. Keep up."

She dragged me from shop to shop. To me, there was no difference in what anyone sold; each clothing store sold identical items: skinny jeans, blouses, tops, thin sweaters, fake jewelry accessories, handbags, slip-on shoes, heels, crop tops, and graphic tees with nonsensical designs like an upside-down palm tree with a surfboard standing upright next to it. Thaleia browsed through each rack, examined each shelf, and sifted through all islands. When she couldn't find anything, she quickly walked out of the store, my one and only queue to hurry and follow her to the next battleground.

We zigged to a sneaker shop, then zagged to a shop whose key demographic were full-bodied, thick-bottomed, small-wasted, busty women. Here, Thaleia only looked at leggings she thought were cute but ultimately didn't find intriguing enough to purchase.

"It pays to be frugal," she proudly touted.

Thaleia tried her luck at random kiosks, looking at earrings, necklaces, and rings. At another, she sampled different perfumes while the saleswoman, who I assumed most likely worked on commission, showered her with praise. The sales tactic worked; Thaleia bought three perfume brands from the over-flattering clerk

"What?! The woman was trying so hard, I thought it would be nice to reward her effort," she said, justifying her purchases.

Next, I followed Thaleia into a hipster store. The walls were black and lined with purple neon lights that made white shirts glow, and EMD music pounded through the speakers. Its main products were graphic tees and weed paraphernalia. It also sold sexual items. Thaleia had fun making me uncomfortable waving floppy dildos in my face, and explaining how anal beads worked.

We visited a few more places until Thaleia finally decided she would just buy her friend a Victoria's Secret gift card. She tried to get me to go in with her, but I fought vehemently against it. I made up an excuse that I was tired (which I mentally was) and would wait for her at the food court.

"Suit yourself. I'll come find you when I'm done. Stay out of trouble," she said.

We parted at the entrance of the store. I could smell the perfume wafting toward me and left before I could be enfolded in the Heavenly scent.

Following the trail of stores and kiosks Thaleia and I left in our wake, I retraced our steps back to the food court. Before I arrived, a kiosk I had not seen on our voyage caught my eye.

A very tall woman, perhaps in her mid to late forties, sat on a stool scrolling through her phone. Her natural platinum blonde hair hung over her eyes like a wet mop, falling and resting on her square shoulders. Her tight skinny blue jeans were ripped and covered in acrylic paint and ink, as was her black combat boots. The metal bands around her wrists jiggled and jangled as she twirled a cigarette in her free hand, putting it to her lips, then, as if remembering she isn't allowed to smoke indoors, removing it from her lips and twirling it all over again. She wore a loose, plain white shirt (probably because she appeared to be so thin and frail, now that I think about it) with a cream colored drop shoulder duster over it.

Unlike the other kiosks that had standard displays and set-ups, this woman only had the stool, two clothes racks, and a large stand with a sign. One of the racks had only white shirts, the other black shirts, both appeared to only have shirts in one size, extra-large. All the shirts had portraits of celebrities crudely drawn and poorly painted. It was as if she found their pictures online, printed them out and tried to replicate them. The ones she proudly showcased were celebrities that "kind of looks like" Beyoncé or Nicki Minaj, "maybe" Lupita Nyong'o, "possibly" Salma Hayek, "could be" Taylor Swift, "has to be" Harrison Ford, Samuel L. Jackson "right?", "no that's" Denzel Washington, and/or "that's definitely" Eminem… or Adam Sandler as a bleach blonde?

Everyone walked past this kiosk. Their eyes never even drifted her way by accident. It was as if she found the Bermuda Triangle of the mall. I would've passed her, too, if it wasn't for her sign which caught my eye It was a black board that simply read, written in white chalk: BUY MY ART BEFORE I'M DEAD and below that #SWFPHANARTS.

I looked at the sign for an eternity. What did she mean? Buy her art before she's dead? Was she dying? Was she going to kill herself? Questions kept popping up like microwave popcorn. I looked at her, ready to ask her. She finally felt me looking, tore her hawk eyes from her phone and looked at me, a boring expression on her face. I flashed a wry smile. I dropped all the questions and bought two shirts.

I found an empty table in the middle of the food court. The table was made for two people, but I barely fit myself. I sat in the plastic chair, placed the shirts on my lap, and put my elbows on the table, pressing my hands against each other almost in prayer. I looked at the empty chair across from me. I closed my eyes, trying to block out the noise and the smell, attempting to disappear into my thoughts. I felt myself cascading down into the darkness behind my eyelids. No matter how far down I tumbled, I couldn't escape the noise.

I climbed back to the surface of my subconscious and opened my eyes. I expected to find the seat empty; I found Evelyn sitting across from me instead.

Chapter Five

I guess this is as good a time as any to stop and tell you about Evelyn. I'm sure that thus far, in context, you've gathered that she is the love of my life. To me, she is the epitome of the word *woman*. I have no right to go into detail about her personal history (though I doubt she'll ever read this, I could never betray her trust; it's her story, not mine), however, I will say that her life experiences shaped her into the person she is: intelligent, strong willed, funny, fearless, caring, selfless and empathetic. In short: *beautiful*. Her hands have helped mold me and shape me. For that reason, I say she *is* the love of my life. Not *was*. When I see or think of the word *love*, I see Evelyn De Las Cruzes. A fact that time, with all of its destructive power, is powerless to change.

I first saw Evelyn at my orientation for The Company. The conference room was packed to the gills and well underway when she burst through the main double doors. All eyes immediately trained on her.

It was an instant, a single moment in a sea of simultaneously dead and living moments that seemed to stretch ad infinitum. She wore a green bomber jacket over a black and white striped shirt, faded blue ripped jeans that tapered off at her ankles, and black flats. Her shoulder length, curled auburn hair appeared wet, shining under the LED lights. The doors closed behind her slowly and silently. She was acutely conscious of all the eyes drinking her in. She flashed an apologetic smile and nervously tittered, her entire face glowing crimson with embarrassment.

The speaker made a joke that broke the tension and urged her to find a place to sit. I watched her as she picked a random row, sashayed through people, and descended into an open seat, out of sight.

Then the moment was over. It came to a sudden, violent halt, and what remained was a memory permanently etched into my mind, covered in several layers of rosy film.

The orientation proceeded uninterrupted. The speaker covered the typical corporate topics: the history of The Company and its founder (or founders), the benefits and joys of being a The Company employee (access to top quality healthcare insurance, dental insurance, and stocks [all of which - they fail to mention, by the way - require disposable income, of which people working for minimum wage, whom for which every day is a perpetual battle to make ends meet due to the ever increasing cost of living, no matter how much the minimum wage rate is raised, cannot afford to invest in] and tutorial videos).

Tutorials and training videos are my favorite part of orientation. No matter what decade they're made, these videos are the most poorly scripted, abominably acted, and visually inept pieces of film ever produced.

Perhaps the most heinous act perpetrated by these training videos is that it - whether purposefully and/or naively - actively misrepresented the true nature of humanity. The employees were always "more than happy to help," and did so with all the patience and personality of a Speak and Spell. The often flummoxed customers were not soaked in the redolence of smug entitlement and apathy; quite the contrary, they were always delightful, appreciative, and grateful for the service. The artificiality was enough to make me want to retch.

After the speaker and his guests finished their presentations, we were paired with partners and given a task to complete within a set time limit. Whoever finished their assignment quickly and efficiently (meaning absolutely no errors) would receive a prize, like a plastic bottle opener that doubles as a pizza cutter that has The Company's logo printed on it. You know, something that is an absolute necessity.

Everyone found the person they were supposed to be with. As luck (or fate) would have it, I was paired with none other than Evelyn. She smiled as she approached me, and I tried my best to keep cool.

"Are you ——— ?" She asked.

Great! I thought. *Here's your chance to make a good first impression. Don't say anything goofy like* "That's my name, don't wear it out," *say something suave like* "I'm whoever you want me to be, beautiful."

However, as I sifted through other comebacks in my mental rolodex, I suddenly became aware that too much time had passed, and I still had not provided an answer.

"Uh... yeah?" I was so panicked, I phrased my response as a question.

"Are you sure?" she quipped, her right brow raised, her lip curled in a slight smile.

Okay, idiot. Say yes and sound confident!

"... yeah?"

Damn it!

She laughed.

"Evie," she said, pointing to her name tag obliquely stuck to the chest pocket of her bomber jacket. Unlike everyone else who simply printed their name in black permanent marker, Evie drew hers with what appeared to be multiple pens of unusual colors. It looked like a mix of calligraphy and street art. Perched above the "i" was a giant butterfly.

She offered her hand to me. I looked at it as if it were some mystic being calling out to me from within a burning bush.

Shake her hand!

I took her hand in mine and shook it. It was soft yet firm, a trait I assume you'd find in a professional femme fatale assassin.

"Nice to meet you... Evie," I managed to say. That was the first time her name on my lips sent a numbing warmth through my body.

"That's my name, don't wear it out!" she said with glee.

The speaker went through the terms of engagement once more before firing off the proverbial starter pistol, sending the room into a buzzing frenzy of excited chatter. Evie wasted no time delegating our tasks. Once the work was divided, we focused on our assigned labor. After a few minutes of assembly, I became overwhelmed by the selfish desire to pull Evie into a conversation, just to hear her speak; the silence was deafening.

The last thing this goddess wants is to hear your pathetic voice.

"What kind of name is ———— ?" she asked, speaking without provocation, as if some invisible force heard my silent pleas. To be sure she was addressing me, I raised my eyes and met her emerald gaze. I blushed like a virgin.

"I have no clue," I admitted. "My mother chose it for me. I assume she thought it would be funny."

"Funny? How?" she inquired.

"I assume she wanted to be a stand-up comedian," I answered, as I inserted a piece of metal into another metal piece until they both clicked.

"But... I don't get it," she said flatly.

"That's why she's a Tax Attorney. She can tell all the bad jokes she wants and charge her audience by the hour."

Evie burst into a sudden fit of laughter.

"Okay," she snorted. "Now I get it." She wiped away tears from the corners of her eyes. I couldn't believe I just made this woman laugh.

"So, what's your deal? How'd you land in this fresh form of Hell Lucifer himself couldn't dream up?" she asked.

"Not a harrowing tale, I'm afraid. I forwent college but found, believe it or not, that my landlord still wanted me to pay to continue sleeping in my apartment," I joked. "Did you know that Publix doesn't just give food away?" I answered.

She laughed again, triggering my dopamine. I was becoming addicted to her laugh. I found myself encouraged to speak further.

"How about you?" I asked her.

Her laughter quickly subsided, and her shoulders slumped slightly. A dark shadow fell over her eyes as she considered the question silently.

"Same," she said softly. "Failed."

Make her laugh!

No words would come. She looked up at me and smiled.

Before I knew it we were done putting together the contraption we were assigned. Not only were we done, but we were the first to finish. Worse, the assembly was impeccably done. We won the prize: a rape whistle that also doubled as a laser pointer... with The Company's logo printed on it.

The speaker asked everyone to give us a round of applause and they responded with a less than rousing smattering as he handed us our prize. Evie smiled wryly and shook her head. She leaned over to me.

"I guess we're a couple of failures, huh?" She whispered.

"I guess so," I smirked.

"There is a silver lining to that, you know."

"You think so?"

"Well, yeah," she exclaimed matter-of-factly. "Failures excel at mediocrity."

We stood on stage, a couple of court jesters, receiving a standing ovation from a group of clapping mechanical monkey's.

* * *

We were given a break for lunch and escorted to the lavish lunchroom. Lunch in Babylon was nothing like lunch in the Plantation. It was organized like a Japanese hibachi restaurant, several tables arranged around a personal chef who made meals on the spot. Whatever you wanted, they had the ingredients to whip it up. Meatballs subs, personal pan pizzas, fresh mac n cheese, sushi, poke bowls, you name it.

The mechanical monkeys ran to these tables, clattering excitedly. I decided to get my meal from one of the abandoned buffet lines.

The outside doors led to a balcony that overlooked a courtyard with three large fountains surrounded by a paved walkway and trees that seemed out of place in Florida. On one side were concrete tables ergonomically designed for lunch.

A group of suits occupied these tables, deep in serious conversation. On the other side were some empty tables. I made my way toward them and then stopped cold.

I didn't notice right away, but sitting at the last table was Evie. She had her head down, scribbling in a notebook, her plate of food pushed away from her, barely touched. Smoke from a lit cigarette between her fingers twirled into the air and vanished. I commanded my body to turn quickly and go back inside but before I could move, she looked up at me and smiled. She tucked the cigarette between her lips and waved me over. I waltzed over to her and as I got nearer, she closed the book and set the pen down on the cover.

"Quite a show in there, huh?" she said.

"Yeah," I chortled.

"You don't mind cigarette smoke do you?"

"Not at all," I lied, but I would've let her put that cigarette out on my pupil if she'd asked. She motioned for me to take a seat. I put my food down and sat down across from her. She examined my plate.

"Turkey sandwich and plain chips?" She inventoried. "You're a simple guy, aren't you?"

"You think so?" I shrugged my shoulders, doing my best to be cool while struggling to unravel the cellophane around the sandwich.

She took a long drag from her cigarette, held the smoke in her lungs, and then exhaled. One of the suits from the other table started to purposely cough. Evelyn's eyes flashed in his direction.

"You alright, man?" she called out to him.

The suit, clearly caught by surprise not expecting her to address him directly, stammered.

"I'm good. I'm good," he tried to play it off.

"You sure? I can put out the cigarette if you want. Just ask. You don't have to do that passive aggressive, coughing shit. Bitches do that. Are you a bitch?"

"No," the suit said flat out.

"So, I can finish my cigarette?"

"Yeah, yeah. Of course. Please."

"Thank you," she smiled.

She went on, continuing to smoke. The suits gathered their trays and important documents, got up and walked back into the lunchroom as she exhaled an exaggerated amount of smoke. She watched them leave, savoring the dirty looks they tossed her way. Once they were inside, she scoffed.

"Idiots," she said, not wanting to give much energy to the swift exchange. "Sorry you had to see that, but dicks like that really make my blood hot."

"The problem is theirs, not yours," I said.

"Nah, it's mine. I don't even like cigarettes. It's a bad habit I picked up in Art School. Doesn't it make me look like a douchebag art student?" she said, striking several poses with the cigarette. I laughed.

"You kind of look like Anna Karina," I blurted out.

"Who's that?"

"Oh, she's...," I blushed. "This... French actress. Well, Danish and French. She was in a lot of Jean-Luc Godard films. You ever heard of a movie called *A Band Apart*, or *A Woman is A Woman*, or *My life to Live?*"

I rattled off.

A smile creeped on to Evie's lips as she slowly shook her head.

"*Pierrot... Le Fou?*" I said softly. I took a bite of my sandwich.

"Ah... you're a film douche," she chuckled. "That's cool! You'll have to show me one of these movies with this French Danish actress I look like."

"Yeah, sure, anytime," I stammered.

Evie flashed another smile. She stubbed out the cigarette on the bench and tossed the butt over the balcony. She then opened her book, took the pen back in her hand and returned to what she was doing. Looks like she was drawing sketches. I sat in silence and watched her work. She was precise and surgical. She used a multicolor pen and didn't make any mistakes. After a while, she began to speak; I guess she could feel my eyes on her.

"What do you think?" she asked.

"About?"

She put the pen down and slid the book over to me. I reached out to grab the sketchbook.

"Don't get any mayo or mustard on that or I will kill you," she threatened. I immediately pulled back and wiped my hands on my jeans. She laughed.

"I'm kidding!"

I looked at what she was working on. It was a full page sketch parodying the tutorial videos from the orientation. A customer service rep and a customer were eating each other politely. She titled it: *A Dialogue Between Two* Real *People* (she italicized the word "Real").

I laughed so hard, Sprite shot out of my nose. She quickly snatched her book back before I messed it up and burst into laughter.

"That bad, huh?" she said.

"Are you kidding! It's great!" I exclaimed, wiping the liquids and mucus from my face and jeans with a thin napkin. "You just did this?"

She blushed crimson and her smile stretched from ear to ear.

"Yeah, it's nothing. It's really easy when you're inspired, you know," she said, motioning to the building and the clapping monkey's inside.

"You really are an artist!"

No sooner did I say that, the smile evaporated from her lips. She opened the book and started going over the lines with a different color from her pen, shading here, and cross hatching there.

"The school I went to didn't think so. So much so, they failed me… right out of school," she admitted quietly.

I stayed silent; I'm sure there was nothing I could say to heal that scar. She took a beat, looked up and smiled with all of her teeth.

"That's okay! These schools, they don't make sense. They teach you one thing like there is no clear definition of art, art is often subjective," she imitated in a proper, monotone voice. "Then they turn around and tell you that what you create with your own hands and your mind's eye isn't. They're clashing ideals!"

She closed her book and reached into her bag for another cigarette.

"I'm sorry. It's just frustrating you know," she puts the cigarette to her lips and lights it. "You spend your childhood and adolescence in school unable to be creative. Then you pay to go to a school to gain that freedom and end up feeling more restrained. Explain that shit to me," she took a long drag and exhaled.

"Guess that's still a sore subject for me," she chuckled. "How about you? You failed out of college you said?"

"Oh, no. I didn't fail. I was doing very well actually. High marks even," I began.

"So, then what happened?" she asked.

"I don't know how to explain," I admitted.

Her eyes pierced mine, patiently waiting for me to explain, and not letting me leave until I did.

"Try."

I thought about it for a moment.

"It happened in the middle of my final semester of college. I was in my dorm, cramming for a test that was worth 15% of my final grade. I was racking my brain, taking notes, trying to absorb all this information. Then something happened. I went catatonic."

"Figuratively?" she asked.

"No," I corrected. "Literally, catatonic. Not for a long-time mind you. Just long enough to notice. I looked at the work before me, highlights of varied colors, notes in margins, books open, and I thought to myself 'Why am I doing this?' I was studying astronomy. Astronomy, like I was trying to be the next Carl Sagan or Neil deGrasse Tyson or something. Not because I was interested in the subject purely for educational purposes, but because it was required of me in order to pass and obtain my degree. If it weren't required, would I have taken it? Then I thought… 'what's the point?'"

I stopped for a second and took a sip of my drink. Evie took a drag of her cigarette and tapped the dangling ash onto the floor. I continued.

"There was none. I had no such aspirations. If I wanted to be an erudite, I could go to a library and discipline myself. School didn't feel like it was about education for the sake of education. I mean, it is, but it isn't its primary purpose. It is the death of individuality. Group thought. There-is-one-way-to-learn kind of thought. It's structured to cripple creativity and critical thinking. Chances are if I would've gone all the way and got my bachelors, I wouldn't know what to do with it. I was an English Major. Why? I never understood Chaucer or the importance of Beowulf. T.S. Eliot confuses the hell out of me. What the hell do I do with an English Major?"

She was listening to every word, nodding along as I tergiversated.

"That's when I understood I was only in school because that was the next step. We're born, and depending on where we're born, we go to elementary school, then middle school, then high school, the next step is college, then you get that career you went to college to get. By 22, 23 years old, we're expected to know what we'll be doing the rest of our lives. That's insane! I sat there, with the books open, highlighted, and annotated notes, and I came to the conclusion that I didn't want to do this anymore. Once I came to that realization, I got up from my desk, packed up my belongings, bid my roommates farewell, and came back home."

I finished my rambling and took another sip of my drink. Evie sat with my words for a few minutes, smoking in silence. Finally, she looked at me and smirked.

"That's you not knowing how to explain it?" she said.

"Never had to give it much thought," I said, my cheeks hot with embarrassment. When I opened my mouth I didn't expect for all of that to come out. "Did my mad rambling make any sense?"

"You didn't know what you wanted to do, but you knew whatever it was, it wasn't what you were doing... is that it?"

"Basically, yeah."

"So, then, what *do* you want to do?"

"Nothing."

She was taken aback by my quick answer.

"Nothing? You have to want to do *something*. You like movies, right? Why not do something with that?"

"I also love reading manga but I'm no Akira Toriyama," I joked. "I love film, yeah, but I have no desire to do anything that has to do with film. Not directing, not acting, not screenwriting, not even film critique. I just want to sit back and enjoy it."

"You're telling me that all you're going to do for the rest of your life is work here?" she asked.

"I hope not, but at the same time, who's to say? All I know for sure is that I have no delusions of a reality that doesn't exist. I don't know if people are born with purpose or not. I can't say for sure whether we choose our purpose based on our experience in life. Some people know what they want to do from an early age, and they resign their life to its pursuit. That's great. It really is. But, just like some people realize their purpose early or late in some cases, it's also true some people don't, for whatever reason. Want proof? Take a look inside," I motioned toward the people inside the cafeteria cheering the chef on as he flipped a shrimp into his pocket.

I blathered on.

"I am a person who understands I will not make an impact on this world in the way others have, others who are in textbooks, others who changed their fields of study. I am just an insignificant speck of space ash catapulting through space. And I'm fine with it."

Christ, man. Shut up.

Evie's curious eyes studied me. I expected to see revulsion in her eyes. I was surprised to find they were brimming with curiosity.

"So, you're purposeless?" The words came out of her mouth as if she were choosing each one carefully.

"Never thought about it that way... but I guess so. Yeah."

Again, she took a small drag of her cigarette, held the smoke in her lungs, then exhaled deliberately.

"And do you think," she began slowly, her eyes peering through the smoke, "you can live a happy and fulfilling life without a purpose?"

I finished what remained of my drink and piled all the trash onto the lunch tray, preparing to throw it all in the garbage.

"I have no idea," I responded. "But this is a decision I made, and I'm content with it. I can still enjoy what life has to offer: blue skies, fall breezes, cinema and music, amazing food, incredible artwork."

She blushed and quickly regained her composure. "Well, forgive me if I don't agree with your view. This," she held her notebook up, "this here, gives my life meaning. I don't know who I am without it. If I ever give this up for *this life*, a life of mindlessly tinkering away for someone else's benefit, that's the day I die." (I will remind her of this later on and she won't remember having ever said this).

I grabbed my tray and stood up from the table.

"Good," I said. "Depriving the world of experiencing your talent would be a real shame. See you inside, partner."

"You're leaving already?" She asked. "We have plenty of time before our break is up. I'd like to show you other things I've been working on. If you're interested?"

I smiled. I could not believe this woman actually wanted me to stick around.

"Of course, I'm interested!" I exclaimed, sitting back down.

She got up from her side of the table, came over to my side, sat down next to me and got close. My heart raced. She opened her book from the beginning and started thumbing through it, speaking excitedly about pieces she was working on and the stories behind them, and I was more than happy to sit and listen.

* * *

The orientation was over. The sun was already descending behind Babylon, leaving the sky a beautiful mix of bronze, violet, and purple. Everyone poured out of the building and rushed to the parking garages, desperate to scurry off into their lives. I sat on a bench on the sidewalk, waiting for the congestion to dissipate. Evie came out of the building, noticed me sitting there and came over.

"Waiting for a ride?" She asked.

"Nah. Just waiting," I responded, motioning to the crowd.

"Oh, ok," she said. Her tone sounded somewhat disappointed or maybe I was imagining it. She came to the bench and sat next to me. "That's actually a good idea. Mind if I wait here with you?"

What the hell is going on?

"Not at all."

I slid over and made room for her. She sat next to me and sighed. We shared a solid moment of silence.

"Got any plans tonight?" she asked.

"Not really," I said. "Just going back to my apartment. Heat up some leftovers. See what movie is playing on TV."

"Not gonna lie, that sounds kinda sad," she said.

"Really?" I asked, genuinely bemused.

"I'm heading to Five Guys - I've been craving their seasoned fries. Want to join me? I don't like eating alone; feels like I'm on display."

"Oh, I don't know-"

I began to stammer but I caught myself and stopped. I looked into her shimmering eyes and suddenly saw our entire relationship play before me:

We'll go to dinner; we'll talk and laugh and learn more about each other. How she comes from a large Puerto Rican family, five siblings of which she is the middle child. We'll finish eating, walk to our cars and she'll tease me about how I insisted on paying because I conform to traditional gender roles. We'll stand in between our vehicles and talk the entire night, and won't notice the parking lot of the plaza is completely empty. We'll exchange numbers and I'll watch as she gets in her car, starts it, blasts Bone Thugs N Harmony, reverses out of the parking lot, waves at me and drives off honking the horn. I'll get home and pace back and forth in the kitchen, wondering if I should send her a text message thanking her for inviting me out to dinner, and just when I've worked up enough courage to do it, I receive a message from her saying she had a great time, and see you tomorrow. Her message leaves me floating in space, over and beyond the moon. We'll see each other on our first official workday at the Plantation and find excuses to work together, or engage in playful competition, who can finish kits the fastest and without error, both categories she excelled

78

at marvelously. Soon after, we'd be eating lunch together every day where she would continue to show me new drawings she was working on, toying with the idea of canvas paintings inspired by painters like J.M.W Turner and Théodore Géricault. I would urge her to go for it, and feeling confident, she would invite me to go shopping with her for art supplies. She did all of her homework. Told me the difference between painting with acrylic and oil. How during the Pre-Raphaelite era, artists would paint the canvas with white or yellow paint to make the image bright. Afterward, I'd invite her to the movie theater. I'd wait for her at the entrance of the Parthenon anxiously, trying not to show my irritation when she arrives three minutes before the showing and then insists we make the long line at concessions. We'll find our seats as the last trailer finishes (some superhero movie), and I'll watch as her eyes light up when Hayao Miyazaki's *Nausicaä of the Valley of the Wind* comes on the big screen, and when Nausicaä asks the injured ohmu for forgiveness through mournful tears, Evie clutches my arm and wipes tears from her red cheeks. When we leave the theatre we run to her car to avoid the rain, but it's no use, we're both soaked. On the way to my apartment, she'll talk excitedly about how Studio Ghibli is lightyears ahead of Disney and won't stop until we park in the parking lot. When I ponder out-loud if it's because of how Japanese cinema challenges its children's imagination instead of spoon-feeding it, she'll kiss me for the first time and send my mind reeling. Soon after we'd never be apart. Some weekends, when we weren't scheduled to work, we'd get up early and go to the park. She'd teach me how to play tennis (and show off her mean back hand and deadly spin) and I'd teach her how to sink a free throw touching nothing but nylon. Other times, we'd go to the public pool, race each other in the swimming lanes and dare each other to jump off the high dive. I'd go first, do a flip, trying to show off, and land flat on my back. I'd scream and cry underwater but emerge with a victorious smile on my face, while she snorts and laughs at my visible pain. She'd go next and lose her top, her breasts exposed for everyone to see. She'd adjust them immediately and rush out of the water to her towel, her face blushed beet red. I laugh and she punches me in the stomach and doesn't talk to me until we get back to my apartment to shower and wash the chlorine from our skin and hair. She joins me in the shower, and we wash each other. We get out of the shower, fall in bed, and make love for the first time. It is beyond description. Afterward I'm in the kitchen making us coffee. I look up and watch her, memorizing every curve on her naked body as she lays on her stomach, smokes a cigarette, and sketches in her sketchbook, her skin glowing in the afternoon light. The scene is straight out of a French New Wave film. After her cigarette, she takes a long nap, and I go out to buy groceries to make her dinner. After dinner, we snuggle under a blanket on the couch and watch *Vivre Sa Vie*. She's in awe of Anna Karina but disagrees that she looks anything like her. We'd be happy like this for some time; however, the happiness will eventually ebb. After years of the same, I'd start to notice subtle changes. She'd no longer smoke, substituting a cigarette for a clicking pen she could click anytime she felt anxious. She'd start taking her lunch period with other co-workers and take her job much more seriously. I'd take her to the movies and she'd fall asleep halfway through. I'd invite her out to dinner, or to the beach, or the park and she would cancel our dates. She wouldn't even draw anymore, and when I asked her about her plans to go to Ringling, she'd snap at me about childish dreams and real life. I know the end is coming, but I love her, and I want to give her the space she seemingly needs to grow. Soon after, she'd get promoted and leave the clean room. We'd no longer have the same schedule so we'd see each other less, and when we did see each other, no matter how close we'd be, there would continue to be an ever widening gulf between us. I'd hold on for as long as I can. Then one day, after an afternoon of window shopping at the mall, we will sit down in the food court. As I mull over what to have for lunch, she'll tell me that our relationship is over. She'll speak at length, but when she says *"There's someone else. It's over,"* I'll feel the ground beneath me shake violently, as if the ground opened up and the flames of hell swallow me. She'll burst into tears. Her green army jacket opened, and underneath a black and white striped shirt. Same clothes she wore when I first saw her all those years back. Her hair, brushed back and tied into a tight ponytail, slick and wet from the rain. The mall, crowded with people trying to find refuge from a storm that had enveloped the sky. Thunder strikes. The entire mall shakes. Or it's the sound of my world crumbling. I won't be able to tell. Evelyn's bulbous eyes will be glassy and swollen with tears.

"Well?" She'll say, crossing her arms and folding her right leg over her left.

I'll lean back and fold my arms across my chest. My head sinks between my shoulders, and my chin digs into my collar bone. I am overcome by nausea. My face contorts with bewilderment. For a second, I don't recognize her. Then it all comes flooding back.

"Did you feel that?" I ask her.

She'll scoff. A scoff heavy with anxiety, annoyance, and disgust. Her eyes no longer retain water and release a few tears from the corners of her eyes. She looks up and wiped them both away with her thumb before they can reach her chin. She shrugs her shoulders.

"Hear what?" She asks. Her voice sounds like it's drowning.

I sense her tone. She doesn't have the patience for my nonsense, so I put it aside. I don't want to say anything that will bring the conversation to an end. I prefer to spontaneously combust than continue to move forward.

"Never mind," I say.

I want to share silence with her, but she refuses.

"Well?" She repeats again.

I open my mouth, but all of the words are trapped in my throat. I shake my head slowly and unfurl my hands on the table as if I am examining them.

"Did you sleep with him?" I have many questions swirling around in my mind; that's the first to squeeze through. I ask it, but I don't want the answer.

She frowns. "Does it really matter?"

Knowing whether the other man touched her, kissed her, penetrated her, would not palliate the pain.

"No," I say.

Again, I extend a moment of silence to her. Again, she passes.

"He said he's going to put me in a house, we're going to travel, see the world...," She pauses, taking a moment before plunging the final dagger. "He's going to take care of me."

The words stab at my ears. The words funneled into my head and disappeared into the depth of my chest. She'd been giving me pieces to a puzzle that suddenly start to form a picture.

"And I can't," I finish the sentence for her.

Evelyn's lips part to speak, but whatever words were born in her mind, perish on her tongue. She takes a pen out of her purse and begins to click the top.

"Do you love him?" I ask her.

Her eyes widen. She tears her eyes away from mine and stares at the floor. The floodgates are collapsing; tears cascade down her cheek. She refuses to wipe them away as they collect at the tip of her chin and fall to the floor. The mall patrons are too wrapped up in their own lives to notice the dark clouds hovering over us.

"I don't know," she says, her voice small.

"Do you love me?" I ask. I have to.

"Of course I do." She says, sharply. She means it.

"But I can't take care of you," I say the words, the puzzle pieces all falling into place. She nods slightly and my chest caves. I can feel my heart disintegrating. I nod my head slowly and purse my lips trying to resist screaming from the agonizing pain. After a long moment of silence, I sigh.

"Okay," I finally say.

"Okay?" She echoes, stunned.

"Okay. I understand. It makes sense," I confirm.

"That's it?" Evelyn is flabbergasted.

"What else is there? I love you. You love me. But you want to be taken care of. You want to see the world. You want a life that I can't provide. But he can. And if that's what makes you happy - and I want your happiness - the logical conclusion *is this*... isn't it?"

Evelyn looks at me expecting me to go on. Instead, she gives me a confirming nod.

"Then... that's it," I punctuate.

"You're not angry? Distraught? Sad?" She'll ask.

My eyes sting, and the nausea gives way to full blown *sick*, but I can't fall apart. Not in front of her. I inhale air through my nose and let it out slowly, regaining control of my faculties.

"Does it really matter?" I say, coldly.

Evelyn is taken aback by my frigid callousness. More tears stream down her cheeks. She wipes them away with the back of her hand and dries her hand on her jeans. She sniffles, and trembles, fighting to keep herself together. We finally share a silence.

She collects her purse and stands up. I remain as still as stone. I simply stare at the empty chair as if she's still there. Evelyn looks down at me as she slings the strap of her purse over her shoulder. She clears her throat.

"Okay then... I guess that's it."

I won't respond. My eyes are blank, sunken in shadows. I grind my teeth. My jaws twitched madly.

Keep it together.

"I got promoted this morning," she speaks to the air. "I'll be heading to Babylon. Purchasing and Logistics department. I start tomorrow."

I remain motionless. I dare not move an inch, trying to keep myself from hurling.

"So... this may be the last time we see each other," She finishes her thought.

Evelyn waits for me to say something, anything, one last time, but I won't. Her shoulders slump.

"Goodbye."

She walks away, leaving behind her Heavenly scent. My eyes well with tears. I close my eyes and bury my face in my trembling hands.

* * *

I saw all of this in her eyes as we sat on the bench at the end of that first day of orientation.

"Well," she said. "You hungry, partner?"

"Yeah..." I smiled. "I could eat."

Chapter Six

"You sleeping?"

Thaleia put her hand on my shoulder and nudged me slightly. I opened my eyes and looked up at her, half expecting someone else.

"Sorry I took so long," she said, shifting her shopping bags from one hand to the other, leaving the other free to adjust her purse strap. "Stopped in Books Galore. I always lose track of time in there."

I scanned the food court quickly; all was as it was before. The chair across from me remained empty.

"You, okay?" Thaleia asked, a hint of concern in her voice.

"Yeah," I began. I felt heavy with lethargy, as if waking up from a long nap. "I was just... thinking..."

"That I owe you dinner?" She finished the sentence with a smile.

I looked at my watch. It was already 6:30 p.m. The sun was descending lower, taking the blue sky with it. She was right; I was suddenly struck with hunger. I looked up at her and smiled slightly.

"I could eat," I said.

"The correct answer is 'You do not owe me anything m'lady, but I would be a damnable fool to deny such a noble request,'" she mocked.

"That's what I meant," I said.

"Yeah, I bet. Come on, Droopy," she commanded. She pulled me up out of the chair and handed me the entire load of shopping bags. "There's a small Thai place not too far from here that's really good.

You'll love it."

She charted a path out of the heart of the food court and made her way to the exit, and I followed close behind.

She wasn't lying. The Thai restaurant was five minutes away from the mall. It was in a small obscure shopping center tucked between a Christian music store and a store that sold handmade beaded bracelets and necklaces. Unlike the surrounding stores, the restaurant had no sign outside facing the main road. It had one solid red door and two large windows, one on each side of the door, with red curtains so thick it made it difficult to see its interior layout. In fact, the restaurant was so small, the parking area was located behind the building.

I could smell the food from outside the back door entrance. Unlike the food from the mall that suffocated me and made me ill, this smell was reposeful.

The moment we stepped inside, we were immediately greeted by the Thai family who ran the establishment: a young woman, an older man, and a stout woman. The young woman helmed the cash register and took incoming phone orders. The older man was the cook. He stood at the high bar, chopping assorted fruits, vegetables, poultry, and red meat, while the stout woman waited on customers and bussed tables.

The stout woman stopped cleaning when she saw Thaleia waiting by the register. She beamed and made her way to us. The stout woman took Thaleia's hands into her own and greeted her as if she were her own flesh and blood. Then she turned to me and did the same, exclaiming excitedly.

She grabbed a few menus and guided us through the restaurant. The walls were dark red and lined with wooden wainscoting. Warm sky lantern lamps hung above each table. The walls were adorned with frames of Thai-themed paintings, and soft jazz filtered from hidden speakers in the ceiling. Even though the curtains from the large windows were thick, they were still thin enough to see the main road outside. The setting was effortlessly intimate.

There were a few customers scattered around the restaurant: a couple in the front corner by the main entrance who were deep in a private conversation, a trio of college-aged young men feasting on their meal and talking amongst themselves, and an older gentleman sitting alone near the high bar, reading a newspaper and sipping a glass of wine.

We arrived at a table for four. The middle of the room was supported by a wooden divider that stretched from the floor to the ceiling. Since most of the customers (except for the older gentleman) were on the other side of the partition, it felt like Thaleia and I had the entire restaurant to ourselves. As we took our seats, the stout woman asked if we wanted anything to drink.

"Two Thai iced teas, please," Thaleia requested.

The stout woman exclaimed gleefully and bowed her head slightly before turning on her heel and going off to retrieve the drinks. Thaleia looked at me and flashed a wide smile.

"Have you ever had Thai tea before?" she asked me.

"No, never. What's in it?"

"There are different ways to make it. Here, it's made with strongly brewed black tea, sugar, and condensed milk. Other places substitute the condensed milk with actual milk," she explained.

"Sounds good."

"Good doesn't even begin to describe it. It's *orgasmic*. It's my favorite drink. It'll simultaneously warm you up and leave you rejuvenated like standing under a waterfall or diving into spring water in the dog days of August. Putting it in the same category as Pepsi and Miller Light is downright blasphemous."

The stout woman returned, balancing a round plastic tray with two glasses filled with ice, a small white porcelain jug, and a large stainless-steel kettle. She placed them on the glass tabletop along with two plastic straws. She then took the kettle and poured black tea into the cups.

"Watch this," Thaleia said.

The stout woman smiled. She moved poetically, lifting the white jug and pouring the condensed milk into the cup. The moment the milk mixed with the black tea; the black tea turned orange. The stout woman performed the same ritual with my cup. When she was finished, she placed the jug on the table.

"Let me know when you are ready to order," she said. Her words were as gentle as a fine morning mist in spring.

"Oh, I already know," Thaleia said proudly. "I'll have the Jumbo Shrimp in red curry, and he'll have the boneless duck in panang curry."

I looked at Thaleia impressed, but still with concern on my face.

"Trust me," she said with a wink.

The stout woman giggled as she took the menus back and tucked them under her arms. She bowed her head again and left to tend to the other customers. Thaleia and I turned our attention to the Thai tea. She loudly sucked her teeth.

"You're so lucky. I wish I could go back to the first time I tasted Thai tea. It changed my life," Thaleia proclaimed.

I inserted my straw into the cup, swirling the liquid around until the milk and the tea were mixed, and took my first sip. The tea hit my tongue. Thaleia was right; the taste was incredible. I looked at Thaleia wide eyed. She smiled back.

"You've been baptized, my son," she joked, blessing me with the sign of the cross. She put the straw in her drink, mixed it, and took her sip. Her eyes rolled back in her head as she moaned with pleasure.

We shared a brief silence.

"*Thank you for treating me to dinner, Tally,*" Thaleia said in a low-toned voice, imitating mine. "Oh no. Please, it's my pleasure. *You're so smart, and beautiful, and generous. Oh, you flatter me, sir. You're an Angel. An*

88

Angel really? *The sun pales in your brilliance*. Oh, stop it."

I chuckled. "Okay I get it. Thank you."

"And?" Thaleia said, her hand motioning for me to continue.

"You're so smart and beautiful," I recited.

"And generous," she reminded me.

"Right, sorry. You're so smart, beautiful, and generous. You're an Angel. A goddess. The sun pales in your brilliance."

"Oh, I didn't tell you to improvise, but 'goddess' yeah I'll take it. Thank you!" She sipped her Thai tea and we shared another silence.

"Speaking of generous," she suddenly remembered. She reached into her purse and took out a small paperback book. She placed it on the table and slid it over to me. It had a black cover with a red moon, and the silhouette of a cat in front of it. The title was in bold white font. It read: *Kafka on the Shore* by Haruki Murakami.

"A book?" I remarked.

"Yeah. My way of saying thank you for driving me around today," she said. "Plus, you told me you haven't read a book in a while and well… that just made my soul cry."

I took the book in my hands and flipped through it before turning it over and scanning over the blurb.

"What's it about?" I asked.

"Storms," she said with a playful smile.

"Storms?"

"Have you ever walked out into a storm?" She asked me.

"Never occurred to me to do that, no," I answered.

"Murakami wrote…," she paused. "You know what, you'll find out."

"Just give me an excerpt," I pleaded.

Thaleia shook her head.

"You'll have to read it to find out. All I will say is that he's a master of magical realism. I swear every time I read his novels I just want to have a drink alone in a bar listening to vinyl Jazz records, hoping it rains frogs. This was the first book of his that I read. The moment I opened the book, I was swept away. But I don't want to hype it up too much. I hope you like it. And if you don't… at least it wouldn't be a waste of time."

"I don't know what to say… thank you," I said.

"Thank me when you get to the end," she quipped with a smile.

"I will."

Again, we shared a silence as we both slurped and savored our Thai teas.

"Wow, you're great at small talk," she remarked, sarcastically.

"Sorry, I'm just enjoying this drink, and admiring this place. I've lived here all my life, and I've never been here."

"You're kidding? The moment I moved here, I drove all around this town. I got lost a few times, but eventually found my way. My father used to say, sometimes you have to get lost in order to find the right path."

"And that works?" I asked.

"I found this place," she said with a smile.

"Then your father's philosophy was sound."

"My father," she said with a soft grin, "he was Japanese. From Okinawa. He grew up reading all types of books, all genres, Sci-Fi, fantasy, pulp fiction, philosophy, you name it. He always had a book with him. He said, 'always carry a book with you, when you find yourself with down time, whip it out and learn something.' He is the one who named me, actually. Guess where he got my name from?"

"A book?" I said.

Thaleia nodded her head and grinned.

"Yeah, when my mother found out she was pregnant with me, my parents were in the midst of a turbulent time in their life. My mother was Black. Not only was she Black, she was also Black *American*, so my father's family really didn't welcome her. They didn't openly mistreat her, they were really tolerable when she was around, but behind closed doors, they berated my father for tainting the family. They were very traditional. My father wasn't."

"Did they disown him?"

"No. They loved my father, but my father loved my mother deeply. She was a great woman, and she brought out the best in him, so my father disowned himself, so to speak. His family blamed my mother, and things were somewhat hectic. When she found out she was pregnant with me, it brought them much-needed joy. That's how my father explained the origins of my name to me. When it came time to name me, he found the name Thaleia, spelled T-H-A-L-E-I- A. He said the name came from Greek Mythology, and Thaleia was a muse of Comedy and Bucolic poetry. And in some translations, the name also means *Joyous*. So that's what he named me."

"I'd bet his family were not happy about that," I said.

"That would be a good wager. Being traditional I think they wanted him to name me something like *Akari*, *Fumiko*, *Yui*, or something, which to be honest, I would've been okay with."

We both sipped more tea, nearly finishing.

"You think our names play a part in who we become?" I asked her.

She playfully sipped on her straw, her upper lip flapping up and down like a fish.

"You don't?" she finally said. "I've done my best to live up to my name. Every time I find myself in a depressing situation or fretting over things I have no control over, I remember my name and do whatever it takes to find joy. Since we only get one chance to experience life, it doesn't make sense to deny yourself a full existence. You're not alive if you're not living. Don't you think?"

"Yeah, " I said. The conversation was starting to veer into an all too familiar area. I tried to turn the conversation into another lane. "So, you're from Japan?"

"Not really. I mean I was born there, but I don't remember ever living there. My mother was a Marine, so we moved around a lot. I mostly remember living in Germany, then South Korea, *which* was fun, but my favorite was Hawaii. You hear how beautiful it is there, but until you see it with your own eyes, you can never really know. You ever been?"

"I've never been anywhere," I scoffed. "I was born in Loblolly Pines and I'll die in Loblolly Pines, I'm sure."

"How do you know?"

I looked up at Thaleia. I wasn't expecting that question.

"What do you mean?" I asked.

"How do you know you'll die here?" She repeated.

"I guess, I don't know really, but, based on my current situation, I'd say it was likely."

"Why?" she pressed.

Why?

Tell her. Tell her you're thirty years old and you've got nothing going on. You work at a dead-end job. You live in a dreadful box of an apartment. You barely have two nickels to rub together. You're a failure. Everyone knows you're a failure. Useless. Waste of life. You lack the courage to live purposefully. Tell her. The world doesn't exist for you. You're in a room with no windows or doors. No escape. You're not a small fish in a vast ocean. You're a small fish on dry land flopping around pathetically in a tiny puddle on a blistering hot day, and the water is rapidly drying up.

"I don't know," I finally answered, shrugging my shoulders.

Thaleia examined my demeanor. I can tell she was deciding whether to continue to press the issue or change the topic. I hoped for the latter.

"How do you want to die?" she asked.

I looked around the restaurant. The couple in the quiet corner had already paid and left. The young men were finishing all the bits and pieces on their plates. The old man was still next to the bar, reading and sipping his wine.

"I don't... know. I didn't know it was a choice."

"Do you think about death?" she asked.

"Well, yeah, but not how I want to die. Do you?"

"Do I what? Think about death or how I want to die?"

"Both," I clarified.

"All the time. Naturally, there are some days I don't. Those tend to be the days where I'm too busy or distracted to think about it. Usually though, when I'm alone and I suddenly find myself with time to think, the thought creeps up on me and seizes my heart. Sometimes..." She paused, almost wishing she hadn't started the sentence. She lowered her voice and finished her thought. "... Sometimes... I get panic attacks."

"Really?"

"Oh yeah. Pretty bad ones."

"Why?"

She poured herself a little more tea and took a gentle sip.

"Of all the creatures on this planet," she began slowly, "we humans are the only beings blessed - or cursed depending on how you look at it - with intelligent thought. Intelligent thought, meaning the ability to contemplate and fret over our own mortality and the meaning of our existence. We're all born to die. Right now, this moment, this table, this room, everything we're experiencing, all this life, this light, the smell of food, the feeling of great sex, our memories, all of it, *all of this*, disappears the moment we draw our last breath. We're thrust into a black abyss, stripped of conscious thought. Pure nothingness. And knowing there is nothing that can be done to prevent it, the feeling is overwhelming."

Her breathing quickened. She closed her eyes and clenched her hands into tight fists as if she were trying to stop herself from spinning out of control. I sat frozen in place, unsure of what to do or how to act. Finally, she took several deep breaths and calmed down.

"Sorry," she said, her eyes still closed.

"It's okay," I said, although I felt like I should be the one to apologize.

"Anyway," she continued, opening her eyes. "I've accepted that I'm going to die. Fine. I have no control over that, but I can control *how* I want to die, even if I know I really can't. It brings me some semblance of solace and control just to think about it," she finished.

"So how do you want to die?" I asked, playing along.

"Watching the sunrise over the Pacific Ocean in Okinawa. My father used to say, even though it's the same sun and the same sky that has loomed over the Earth since the dawn of time, when you watch the sunrise from the Miyako Islands, you feel like you're on a different planet. I've always wanted to know if that was true."

"Sounds remarkable."

"Probably. Probably not. Either way, it's a comforting thought."

Thaleia swirled her straw in what was left of her Thai tea. She seemed to let another thought play out in the silence of her mind. She looked at me, took a deep breath, exhaled, and smiled.

"Your turn," She said.

"I've never considered it."

"Give it a shot."

"Right now?"

"If not now…"

"I can't."

"Why not? Does it make you uncomfortable?"

"No. Not really. Like you said, death is an inevitability, but how you die isn't, no matter what I prefer. I could choke on my dinner, my building could collapse while I'm sleeping, I could succumb to a sudden illness. No matter how comforting the thought, you can't control how you die."

"What about suicide?" she asked.

I was taken aback.

"What about it?"

"Isn't that a way to control how you die?"

"Not really," I began to explain. "Suicide has nothing to do with when or how you die. It's not about controlling life but taking control of pain."

Thaleia's eyes reduced to an inquisitive squint.

"For someone who doesn't give death a second thought, you sure came up with that explanation fairly quickly."

Thaleia's eyes pierced my gaze so strongly that I couldn't sustain it much longer and looked down at the table. Thaleia stopped messing with her drink and leaned back in her chair and crossed her arms, visibly bothered.

"You've contemplated it?" she asked. Her voice was a loud whisper.

I didn't answer. I fiddled with a napkin, drying up wet spots on the surface of the g;ass table. That was all the confirmation she needed.

"Why? And please don't say it was over some dumb Daisy Fay bitch, or I will lose all respect for you."

I looked up from the table into her inquisitive eyes and smirked dispassionately, shrugging my shoulders.

"Nothing like that. I was just... in excruciating pain."

Thaleia seemed to absorb my words. She leaned forward and continued to play with her drink.

"So, why didn't you go through with it?" she asked.

I pursed my lips.

"I didn't say I didn't."

The table fell silent. The stout woman returned with our meals and placed each of our respective entrees before us. She refilled our Thai teas and asked if she could get us anything else. When Thaleia kindly declined, she went back to cleaning the other vacant tables.

Thaleia and I didn't break our gaze, both eyes locked on the other, like we were playing a quiet game of chicken. The tension was broken by the amazing fragrance of the curry, forcing us to both suddenly remember we were starving. We ate and enjoyed our food, opting to discuss lighter topics.

* * *

The sun had long descended into the sea, and a waning crescent moon had taken its place, creeping up into the starless night sky as we arrived back to Perdition Towers. I followed Thalia into the stairwell, climbing the steps to our floor and our respective apartments. We hadn't spoken the entire ride back. I'm sure me opening my mouth like a moron had something to do with it. I had to say something to break this ice.

"I've never had fried ice cream before," I said.

"There is a reason why it's the only dessert on their menu," she replied. "How was the duck?"

"So tender. Come to think of it, I don't think I've ever had duck either," I said.

"A lot of firsts for you today," she quipped.

My face flushed red. Thaleia unlocked her apartment door and pushed it open gently.

"Stick with me, kid. Life can only be understood backwards, but it must be lived forwards," she said.

I stared at her perplexed. She rolled her eyes and shook her head slightly as she pushed her door open.

"Do me a favor, look up Kierkegaard sometime," she said with a wink. "Goodnight, Perv."

"Good night, Thaleia," I said, unlocking my door.

She walked over to me and hugged me tightly. I was struck with her sudden warmth and froze. She held on to me for what felt like an eternity. Finally, she let me go and walked back to her door.

"You better be alive tomorrow," she threatened.

"We'll see," I said with a smile.

She let out a hardy guffaw.

"That's not funny," she said. "Don't forget to read that book."

"I won't."

She entered her apartment, closed the door, and locked it. I remained in the hallway alone for a moment before finally retreating into mine.

I stood in the entryway, absorbed in the silence of my apartment. I could hear Thaleia moving in hers and tried to imagine what she was doing. I grabbed a clean glass from the cupboards, dumped a load of ice in it and filled it with water. Before I could take the tiniest sip, my phone rang and vibrated in my pocket. I dug it out and looked at the screen. It was my mother. I answered immediately.

"Hello, Mother."

"Bendición, hijo," she greeted in her usual monotone voice. "Happy belated birthday. Sorry I didn't call yesterday. I was tied up with a few clients," she explained.

"It's okay. You know I don't like to make it a big deal. It's just another day," I assured her. Though given the day's events, it wasn't just another day.

"I know, but still, I'm your mother, I shouldn't've forgotten," she argued.

I noticed a shift in her tone. It was remorse, a feeling unfamiliar for her. I put the glass of water down on the table and leaned against the counter.

"Something wrong?" I asked, concerned.

She dragged out a long sigh over the phone.

"Your father is dead."

Chapter Seven

The autumn sun was suffocating. My mother and I stood on the sidewalk next to a busy street. Dressed in reserved office attire, a gray skirt, white blouse, gray coat, and black high heels, my mother consulted her thin silver watch. Each time she looked, she became more impatient, stringing together a lengthy line of Hispanic cuss words, each as colorful as the last. Her hair was done up, a blowout that made her hair look like a wig. Large silver hoop earrings hung from her ears, and her face was painted with all types of make-up. All of it was being undone quickly by the humidity, a fact that only served to make her that much more irritable.

Nipping at her impatient heel, I found refuge from the glaring sun under the hoodie of my plaid, sleeveless shirt, stomping my feet randomly trying to see how long the lights on my Ninja Turtle sneakers illuminated for before turning off.

An old four door Volvo careened up the street. It was a flat gray color with faded patches of orange rust. The rust damage was extensive; there were several holes where the rust was eating away at the metal. Two of the tires had white walls, the other two were completely black. One of the tires was missing a hubcap, while the other three looked just about ready to fall off and live their own life. The back window was missing but was taped off with translucent plastic.

The Volvo screeched to a stop, causing several trailing cars to brake and swerve in order to avoid near collisions. The cars went around the Volvo, honking their horns and flipping off derogatory signs, cursing the driver of the Volvo, who didn't really seem bothered. With nowhere to park, the Volvo just flashed the hazard lights.

"Dios mio," my mother murmured under her breath, rubbing her forehead with her hand, shaking her head in embarrassment.

A man emerged from the car. He was much darker than me and very tall. To my young eyes, all adults were tall, but the man was taller than anyone I'd ever come into contact with in my short life. The man wore black sweatpants and a black sweater. Both were faded and oversized, like the man borrowed them from a much larger man. He wore a red baseball cap, torn at the brim, the lip bent so sharply, it cast a deep shadow over his eyes. His white shoes were the only things that looked clean and cared for. Tuffs of his hair stuck out from under the baseball cap, and his wiry beard was so thick and dry, I could barely make out his face (even now as I recall this memory, all I see is a black void).

The man looked both ways as he crossed the street, ignoring the aggressive remarks from the passing drivers. He waved over to my mother, who waved back instinctually. He was quite winded when he reached the sidewalk.

"Don't say anything," he started to say.

"I won't. Because I don't have the time, and also I know you could care less," my mother snapped.

"That ain't true, mami," he pleaded, but my mother was not in the mood.

"Ya, callate," she snipped. She turned her attention to me and her face softened into a smile. "Papi, tengo que trabajar, so vas estar con tu Padre hoy."

My eyes looked up at my mother, then drifted up toward the man, swirled in confusion. *This man is my father?* My father looked toward the road, visibly uncomfortable and suddenly aware of where he was parked, avoiding my gaze. He finally looked back and tittered.

"You don't remember me, huh little man?" he said.

I looked back at my mother; I did not want to go.

As if she could read my mind, my mother eased my unease.

"I know, mi amor. Es un día. Estaras bien," she stood up and looked at my father. "If anything happens, call me. You do have a phone, don't you?" she asked him.

"Of course," he confirmed, trying to sound firm but failing.

Her brow folded with worry. Nonetheless, she hugged me tight, showering my forehead with a barrage of kisses.

"Porta te bien, mi amor," she said. She stood up and got close to my father, glaring into his eyes with menace. "If anything happens to him, I'll cut your balls off."

My father's Adam's apple bounced from the weight of the gulp he managed to swallow as he nodded his head.

"You got time for all this flirting?" he joked.

My mother scoffed with disgust and looked at her watch again. She turned to me, winked, then power-walked into the building behind us, leaving me and my father alone together. I'd hoped she would stop and turn around, but she didn't.

A cacophony of loud horns pierced my ears. My father's double-parked vehicle had caused a massive traffic jam, and the drivers passing around took their turns hurling colorful profanities his way. I felt my father's heavy hand fall on my shoulder.

"We better bounce, kid. Last thing I need is a cop pulling up and giving your old man a ticket," he said.

I couldn't bring myself to look at him, yet I allowed myself to be guided across the street and into his car.

I crawled into the front passenger seat. The car was just as unimpressive on the inside; the interior was all beige: beige seats, beige steering wheel, beige dashboard, beige floors, beige armrests, beige ceiling. Old papers, fast food wrappers, and empty coffee cups littered the backseat and the floor. I put my seatbelt on and made sure to tighten it.

My father wasted no time in getting the car moving. I lowered the window to let in some fresh air. We drove in silence for a few minutes until my father cleared his throat.

"You've gotten big since the last time I saw you," he said.

I didn't respond. I leaned against the passenger door and stared out the window at the passing scenery.

"What are you, seven? Eight now?" He asked.

"Ten," I corrected him.

"No way!" He exclaimed. "Ten? You're big for ten. I bet your mom and your abuela got you eating that arroz con pollo, and those platanos, huh?" He laughed. I remained unresponsive, looking out of the window. His laughing died away and he cleared his throat again.

"I know I haven't been…," his thought trailed off. "You want to do something? Get some ice cream? You ball? I got a basketball in my trunk. Want to go to the park and put up some shots?"

Still no response.

"You're right, it's too hot for that," he said. He thought for a second. "How about going to the movies?"

My ears perked up and I looked at my father for the first time. His cheeks expanded with a wide grin.

"Oh, so, that's it! You like movies! Have you seen *The Matrix* yet?" he asked. He had me on the hook.

"No," I said softly. "My mom says it's too scary."

"What? She's crazy! I'm pretty sure it's not a horror movie."

"Have you seen it?" I asked.

"Not yet. But I was thinking about going today. You want to come with me?"

"What about my mom?" I asked.

"What about her? Remember this life lesson me hijo," he said in broken Spanish, "What she don't know, won't hurt her." He turned his head slightly toward me and winked. "So? You down or what?"

I couldn't help but smile. "Okay!"

My father put his heavy hand on my head and playfully pushed it to the side.

"That's my big head lil' boy!"

A smile stretched across my face from ear to ear. *Is this what it's like to have a father?*

"Are we going to go now?" I asked, unable to mask my excitement.

"Well, your pops has to make a few stops first. Then we'll go. Is that cool?"

"Yeah," I reluctantly accepted. I sat back in my seat with my back straight.

"What music you listen to?" My father asked me.

"Whatever my mom is listening to," I said.

"What, salsa and merengue?" My father scoffed. "I see. She's fulfilling only half of your Afro history. Do me a favor, pull up the armrest."

I did as instructed, reached for the beige armrest and opened it up. Inside were cassette tapes. I could tell my father treasured these dearly; they were the only things in the car that were meticulously organized.

"You got it open?" He asked.

"Yeah," I confirmed.

"Okay, take out the first tape labeled Mix #1 and pop it in the deck," he continued to dictate. I did as I was told and inserted the tape carefully into the center console deck.

"You ever heard of Pac?" He asked.

I shook my head.

"Okay," he began, "I want you to listen to what he says. Close your eyes and let him paint the picture."

I did just that. The sun was so bright the back of my eyelids glowed red and orange as the warm wind whipped at my cheeks. I strained my young ears, waiting for the music to start. It finally came on and a voice began...

"*I hear Brenda's gotta baby...*"

* * *

I don't know how long we'd been cruising around for. We drove from place to place. My father went to an apartment complex, told me to wait for him, and disappeared for minutes on end. When he returned, it was back to the road. All the while, he kept changing out different cassette tapes, explaining each artists' contribution to Hip Hop.

He played Rakim ("he changed the way MC's delivered their punch-lines and stacked their syllables"), LL Cool J ("Cut Creator has the sickest scratches ever put on wax"), Notorious B.I.G. ("He died seven months after Pac. Stupid. The media killed them if you ask me"), Eminem ("That Detroit boy is a student of the game. Listen to that cadence, his schemes, his use of entendre. Whatever this Hip Hop thang is, the kid got it!"), Big Pun ("I thought Pun was this featherweight dude until I heard him tear up this Snoop and Dre *Deep Cover* beat. Syllable assassin!"), Jay-Z ("Rags to riches. A prime example of what it truly means to have a growth mindset"), Nas ("the purest rhymes, every bar is a gem of knowledge"), and Black Thought ("The man is a poetic prolific prophet. Preach on!"). This, too, went on.

We soon stopped at a dive restaurant. It looked run-down, but it was full of people. So full in fact that we had to sit outside. The staff seemed to be on friendly terms with my father; they knew exactly what he wanted, and we didn't have to wait long for our burgers and fries.

I watched as my dad scarfed his food down. While I ate, my father chatted up with the waitress, who came outside to smoke. She looked younger than my father, but not by much. I thought my father's skin was dark, but her skin was the darkest I'd ever seen on a person. Her black hair was shiny and so curly, it bounced with the slightest move. She wore a stained white apron and gloves. She leaned against a wooden post. Her full lips formed like she was going to whistle, but instead, she blew her cigarette smoke out toward the parking lot away from our food.

"You seen him?" my father asked her.

"Last night actually. At Mike and Daisy's," she replied.

"The hell he doing there?"

"What you think," she quipped.

"I thought they got clean?"

"They did."

"Then what happened?"

"We all got our demons, Kai. You know that," she said. "We fight them every day. Some days we don't have the strength. That's when they…," she decided to stop talking, letting the words wander off with the smoke.

My father remained silent for a minute. He shifted uncomfortably in his seat and looked at me. I pretended to focus on my food.

"You think he's still there?" he asked her, keeping a careful eye on me.

"If I was a betting man, I'd put all my money on it," she said. She finished the cigarette and tossed the butt out somewhere in the parking lot. "You thinking about going over there?"

"I don't have a choice."

"The saddest sentence ever uttered."

She sat down on the bench next to my father, grabbed his hand and stared at it lovingly. Tears began to form in her eyes and her chin began to tremble. My father caught my eye as I watched all this unfold, chewing a sizable portion of my burger. He quickly turned to the waitress and wiped the tears away with his thumb just as they spilled

104

over the bottom lid and onto her cheek.

"Hey, hey, come on. What's wrong?" He whispered, concern in his voice.

"What isn't," she both scoffed and sighed. "I'm sorry."

My father kissed her forehead and hugged her tight. She buried her head in his chest and sobbed silently. My father stroked her neck and back with his free hand, cradling and shushing her softly like a newborn baby.

"Come with me," he whispered to her.

"Where?" she said from deep within his chest.

"Wherever you want to go."

She broke free of his embrace and composed herself. She looked at him and smiled, wiping the tears from her eyes.

"Montana," she sniffled.

"Montana? Why?"

"Because it's not here," she chortled.

"Alright. Montana, it is. Let's go."

"Really?"

"Yeah, sure! I'll wear cowboy boots, stick my arm elbow deep in a cow's ass, ride a horse." The waitress burst into laughter; this made my father smile.

"What's so funny?" he asked.

"Your ass riding a horse?" she said between snorts.

"Yeah? What's up?"

"Have you ever seen a horse? They're gigantic. You'd piss yourself."

"Maybe. But I'd piss on myself for you."

She laughed even harder.

"Oh wow, you'd really piss on yourself for me. I'm honored. You're such a charmer," she joked. The tears had all but evaporated. The two adults shared a silence as they gazed longingly at each other. She looked back at the inside of the restaurant. The smile faded away like a cloud of smoke in the wind.

"I have to get back," she said.

"No, you don't. We're going to Montana," he said.

"Well until we do. I have to get back."

"Why?"

"I don't have a choice," she said. She forced a smile to her lips and let go of his hands. She placed both hands on his cheeks and kissed his lips tenderly. Then she got up from the table, straightened out her apron, and turned to me.

"Bye handsome," she said. With that, she turned around and headed back inside the restaurant.

"Finish your shift and we'll leave tonight. I'm serious! Golden skies and Amber waves of grain!" My father called out to her. She only waved before disappearing inside. When she was out of sight, my father turned to me, his eyes still transfixed on where she was.

"What do you think about her?" he asked.

I looked toward the restaurant and back at my father. I didn't know what to say, so I simply shrugged my shoulders.

After our late lunch, we were back in the car again, cruising and listening to music. NWA, De La Soul, The Pharcyde, Pharaoh Monch, A Tribe Called Quest, Outkast, Mos Def, Common, Ice Cube; my father was going deep into his collection. Soon, my father grew stultified with the boom-bap. He decided to listen to Led Zeppelin's *Stairway to Heaven*, Jimi Hendrix's *Voodoo Child*, Nirvana's *Rape Me*, Pink Floyd's *Money*, and The Eagles' *Hotel California*. That's all we did for the next few hours, drive and listen to music.

The sun was coming down, and the further it descended, the more I began to lose faith we were ever getting to the movie theater. My father popped in one more tape but, this time, no explanation followed. The air in the car shifted, and my father's eyes went blank as if his soul retreated inward into his body; the person at the wheel now was just an empty husk.

We arrived at an apartment complex that looked like abandoned ancient ruins. A few people were walking around like aimless zombies. My father parked the car in a far obscure corner and cut the engine off. The music continued to play and my father just sat there listening, eyes closed, letting the words penetrate his body. I sat in silence, watching my father disappear and listening to a song that - at the time - I didn't understand. Something about a man killing a man and life just beginning and throwing it all away. All I could catch clearly was *"If I'm not back again this time tomorrow, carry on, carry on as if nothing really matters."*

Just like that, my father was resurrected, only the person that came back was not the person who I'd been riding in the car with all day. He lowered the volume to the song as the tempo changed and looked off somewhere in the distance.

"Open the glove box in front of you," he said, his voice sounding like it came from the bottom of a deep well.

I pulled the handle, and the glove box violently fell open, causing papers and trash to fall out. However, among that debris, I felt something heavy fall on my lap; it was a .35 caliber revolver. The snout was silver, and the handle was dark wood. I looked at my father, who was still looking off in the distance.

"You got it?" he asked, impatiently.

My throat was dry. No matter how much I tried to generate saliva, it just felt like sand and rubber.

"Yes," I managed to croak softly.

He stuck his hand out, palm, riddled with marks, calluses, and scars, turned upward. I picked up the gun carefully; it felt like a cannon in my small hands. My hands shook under its weight as I placed it into my father's hand. Once the cold steel touched his palm, my father looked at it and examined it like a sword that needed sharpening. He took a small breath and exhaled quietly.

"I'll be right back," he said. "Do not, for any reason, get out of this car. Stay here. Listen to music. You know how to work the stereo. Turn it up if you want. But do not get out of this car. You hear me?"

I nodded my head slowly.

"I can't hear you," he said, so sternly it took me by surprise. "Say you understand."

"I understand," I responded meekly. My father tossed me a quick glance. Then, he pushed the door open, jumped out, tucked the gun under his shirt and into his sweats, closed the door, and walked off briskly.

I watched as he passed a group of guys all dressed like they were on their way to play basketball. They tossed the basketball between them as they talked and joked. My father approached one of the apartment buildings. The apartments were all designed to look like townhouses, but they were all connected. He climbed the steps to the second floor and knocked firmly when he reached the door. My father adjusted his hat and threw the hoodie over it. After a few seconds, he pounded on the door so hard I could hear it from inside the car. I hoped the door wouldn't open, I didn't know what was on the other side, nor did I care to go to the movies anymore. I was scared, and I wanted my father to come back and tell me more about music.

The door opened.

It didn't open wide but just wide enough for my father to force it open with his body. He whipped the gun out quickly and discreetly, pointed it at whoever answered the door, and made his way inside, closing the door behind him before anyone could see the interaction. I trembled.

Time seemed to slow to a snail's pace. I could no longer hear the music playing, only my heart thumping between my ears. It felt like my father had been gone for eons. I took a few deep breaths, unlocked the car door, and got out.

I hustled toward the apartment, careful not to draw any attention to myself. Light on my feet, I took the steps two at a time until I reached the top. Once there, I put my ear to the door, however, all I could hear were muffled voices. One, was angry and aggressive, while the other sounded like a wounded cat dying alone in a back alley. There was music blaring from inside. Nothing I had ever heard before, it just sounded like noise with a screeching guitar. I heard what sounded like hollow trees falling to the earth and glass shattering. My heart was coming up into my throat. I gulped trying to get it back down, but it wouldn't budge. I tried peering into the window, but it was covered up with old newspaper. There were only a few sections that were ripped slightly through which I could see, but I had to get on my tiptoes to get the best view possible.

The apartment was an absolute mess. There was trash everywhere, chicken bones, fast food bags, empty jugs of water, and dirty syringes. The couch was missing legs on one side, so it was completely lopsided, with stuffing coming out of the seams and stained with God knows what. I saw a bag of dog food but didn't hear any dogs barking inside. Dirty dishes were piled on every surface of the kitchen counter. Everywhere except the sink which was filled with more trash.

Someone was sitting on the floor, leaning against the slanted couch. I couldn't see this person's face, but I could tell by the build that it was a man who looked sickly thin. My father was pacing around the apartment like a mad man flipping things over and violently swiping the trash off of the kitchen countertop with his arm.

I still couldn't make out what they were saying, only a few words or sentences every now and then.

"Where is it?" My father yelled over the music.

The man on the floor whined and moaned incoherently. My father continued to thrash around. His back was turned to the man on the floor, so he didn't notice when the man reached under the couch and pulled out a shotgun. I wanted to bang on the window, but I was paralyzed with fright. I stood there frozen, reduced to a mere observer.

The man cocked the gun. The sound made my father spin around, but to my surprise the sight of the gun didn't unnerve him.

"Do it!" He yelled, goading the man to pull the trigger.

"I will!" The man responded.

"Go ahead!" My father smirked. "But I'm warning you, don't miss.

The man was shaking so much, he couldn't keep the shotgun steady. The man finally buckled and pulled the trigger. Click. No bang.

There was an immediate pause afterward. I felt like I was watching a movie, and the VHS just froze on an image. Suddenly, my father descended on top of the man like the wrath of the Old Testament God, assaulting the man with a barrage of punches, each landing with heft and ferocity. My father ripped the shotgun away from the man with relative ease and smashed his nose in with the butt of the shotgun. The man wailed as his nose gushed blood. My father raised to his feet, tossed the shotgun aside, and removed his own gun from his trousers. I could hear the man panting, sobbing, and pleading for his life.

"Last chance," my father said.

The man, blood pouring from his nose like a faucet, pointed to the kitchen. My father grabbed him by the collar of his filthy shirt and forced the man to his feet, giving me a better look at him. The man was a walking corpse. His skin looked like it was coated in a thin layer of chalk. His jeans were small enough to fit a child, but they somehow were too big for this man, and his yellow shirt was pale and shredded like the man was buried in it for weeks and emerged from the dead wearing the same clothes he died in.

My father put the gun to his head and pushed him hard into the kitchen. The man fell over the dishes and knocked them over. Annoyed, my father pulled him back up by his shirt and guided him through the kitchen.

Roaches scattered as the man opened all of his cabinets. His patience running thin, my father dug the gun into the back of the man's scalp. He then leaned in closely to the man and whispered something that made the man completely break down into tears. My father shook some sense into him, and the man finally conceded. He removed a coffee canister from the cabinet that was behind a false back. My father snatched it from the man and opened it. The man tried to grab it back, but my father pushed him to the ground with all the ease of a rock falling on a piece of paper. My father reached into the canister and extracted several large wads of cash. He stuffed them all in his pockets. A look of disgust befell his face as he removed something else wrapped in plastic. My father muttered something to the man who remained on the floor writhing in frustration and agony, physically and mentally. My father took whatever was wrapped in plastic and put it in his pocket.

As he turned to leave, the man jumped up from behind the counter with a butcher knife. My father caught him just in time and averted the wild strikes. He pushed the man back to the ground, pointed his gun at the man, and shot him.

A yelp escaped my throat before I could clasp my hands around my mouth. It was too late; my father heard something and looked up in my direction. I did not wait to be caught. I leapt down the flight of steps with the grace of a gazelle and galloped to the car. The car looked so far, but before I knew it, I was in it, putting on my seatbelt, sweat permeating through my pores, and my young lungs struggling for air. It felt like my body teleported from one place to another. I looked back at the apartment building and saw that my father had yet to exit.

The lights to the apartment turned off and the door opened. My father let himself out, hoodie still covering his face. Against the pale early night sky, my father looked like a faceless reaper floating through the parking lot. He pulled something out of his pocket and tossed it by the trees near the fence. I did my best to calm myself down and appear normal. I turned the music up a little bit and pretended to be looking off into the distance when my father got into the car and shut the door.

He stared at me, burning a hole into the back of my head until I turned around, and our eyes met; neither of us spoke. He handed me the gun; it stunk of gunpowder and smoke. I put it back in the glove compartment and shut it away. My father took a deep breath and exhaled it all at once.

"You ready to see *The Matrix*?" He said coolly. The face I had grown familiar with had returned.

I nodded, hypnotically.

My father grinned, started the car, backed out of the parking spot, and drove into the night.

The movie theater was packed, not an empty seat in the house, yet my father managed to get perfect seats, dead center of the entire theater, perfect angle for sound and sight. I was blown away by the movie, but every so often, I would look up at my father, who was stuffing his face with a monstrous tub of popcorn and chugging down a large Sprite. The silver screen lit up in his eyes, his soul entranced by the passing visuals, the rest of the world melting away into oblivion. I smiled and turned my attention back to the screen, checking back occasionally to etch this moment to memory.

As we exited the movie theater, I was surprised to find my mother already waiting for us by the ticket booth. I ran to her, weaving through the dispersing crowd. I hugged her torso and immediately started going on about the movie.

"I don't get it. The cat was a glitch?" she said with a smiling frown.

My father threw away his trash in the nearest bin. He timidly approached my mother with his hands shoved in his pockets.

"I didn't want him to watch this movie," she said.

"Really?" He feigned, picking earwax out his ear with his little pinky. "Didn't know. Oh well. That movie was insane! Right, kid?" He smiled and winked at me. I couldn't help but smile back.

My father pulled the wads of cash (which were now folded and banded neatly) out of his pocket and handed it to my mother. She refused to take it, but he stuffed it in her purse anyway.

"For him. Okay. Please. I owe more. I know that. But... you know," he trailed off.

My mother didn't say anything. She simply sighed and nodded slightly. We shared a moment of silence. Then my father rubbed his hands on his pants and looked away from us and toward the busy road.

"Welp," he began, "I better get going."

The smile disappeared from my face. Before today, I had no idea who this man was. If I passed him on the street, I would've never recognized him. But at that moment, I knew who he was: My father. We listened to music, saw a movie, and ate a bunch of junk. I didn't know if this is what it was like to have a father, but I felt an invisible thread that tied us to one another. And now that thread was fraying.

Before I knew what was happening, welts of tears bolted down my cheeks. I let go of my mother, ran to my father, and wrapped my arms tightly around his knees. I buried my face in his pants and began to openly weep. My mother turned her head, her eyes welling with tears of her own. She didn't want me to see her pain; she swallowed it all down and kept it there. My father stood momentarily stunned.

"Hey. Hey. Little man," he pleaded awkwardly. "Come on. Don't cry. Your pops has to go."

He patted my head gently and lovingly. Moviegoers passed by the scene with curious eyes but didn't linger on the private moment. I tried to stop crying but I couldn't. My father managed to pry me from his body and returned me to my mother. I hugged my mother and buried my face in her skirt.

My father put his hand on my shoulder.

"Look at me," he asked.

I wouldn't.

"Listen," he sighed. "I'm sorry I haven't been around. That's on me. I have my own stuff to deal with before I can be a good father to you. But, that doesn't change what I know in my heart. And that's this: wherever I end up - and if you remember anything from this day, I want you to always remember this - wherever I end up, you will always be my son. And til my last breath, I will always love you."

I'm sorry. I'm lying. I would've wanted my father to say that, but he didn't. I have found that when the pen is in your hand, the temptation to manipulate the truth is all too powerful. In truth, what was really said was as follows:

"Look at me," he asked. I wouldn't.

My father opened his mouth to say something, but the words failed him. Instead, he rubbed my head one more time and slowly backed away from me and my mother.

"Take care of yourself," I heard him say to my mother.

"You, too," she said.

I turned my head and watched my father walk down the sidewalk, hands in his pockets. I hoped he would turn around, just so that I could see his face one more time.

He didn't.

All I was left with was the lasting glimpse of the man who was my father mosey up the road and disappear behind the mist of a brisk autumn night.

Chapter Eight

"Are you still there?"

My mother called out to me from the other side of the phone line. I took three generous gulps of icy water and wiped the residual water from my upper lip with the back of my hand.

"Yeah," I casually reassured her.

"Did you hear me? Your father died," she repeated.

"Richard died?" For some reason I couldn't understand what she was telling me.

"No, not my husband. Your father."

Father. That word was foreign to me. It was like trying to swallow an old catcher's mitt; it didn't quite fit in my mouth.

"Oh," was the only word that came out, followed by "Okay?"

I could hear my mother draw a shallow breath on the other end of the line. Either she was waiting for me to inquire more, or she was looking for a way to move the conversation forward. She chose the latter.

"He was in jail for fighting," she continued. "His brother told me he was only supposed to be there one night. To sober up apparently. According to the police, he was alive at lights out. He was dead the next morning. It appears he vomited in his sleep and suffocated."

"Really," another word I managed to conjure up.

"Your father suffered from epileptic seizures. Did you know that?"

she asked.

I shook my head over the phone, watching as the ice in my cup slowly melted.

"No. I don't know anything about him."

My mother fell silent. I drank what was left of the water in one swallow and placed the cup in the sink.

"Is that all?" I asked.

"¡Niño!" my mother exclaimed, her patience reaching its breaking point. "¡Por favor! Don't be like that."

"Like what?" I was starting to get annoyed.

"He was your father."

"Technically."

"When are you going to let go of that grudge? You can't keep hating him."

My face was hot with simmering rage. When my mother scolded me, she had a knack of making me feel like a little boy. I managed to settle myself before I said something rude and disrespectful. I took in air through my nostrils and exhaled silently, as to not let my mother know she was getting under my skin. I needed to get my point across rationally, without emotion, or she was going to take any word that came out of my mouth as the rantings of a child.

"I can't hate or hold a grudge for someone I don't know. I've only met the man two times in my life, one of which I remember. We never had a relationship. He may be part of the reason I exist in this world, but what you're asking me to do is grieve for a stranger, and I'm sorry, I can't do that," I explained calmly and rationally.

My mother was silent for a moment. Then I heard her sigh slightly.

"Esta bien, hijo, esta bien," she didn't want to argue. Her tone was a mixture of genuine disappointment and utter sadness. It occurred to me at that moment that my mother was not upset with me. It was something else. Though I had no real memories of my father, my mother did. They were separated for nearly thirty years, but they had an entire life together before me. A life, I surmised, my mother must have still held dear to her heart and reflected on in quiet moments.

"Okay..." she found her second wind. "I'm guessing you wouldn't be interested in attending his memorial, then? It's in DeFuniak."

I paced around the kitchenette, opening random cabinets, the fridge, the oven, my not-so- subtle way of telling my mother that I'm ready to end this conversation. The longer it went on, the more irritable I was afraid I'd get.

"DeFuniak? That's a real place?" I quipped.

"His hometown. Born and raised... And. Died. Now. I. guess," she said the last five words one at a time, as if a period followed each one.

"Are you going?" I asked her.

"What?" My mother remarked. Her voice was growing distant.

"The memorial. Are you going?"

"No. No. But I will go with *you* for support," she replied.

"Yeah, I'm not going. The whole thing would just make me uncomfortable."

"I understand," she said, again, unable to conceal her disappointment. "Will you at least come pick up this package they sent to you?"

My spine stiffened.

"Package?"

"Yeah it arrived this afternoon. They didn't have your address, so they directed it to me," she said.

"What is it?" I asked, no longer hiding my irritation.

"¿Que se yo? It's for you so I didn't open it. It's pretty heavy though. Richard had to bring it in for me."

I stayed silent.

"¿Lo quieres, si o no?" she demanded to know; now *her* patience was running thin.

"Yeah, fine," I conceded. "I'm off the next couple days. Let me know when you're home and I'll come by."

"Okay," my mother said, sounding somewhat victorious. "I should be home by tomorrow night so come by the next day."

"Okay, see you then."

"Okay, mi amor. Good night. Bendición," she said.

I was ready to hang up when a question sprung into my mind.

"Wait. Wait. Hello?"

"Yes?"

"When did he die?" I asked.

My mother was silent. I could hear her breathing but couldn't tell if she was hesitating or trying to remember the date. Finally, she cleared her throat.

"Yesterday," she slowly confirmed.

My brow furrowed. My mother misconstrued my silence for solemn dismay.

"On your birthday... I'm sorry," she said.

"No, it's fine. I'll see you later."

We said our final goodbyes and hung up. I put the phone down on the counter and stared at it for a second, letting the information settle. After a moment of quiet reflection, I moved to the sink, dumped the ice out of my glass, and washed my cup, drying it with a hand towel and putting it away.

I picked up the book Thaleia gifted me, rounded the kitchenette and sat down on my futon. I opened the book with the intention to read the first chapter, but I couldn't focus on the first sentence. I closed the book and tossed it on the coffee table next to the notebook and the pen already resting there. I stared at them both when a thought occurred to me. I took the pen up into my right hand and the notebook into my left, opened it, and began to scribble down my father's physical features.

I tried to picture my father in my mind, but I could only see his body type. He wasn't thin, but he wasn't overweight. He was naturally athletic, like a person always on the move. He had dark skin, darker than me, and large hands. And he was tall, at least from what I remembered. Yet, even though I could see all of this: his body mass, his height, his skin, his hands; try as I might, I could not configure my father's facial features. It remained a blank face with ears.

I finished jotting down the descriptions, sat back, and reviewed my work; it was barely enough to fill half the page. I ripped the page out of the notebook and balled it up. I closed the notebook and placed it and the metal pen back on the coffee table, got up from the futon, and tossed the balled-up paper in the trash. I returned to the futon, sat down, turned on the television and watched some sports highlights.

* * *

I woke up before my alarm again. As had become customary, I lay in bed for a few minutes trying to capture the fleeting images of what I dreamt before they fluttered out of reach. I tried to remember something - *anything* - but the moment my alarm came to life, I gave up and convinced myself it was a dreamless sleep.

That settled, I dismissed my alarm, got out of bed, and changed into comfortable shorts and a dry-fit hooded t-shirt. I opened my sock drawer and found it nearly empty, except for one pair. The pair was mix-matched, one white, one black. The white sock was ankle length, and the black sock reached up to the back of my calf. This meant it was time to do laundry, which I had already planned for that day anyway. I slipped the socks over my large flat feet, folding the black sock to match the length of the white sock, and shoved my feet into a pair of old black running shoes. Before I started the errands for the day, however, I felt the need to go to the park near my apartment and shoot some hoops. This was not typically part of my day off routine, but I found that putting up some shots alone and emptying my mind would help me make sense of the many heavy thoughts that were perched on my shoulders like a couple of anvils.

In an attempt to rid myself of the residual dreariness that lingered from sleep, I went into the bathroom and splashed cold water into my face. Then, I stood over the sink in the kitchenette and drank two glasses of tap water.

On the second glass, I smelled an unfamiliar odor. It smelled like decaying onion and garlic. I could not recall the last time I cooked with either of those things. I assumed it was coming from the trash bin at the corner of the kitchenette. I opened the lid and scanned through it. The trash wasn't full; it was filled with potato peels, discarded ramen noodle containers, and empty meat packets. It smelled a little foul, but it definitely was not the particular rotten smell that was hitting me. I removed the trash bag from the bin, tied it up with several knots, and put it by the door. I grabbed my phone, found my off-brand earbuds (confirming they had enough charge), grabbed my keys from the counter, grabbed the trash bag, and left my apartment.

I stood in the silent hallway, and looked at Thaleia's door. I briefly considered asking her if she was interested in joining me but tossed away the notion just as quickly. She didn't really seem like a morning person, and I wanted to be alone anyway. I took the trash bag downstairs, tossed it in the dumpster, got in my car (it started up right away) and drove out of the parking lot onto the main road, already crowded with people making their morning commute.

I frequent the park often during the week and even then it's never empty. More often than not, there are always people, older men and women playing tennis or pickleball, or jogging on the path, or walking their dogs. Hardly anyone used the basketball court or the soccer field. That morning was no different. The sun was still on the rise but not fully visible. The sky was in transition from mauve to dark blue, and the rays from the morning sun turned the bottom of the stacked stratus clouds several exuberant shades of orange.

The basketball court was nice and smooth concrete. Barely any cracks or dips that cause the ball to bounce awkwardly. It had recently been repainted, so it looked nice and new. Yet what appealed to me most about this court is that the rims were the official height of real NBA rims (ten feet), and the stanchion was solid concrete, so when the ball bounced off the rim, the basket didn't vibrate and shake. I have tried all of the courts in my hometown, these were the best, hands down, and lucky for me, it was also the least popular.

I parked, retrieved my basketball from my trunk, stuffed the head-phones in my ears, adjusting them until they were comfortable, and found a good Lo-Fi Hip-Hop playlist. I stood at the free throw line, stared at the rim, and began to empty my mind of all thoughts: Evelyn was waiting on an answer from me regarding the open position in Babylon. My father was dead, however, apparently he left something of an inheritance. Then there was the enigma, Thaleia, my young, attractive, and somewhat unceremonious neighbor who, up until two days ago, I never knew existed. What made her case so strange was that she had appeared to be my neighbor for a while, though I was sure that my neighbor had committed suicide on a thunder-less night two days prior. Does this mean that I imagined finding my neighbor's headless body? I know what I saw, but I never did touch and confirm it. Could it have been a dream? I felt the door, I heard the storm, I smelled the ammonia in the apartment. Not to mention I have the notebook and the pen I took from that apartment. There is no way I could bring ethereal objects into a corporeal world, and if there is, I've heard of no such case. Is it possible, then, that I bought these items myself and simply forgot? It was probable but not likely; I had no aspirations to journal my uneventful life. I do not purport myself to be a thinker like Aristotle, Plato, Socrates, or Marcus Aurelius, nor did I consider becoming a novelist, playwright, or poet as a vocation. I had no such burning ambitions, and therefore would have no urgency or need that would compel me to buy a notebook and a pen in the first place.

Have you considered... that the real problem is... that you... are losing... your mind?

My shoulders shrugged. I certainly did not feel I was losing control of my mental faculties; however, insanity was the only possibility with the most valid rationality. If I were, in fact, going insane, there was not much else that could be done to stave it off. I would lose my sanity and accept it.

Three deep breaths. That's what it took to quiet my thoughts. Three deep breaths. I held the last one, exhaled slowly, draining all questions from my mind, and put up my first shot.

* * *

It was mid-morning when I returned to my apartment. I emerged from the stairwell onto my floor, drenched in sweat, my shoulders, and thighs sore. Thaleia was standing at my door, knocking aggressively, her demeanor dripping with impatience. She wore a soft white cotton half top hooded sweater sprinkled with pink and red hearts of assorted sizes that exposed her stomach just enough to be curious, baggy blue windbreaker pants that tapered off just above her ankles, and bright white Puma's. Her golden curls were done up into cornrows, with her excess hair braided into two ponytails that fell over her shoulders.

I walked up the hallway, my confidence failing me the closer I got to Thaleia. She knocked on my door again but stopped midway when she finally noticed me skulking up the hall. She slapped her hands against her hips and sucked her teeth.

"Geezus! There you are! Where the hell have you been?! I was about to kick the door down!" she began.

"Good Morning to you, too," I said with a wry smile.

"Yeah, yeah, good morning," Thaleia tossed out coldly.

I reached my door and stood before her. "What's up?" I asked.

Thaleia looked around the empty hallway.

"I'm sorry, are we supposed to talk out in the open like uncivilized animals?"

"Implying there are civilized animals?" I mused.

Thaleia was not amused. She folded her arms across her chest and let me sit with that remark.

I chortled slightly and dug into my pocket for my keys. The second the door was unlocked, Thaleia pushed her way in with authority, breezing past me, and leaving an intoxicating aroma of shampoo, soap, and gentle perfume briskly trailing behind her.

"Okay, so listen-Whoa!" she exclaimed. "Your apartment is super clean! Makes my place look like a pig pen. Are you a serial killer?"

I was amazed by how fast Thaleia went from sour apple to sweet peach at the drop of a hat. I closed my apartment door and dragged myself into the kitchen.

"Coffee?" I asked, going into my cabinet and retrieving my cafétera.

"What? No. I don't have time for coffee," she said as she flung her purse on the futon and helped herself to a seat at the foot of my bed, crossing one leg over the other as if to remind me she is a lady first and foremost. She bounced playfully on the mattress, testing the springs.

I hadn't had a woman in my apartment since Evelyn. The thought crossed my mind as I poured myself a generous glass of tap water and swallowed it all in three swift gulps.

"Water?" I asked Thaleia after the last swallow, my voice sounding like I was coming up for air. I didn't have the energy to make it a full question. All I could manage was one word and the inflection, and even that required some effort.

"Is that all you got?" Thaleia said as her eyes continued to scan the room in wonderment, as if she were standing at the heart of the Sistine Chapel.

I opened my fridge and took inventory. I didn't have much to offer.

"I've got Orange juice," I called out.

Thaleia's face twisted dismissively.

"Add some Vodka and call me Capote," she said.

"I don't have liquor," I informed her.

"Oh... never mind it's too early anyway," she said, disappointed.

"You *can* drink it as is," I informed.

Thaleia said nothing, just shot me a perplexed expression. With nothing else to offer, I poured her a glass of water from the same cup I drank out of, added some ice, crossed the room, and put it in her dainty hands. She grabbed the cup without reservation and took a turtle's sip.

I stepped back and waited for Thaleia to begin explaining why she was in my apartment so early, but she seemed lost in thought. I crossed my arms and cleared my throat.

"So," I began. "... what's up?"

"Oh right!"sShe exclaimed, suddenly remembering her previous urgency. "My Jeep! The mechanic called me yesterday and said it's ready for pick-up. I can't find anyone to take me to get it. I hate to be a bother - again - *again* - but it seems like you are the only person I can count on. Can you do me another solid? I'll even treat you to breakfast."

I shook my head.

"Thank you but I can't. I have errands to run," I started.

"I just need you to drop me off. That's it. Then you can go about your day, and you don't have to worry about me bothering you ever again," Thaleia pleaded.

"You're not bothering me," I groaned.

"Yes I am. You have your entire day planned and I'm the monkey

124

throwing a wrench into your well-oiled machinations, I get it."

Thaleia suddenly stopped talking. She stood up from the bed, took one more sip of the water and set it down on the cheap coffee table.

"You know what," she said. "It's fine. I'll figure it out. Thanks anyway."

Thaleia grabbed her purse from the futon and made her way to the front door. Just as she reached the kitchen, my shoulders slumped.

"Hold on," I called out.

Thaleia stopped and turned around waiting for me to say something.

I rubbed my beard. The words were all formed in my mouth, I only had to part my lips and let them spill out.

"I like eggs Benedict," I finally said.

Thaleia crossed the apartment, threw her purse back on the futon and hugged me tight.

"You've got to manage your White Knight Complex. It's not healthy," she said. She let me go and held me at arm's length. "Wow you are soaked. Is it raining outside?"

"No. I was exercising," I confirmed. "Do I have time to get decent?"

"Sure. Go ahead. They won't be open for another half hour."

I expected Thaleia to wait for me back in her own apartment so I could get ready in private. Instead, Thaleia made herself comfortable on the futon, picked up her glass of water and continued where she left off.

"I'm going to hop in the shower, so...," I hinted, expecting to excuse herself to her apartment until I was ready to go.

Thaleia brought her phone out of her purse and began fiddling with it.

"Okay," she said, not moving a muscle.

The hint was dead on arrival. I grimaced, grabbed some casual clothes from my drawer and proceeded into the shower and locked the door.

When I finally emerged from the shower, I found Thaleia in the same spot on the futon, the back of her head perched on the back support, either resting her eyes or completely asleep. I quietly tossed my clothes in the hamper and grabbed my sneakers. I sat on the foot of my bed and forced my large bare feet into my shoes without untying the laces.

"You jerk off in there?" Thaleia suddenly asked.

Startled, I scoffed and shook my head, a smile curled on my lips.

"Not today."

Thaleia lifted her head and opened her eyes looking directly at him with a playful smile. "There's still time."

"Nah, I'm good," I assured her.

"Too shy?"

"Too hungry."

I stood up and looked at Thaleia, motioning for her approval on what I was wearing. She immediately burst into laughter.

"What the hell is that shirt?!" She said through chokes. "Is that Black Stalin?" she asked, referring to the shirt I bought from the mall.

"I think it's supposed to be Malcolm X," I said.

She laughed even harder.

"Oh my God!" she exclaimed, wiping the tears from her eyes. "That's beautiful and horrifying at the same time."

"I'm glad you think so," I said. I opened my drawer and tossed her a shirt of her own. She held it up and stopped laughing.

"You didn't?"

I smiled and crossed the room to retrieve my laundry hamper. Thaleia took her sweater off eagerly, exposing her white tank top underneath, and slipped the shirt on quickly. It fit her big, but she still managed to pull it off. She looked down at the picture and laughed.

"Is this Rosario Dawson, or Frida Kahlo. Ugh! I don't care, I love it!" she gave me a tight hug and ran to the bathroom to look at herself in the mirror.

"I legit might never take this off!" she called out from the bathroom.

I dumped the dirty clothes from my hamper into a forest green burlap sack, then placed the sack into the empty laundry basket. She returned from the bathroom, grabbed her water, drank a little more, then emptied the rest into the sink and left the cup on the counter.

"That is the 'errands' you have to run today? Laundry?" She asked with a snort of derision.

I nodded my head with a smile, opened the door and stood aside for her to be the first one out. She grabbed her purse and her sweater, and headed toward the door when my phone, sleeping on the windowsill, screamed in alarm.

Thaleia doubled back and grabbed the phone for me. She turned off the alarm and the screen returned to a picture of me and Evelyn.

"Mercy me!" she exclaimed. "She is stunning. Is she your girlfriend? You better not tell her you've been flirting with me," Thaleia began. She handed me the phone and I put it in my pocket.

"No. Not my girlfriend," I said, my face flashing hot.

"Uh huh," Thaleia assessed the immediate change in my expression. "Looks like I picked at a festering scab. Apologies."

I didn't respond, I just stood at the door waiting for Thaleia to step out of the apartment so I could lock the door and avoid this conversation. A shadow fell over my eyes. I pursed my lips.

"Shall we?" I pleaded, my voice low and faint.

Thaleia finally accepted the hint. She smiled, either out of empathy or pity.

"*There is no remedy for love but to love more,*" she cited.

She squeezed my shoulder tenderly and walked past me, allowing me to finally close the door behind us.

* * *

Thaleia spoke on the phone the whole ride to the mechanic shop. When we arrived, there was barely anywhere to park. All types of vehicles heavily occupied the parking lot, and they all were either missing parts, were on jacks missing wheels, had their hoods open, and doors missing; the place looked more like a chop shop than a mechanic shop.

I dropped Thaleia off at the entrance and had no choice but to park in the building next door where they apparently did accounting; there was no shortage of parking spots there.

I cut the engine and waited for Thaleia to emerge. While I waited, I flipped through radio stations and landed on talk radio, but quickly lost interest when they started talking about what unfortunate celebrity got cheated on by another. Minutes later, Thaleia emerged from the shop, she scanned the area, found me, and stomped over, her face contorted in anger. She reached me in a huff and practically threw herself into the passenger seat. She slammed the door and crossed her arms.

"Cocksucker!" she yelled. I was taken aback by her sudden outburst; her voice was so high pitched, my ears rang.

"What happened?" I asked, concerned.

"That incompetent, phony, *asshole*, told me the car was ready last night. I come in, and now he tells me that they still have to put in some *fucking* part, and it's going to take like three *fucking* hours!" Her face was red with rage and her eyes began to well with tears. She quickly wiped the tears from her eyes and fought a bout of sniffles. "Great. Now I'm crying like a hysterical Valley Girl. You know why I'm crying? Not because I'm upset. I'm crying because I can't punch him in his smug ass-tonguing, cock-gagging face!"

She wiped her tears again and took three slow deep breaths. After the third one, her bronze color returned to her cheeks. She looked at me and buried her face in her hands in embarrassment.

"Oh God! I'm acting like the bipolar women in Raymond Chandler novels," she said, calm creeping back into her trembling body.

"No, I'd be livid, too," I admitted.

She took another deep breath and exhaled. "Sorry for cursing so much," she said with a slight waver in her voice as she struggled to regain control of her trembling nerves.

"It's all good. Don't apologize for raw emotion," I assured her.

A strange look befell her face; she stared at me as if she saw a ghost. She quickly averted her eyes and returned to anguish. She buried her head in her hands and groaned angrily.

"No, it's not fine. It's a bad habit. 'A sign of poor intelligence and a lack of vocabulary.' My father used to say. Now I think I do it just to piss him off." Her train of thought veered off as she stewed in her frustration, releasing a heavy sigh.

"Well," I began, "You want me to go *fuck* that guy up?"

Thaleia looked at me shocked then suddenly broke out into a fit of laughter. She punched me in the arm and wiped the final tears from her eyes.

"Wow! Whoa! Well, well, well. Check out the serpent tongue on you!" she exclaimed.

"I have my moments," I quipped. "Y-you want me to?"

Thaleia shook her head and beamed at me.

"You wouldn't do that. You're a nice guy," she said.

"Yeah, you're right. I actually nearly soiled my shorts just now," I chortled.

"What would you have done if I said 'yes'?" Thaleia asked, laughing.

"I would've had to follow through. I'd come back with a torque wrench shoved up my ass, but hey, at least I kept my word."

Thaleia laughed even harder. Her laugh sent a warmth spreading through my chest.

"Look, we got three hours, right?" I said.

"Ugh, supposedly," Thaleia confirmed, wiping the residual tears from the corner of her eyes with the knuckle of her index finger.

"Let's go get some breakfast," I suggested.

"And if they don't call by the time the eggs and bacon are gone?" she asked.

"Then I guess you'll be coming with me to do my laundry."

Thaleia smiled.

"I get to see your delicates? Say no more."

I started the car and navigated my way out of the parking lot and back into traffic.

There was no shortage of restaurants in my small town; it was mostly designed to cater to wealthy retirees, so all the upscale breakfast places were too expensive for us lowly paupers. Thus, Thaleia and I found ourselves at the only IHOP in town (Unfortunately, we did not have a Denny's), located right off the main highway, wedged between a Shell gas station and a 7-Eleven, and across the street from a RaceTrac, Hooters, and a flop house motel for big rig truckers passing through town.

When we arrived at the IHOP, we were immediately treated to a concert of smells that smacked us in the face in the following order: burnt coffee, cigarettes, applewood bacon, urine, puke, shame, and regret; ironically enough, we did not smell any pancakes.

After five minutes of waiting, we were finally approached by the hostess, a ghostly white woman with dark mascara encircling her insouciant eyes. Her lips were slathered in purple lipstick in a poor attempt to cover up the wrinkles etched around the crusty borders of her mouth from decades of smoking, and her jowls swung mercilessly from her jawbone. The hostess greeted us with all the enthusiasm of an Anhedoniac. Even through her bleach-stained, shit-brown apron and unkempt black polo shirt, you could see her protruding belly and sagging breasts that no bra could save.

The hostess sat us at a booth near the kitchen, tossed two menus on the table, and walked away before we could thank her.

"You get what you pay for," I quipped, grabbing the menus and handing one over to Thaleia.

"I don't blame her. If God cursed me with the body of an anorexic stork who was both pregnant with stomach cancer and had absolutely no ass, I'd be a miserable bitch too," Thaleia said. "If I were you, I'd stick to water. They probably sweeten their coffee with mountain dew and meth."

I kicked my head back and expelled a hardy laugh. Thaleia stared at me with a triumphant smile and waited for me to regain my composure.

"So, you do laugh? I was beginning to worry you had no sense of humor," she said.

"Well... if you're not laughing, you're crying."

We both scanned the menus for a few moments. Then Thaleia slapped the menu down on the table and grinned.

"Got it!" Thaleia proclaimed, as if we were in a race and she stood victorious.

"Already? What are you getting?"

"Three pancakes, three eggs, three pieces of bacon, three pieces of sausage, home fries, and wheat toast with butter and strawberry jelly on the side," she rattled off.

"I don't see that in here," I said, flipping the menu around in my hands.

"It's not. That's just what I want," she said, as a matter of fact.

"You want to throw in a piece a fruit or something?"

"I'm getting *strawberry* jelly," she affirmed.

"You're not going to eat all of that," I scoffed, returning my eyes to the menu.

"Oh, honey, yes I am. If you haven't figured it out by now, I *love* to eat."

"Yeah, I see."

"If I had to choose between sex and food - food every time, no question. The second a fork full hits my tongue, it's instant love. Sex is haphazard. Food never misses. So, I eat. Not that rabbit food. You ever had Kale? It tastes like grass! Disgusting. I'm going to eat! Eat 'til I'm fat. Fat and happy, baby. Believe me, whatever man, or woman I end up with will love every single pound of me."

My eyes jumped up from my menu. I looked at her, my brow scrunched in confusion as if my ears stopped working right when vital information was being spilled. Thaleia took the menu back in her hand and trained her eyes upon it, noticeably irritated with herself. She clearly had not meant to let that slip, but it was out now.

"Wait. What?" I asked.

"What?" She parroted with a coy smile. Her face was red.

"*Whatever man or woman,*" I quoted, quietly.

"Hey, look at that, your ears *do* work," she said.

The Hostess returned with two cups of ice water. She placed them on the table, tossed two straws next to them, and walked away again as if she were purposely trying to avoid serving us.

"You're...," I couldn't finish the sentence. I didn't want to presume anything.

Thaleia removed the straw from its wrapper and dipped it into her water. She took a quick sip and grimaced. "Is that what I said?"

I stared at her confused.

"It's not complicated," she began, somewhat hotly. "If I fall in love with someone, I have to be romantically, emotionally, and sexually attracted to the person."

"That sounds like *regular* love," I said.

"It sounds like *love,*" she swirled the straw around the cup and took another sip. "Do you believe we have souls?"

"I don't know," I answered, exasperated by the question.

"I'm never going to get a simple yes or no out of you will I?" she said, shaking her head.

"You're not asking me if the sky is blue. The question of the soul is complex. My short answer is *I don't know*," I said.

"You're starting to make me sorry I asked," she laughed. *"You don't know?"*

"If I believe we have a soul, that means I believe there is a God or a higher power," I explained myself.

"You saying you don't believe in God?" she said it as more of a statement that needed confirmation than an actual question.

"I didn't say that. I just said *I don't know*," I remained vague.

Thaleia stared at me with suspicion, her mind turning over the few conversations we've had.

"Didn't you tell me you were Catholic?"

"No. You assumed I was," I corrected her. "I was raised in the Catholic faith. That doesn't mean I'm a devout Catholic."

Thaleia nodded her head slowly as if trying to restructure the moment in her mind. After a few seconds she shrugged her shoulders.

"Whatever," she conceded. "I'm not trying to enter into a theological debate over cold rubbery eggs. Let's assume, okay, that within every living human being is a ball of light. And since we're floating around this fictitious world in which there are balls of lights inside of people, let's also say I have the ability to *see* that ball of light in everybody. Now, though everyone has these balls of lights hovering in their chest, there are only a select few whose ball of light shines so bright, it engulfs their entire body. *That's* what I'm attracted to. The beam of light coursing through a person's soul. What physical form that beam of light is in is immaterial."

She took another sip of her iced water and frowned as she forced the tasteless drink down.

"Is that a problem for you?" she asked, her eyes concentrating on the contents of her cup. I could hear a hint of concern in her voice.

It was a flash but, within that moment, I swore I saw a faint purplish

133

aura surrounding her body. A smile bloomed on my lips.

"Depends," I responded in all seriousness.

Thaleia met my piercing stare, waiting for me to bring the axe down on her neck.

"On?"

"This *ball of light*, do you see it in me?" I asked.

Thaleia couldn't hide her joy. Her cheeks flushed crimson and the corner of her lips stretched from ear to ear.

"Yeah," she said. "It's the size of a thumbtack, but it's definitely shining."

We put our orders in and finally got served. I couldn't get eggs benedict, so I settled for a simple egg sandwich with ham and cheese, and fries on the side. I ate my sandwich and a few of my fries. I spent the rest of the time marveling at Thaleia as she indeed cleaned her plate (and the rest of mine). She wasn't lying about food being better than sex; every time she took a bite of her meal, she moaned orgasmically. With our plates clean, we embarked on another journey: awaiting the check.

"So," Thaleia began, slurping down water, "You hear I'm into men and women, and you don't have any questions? Most guys would have a million by now."

I drank the rest of my water and sucked on some ice before crushing them with my teeth.

"I wouldn't know what to ask," I admitted. I gave it some thought and, after some consideration, chose my first question.

"When did you know?"

"I don't keep a diary so I can't give you an exact date, unfortunately," I could see Thaleia actively combing through the memories held deep in her heart. "I mean, I've always liked boys, I know that. I definitely wasn't shy about letting my *Our Lady of Charity* classmates see my panties under my plaid skirt by the merry-go-round," she was tickled by a mischievous memory for a second before finally returning to the matter. "Girls, though - *women* I should say," she trailed off. "I don't know."

She trailed away for a moment and played with the stale crusts of bread that remained on the desolate porcelain plate, breaking them into small pieces.

"Honestly, I wish I had a crazy story for you like I went away to band camp and got into a pillow fight that turned into an all-out lesbian orgy but, it wasn't like that."

"I wasn't expecting it to be," I laughed. "You ever been in love?" The question came without resistance. I hadn't realized it came out until the words hung in the air.

A smile crept on her lips and her cheeks flushed crimson, assailed once more by memory.

"She snuck into my life like a beautifully violent thunderstorm on a cloudless sunny day and left it just as suddenly," she said. "Leaving me with the aftermath. Forever changed," she took one long sip of her water. "Forever changed."

Her thumb traced her lips gently, the memory finally fading from her distant eyes. She expelled a satisfactory sigh and turned her attention back to the table. I had a few more questions lined up, but her response was so perfect that adding one more paint stroke would mar the entire portrait, so I left it all in the air.

* * *

With our stomachs fed, the check paid, and still no word from the mechanic, I had no choice but to drag Thaleia along with me to the laundromat.

I can't say why, but I've always enjoyed going to the laundromat. On the weekends, the laundromat was packed with people, which made it nearly impossible to get free washers or dryers when you needed them. During the week, there was hardly anyone. I always went during the week.

Thaleia's mood seemed to be rising with each passing moment. She delighted in torturing me over my choice of underwear.

"Boxer briefs?! Do you hate your testicles?" she exclaimed, loudly, "Hey, someone was too impatient to wipe properly!" She mercilessly teased.

Even though the only person in the facility besides us was the Old Guatemalan proprietor, I did my best to temper my embarrassment. For Thaleia it was all fun, until the clothes were all divided and in their respective washer. Then, boredom emerged from the depths of immobility.

I took the free time provided to go through my phone and pay all pending bills for that week, while Thaleia read a book on Greek Mythology for half an hour. However, boredom soon gripped her and she shuffled restlessly in the red plastic seat next to me. Unable to bear the silence any longer, Thaleia heaved an exaggerated groan like a reckless grenade.

"Where's your book?" She asked.

"My what?"

"*Kafka on the Shore?* Did you bring it? I could use some of that Murakami magic," she asked, reaching her hand out.

"Oh... I didn't," I admitted.

"What? This is the kind of moment books are made for," she scolded.

"You're right. I'm sorry. I'll bring it next time," I said.

"*Next time* doesn't help me right now," she leaned back in her seat, crossed her arms and pouted. "So disappointing."

The machines churned from one cycle to the other, while other garments tumbled along in the large dryers.

"Do you enjoy this?" she spouted.

"What?"

"This!"

She motioned to the empty room. The Old Guatemalan owner sat at her desk/office sorting small packets of detergent and softener while watching a daytime soap on her monochromatic portable TV. The machines whirled and rattled as they did their job, sloshing and spinning the clothes in a generous froth of soap and bleach. A rather large and bulky Sylvania tube television from the 1990's hung above us strapped to what passed as a wall mount; every second that passed a threat to our life if the mount decided to succumb to its massive weight.

I shrugged my shoulders.

"What's wrong with *this*?" I asked.

"It's just all so… dull and monotonous," she admitted with an air of utter disgust.

"Hey, lawns need to be mowed, dishes washed, and dirty clothes laundered, regardless of monotony. That's life. It's an adventure for the few, and a bitch for the many."

"So, we just sit here and do nothing?"

"What do you usually do when you do laundry," I asked.

She picked up her book and showed it to me.

"Right," I chuckled.

"Additionally," she started, "I don't drive halfway across town to a laundromat when there is a perfectly good laundry room in my own apartment building. Which - by the way - why *aren't* you using the one in the building?"

"To avoid my neighbors," I grinned.

"Ha ha," she said, "what are you doing?"

"Paying bills."

Thaleia gagged exaggeratedly.

"Ew! You're being an adult? On your day off ? Who hurt you?"

"Bills need to be paid."

"Yeah, yeah, yeah, I understand," she said, dismissively, "but, look," she grabbed the bottom of my chin and forced me to look up and out of the giant windows of the laundromat to the world outside, pointing to the sky. "A day this beautiful is wasted indoors."

I had no response for her. The day was beautiful. The sun was perched so hgh in the middle of the cobalt blue sky, not even the clouds could reach it. Thaleia rose to her feet, turned to me, and extended her hand firmly.

"Give me your keys," she commanded.

"What?"

"Your car keys. Hand them over."

I didn't protest. I dug into my pocket and placed the keys in the palm of her hand. Before I could retract my hand, however, Thaleia snatched it, pulled me to my feet, and pushed me toward the front door.

"Wait, what are you doing?" I asked, still allowing myself to be led.

"We're out of here!"

My body tried to stop but she already had all the momentum on her side, rendering me powerless against her force.

"My clothes," I weakly protested.

"Are clothes," Thaleia said. "I assure you they'll be here when we get back."

"I have to put them in the dryer first."

"Don't worry about it, Auntie here will take care of it, right Auntie?" Thaleia winked at the Old Guatemalan owner. The Guatemalan owner smiled and nodded her head softly. Perhaps she had a soft spot seeing her own youth in Thaleia and me play out before her eyes.

Thaleia shoved me in the passenger seat and slammed the door. She bounced over to the driver side and hopped in. I reached for my seatbelt as Thaleia adjusted the driver seat and mirrors to suit her needs.

"Where are we going?" I insisted.

Thaleia plugged the key into the ignition and got the car to start with ease. She exclaimed excitedly.

"I'll give you a hint: It's twenty minutes from here," she teased.

"Some hint. There are plenty of places that are twenty minutes from here," I whined. I did not like this game.

"Guess!" Thaleia commanded. She was already cutting up the busy road, darting through traffic.

"The movies? The mall?" I began to list random places.

"It's outdoors."

"An outdoor mall? The park?"

"You should give up, you'll never get it," she said, aggressively turning the steering wheel. "Give up?"

"Yes. Please end this."

"Sorry, no quitters in this car. Keep trying," Thaleia laughed.

"I'm terrible at this," I complained.

"Come on! Don't stop! Keep going!"

"Can't we just go back. I can't afford new clothes - Geez!"

Thaleia slammed on the brakes and swerved to avoid a car that came to an abrupt stop. She leaned on the horn angrily, rolled the window down and began insulting the other driver as she passed him by, then zoomed off not waiting for a retort from the stunned driver.

"It's noon on a Friday! Why the hell are there so many people on the road?! Don't they have jobs?!" she ranted.

As she was grumbling curse words under her breath, she cut into the other lane without indicating, garnering a symphony of honking. I clutched the dashboard for dear life as Thaleia swerved all over the road like a confident drunk. My breakfast was working its way up for an encore.

"I'm starting to understand why you're having car troubles," I half-joked, clutching on to the car grab handle for dear life.

"You guess yet?" Thaleia boomeranged back to the quest.

"I don't know the - the beach?" I stammered.

"Aw no. I look great in a two piece, but I'm not much of a swimmer," she lamented.

She turned into a side street that was not as crowded as the main road and finally started driving like a respectable motorist. I slowly let go of the grab handle and settled into the passenger seat. The carpet was now filled with water as all her twists and turns forced the water from the evaporator drain to flood onto the passenger floor. I positioned my feet on the sides so as not to get my shoes wet.

"I found this place on one of my random excursions around the town," she said.

She turned into another street, this one was more narrow than the last. Small houses sparsely lined the road.

I looked out the window and saw a plane soaring overhead in the opposite direction. The plane broke the sound barrier above us, making the car tremble.

"Wow, that's got to be annoying to hear all day," I said.

Thaleia only smiled. She turned into a gravel road and drove until she reached a clearing at a dead end. She parked the car and got out. I unbuckled myself and followed suit.

We were surrounded by a thicket of trees. Thaleia walked to the edge of the clearing and climbed over the metal railing.

"Are you coming or what?" she called out.

I jogged over to her, climbed over the railing, and followed her into the forest.

We followed a narrow dirt path for about half an hour. Every so often a plane would boom overhead, sending a strong gust of wind through the towering trees, showering us with falling leaves and pine needles.

"Where are we going?" I asked.

"You'll see," Thaleia said, playfully.

I'm not much for walking so this little hike already had me winded and dripping sweat. I didn't like the beach but part of me was beginning to hope that the destination was the ocean so I could take a quick refreshing dip.

Finally after another fifteen minutes or so, we reached another clearing. Thaleia turned to me with a grin she could barely contain.

"We're here," she said.

I followed her out of the forest into the clearing. There were metal electrical boxes scattered about in the parched brown grass. Past the electrical boxes was a chain linked fence with spiral barbed wire. Past the fence, was an airport.

The airport was not big enough for commercial and international flights. It looked to be all local and some domestic. Planes of all sizes from cessna's to small sea planes were being towed around the runway.

Thaleia grabbed my hand and escorted me through the electrical boxes. There were some empty beer bottles and discarded fast food containers about. We found a concrete base and sat down.

"An airport?" I said.

"Yeah," Thaleia confirmed. "Let me guess, you didn't know this town had one?"

I smiled and nodded. "How often do you come here?" I asked.

"Not often," she said. "I don't ever really plan to. It just happens sometimes, when I happen to be around."

She adjusted herself and sat cross legged, her eyes never breaking from the action playing before us in the airport.

The sun was in peak position over the airport as another plane lined up on the runway and took off into the sky. The warm air rushed around us, surrounding and penetrating our bodies, sending euphoric sensations through our veins like quality heroin.

"I can sit here for hours," Thaleia began. "Just watching the planes take off, imagining where each one is headed to." She picked up a pebble and tossed it, watching it disappear in the brown grass. "Europe, Africa, South America."

She tossed another pebble further out in the distance.

"Then I imagine myself in the plane. Sitting in the window seat, looking out, down at the Earth as I lift into the clouds out of sight. Living the many possible lives I could live. Running with the bulls in Pamplona, strolling through the streets of Marseille, spelunking in the Ivory Coast, sailing the shores of the Greek Islands. "

Another plane hurried down the runway and catapulted into the sky above us, stirring the dust and dirt around us.

"Every time I find myself here, watching the plane's journey on, I'm reminded of what Sylvia Plath once wrote. *'I can never read all the books I want; I can never be all the people I want and live all the lives I want. I can never train myself in all the skills I want. And why do I want? I want to live and feel all the shades, tones, and variations of mental and physical experience possible in my life'...*," Thaleia looked down, a somber expression enveloped her countenance. She grimaced slightly, "... *'And I am horribly limited.'*"

Her breathing grew deeper. She closed her eyes tight and began to tremble. Her hands balled into fists as she began to hyperventilate. I scooched closer to her and covered her fists with my hand. She clutched onto my hand tightly, as if she was afraid if she let go, she would fall to her death.

She finally regained her composure but held on to my hand. She opened her mouth to say something; I could see the letters and words dangling from the very tip of her tongue. After a few seconds, she closed her mouth and swallowed the words. Guess whatever needed to be said was better left unsaid. We sat in silence, hand in hand, watching the sun begin its descent.

Thaleia allowed her head to fall on my shoulder, exhaling a satisfactory sigh.

"Why did you try to kill yourself ? she asked suddenly.

The question didn't surprise me. I can tell she'd been wanting to ask me that ever since the topic came up when we had Thai the night before.

"Was it because of her?"

Her. She meant Evelyn. A deep breath expanded my chest as I prepared and organized an answer. I knew the answer, but to articulate it aloud, I found it quite difficult.

"Her?" I said, trying to buy myself some time.

"The beauty you have as the lock screen picture on your phone," she said. She suddenly lifted her head from my shoulder and shook her head, apologetically. "You know what, I'm sorry, that was - you don't have to answer," she said, retracting her curiosity.

"No, it's okay. I just don't know how to answer your question in a way that makes sense."

"I don't need to know *how*, just *why*. If you're afraid I'll judge you. I won't. I promise," she assured me.

"Nah, that's not it," I said. "I should be judged."

"Not by me," she said, sternly. "Please, don't worry if it makes sense," she advised. "Just speak."

"Okay," I said. She rested her head on my shoulders again and waited for me to continue. I exhaled.

"The short answer is no. It wasn't because of her," I began.

"And the long answer?" She implored.

Thaleia lifted her head from my shoulders and looked at me. Her eyes were begging for the long answer and I felt compelled to oblige. I nodded. Thaleia returned her head to my shoulder. Another plane passed above us.

"I am not passionate about anything," I continued, choosing my words carefully. "So, if I am not passionate about anything, if I have no purpose for existing, why exist?"

I looked down at Thaleia but she didn't move her head from my shoulder. Her way of telling me to continue.

"Imagine sitting in a small room. There are four walls, a floor, and a ceiling. A cement box with no windows and no doors. You can hear life outside of those walls, you can even interact with everyone outside in that life, but you can't see it, taste it, touch it. The people out there, passing by your box, they have no idea you're in there. Just you, alone in the box with a soft white 40-watt bulb to give you light. It isn't bright, but it's bright enough to illuminate the room. The room is compact, but since you're the only one in it, it's sufficiently big enough for you.

"Then one day, you realize that you're not alone in the room. You discover a thought. A tiny seedling, no bigger than a green pea - no- a bread crumb. You pay it no mind because the room is big enough for you both. However, over time, the thought grows. The seed sprouts roots. The roots grab hold of the cement floor. The seed becomes a sapling, then a small tree. The leaves come in and the branches reach up and stretch out. Still, you don't mind. You can co-exist. There's still room, though there is less of it, you just shift around and pick a free space, settle in.

"Still, time continues forward, and the tree, no longer able to grow upwards, now expands outward. The leaves thicken, the branches multiply, the trunk hardens, the roots tear up the floor. The lone light in the room struggles to shine through the thicket of leaves, until it no longer can and dies off. Now you're pinned against the wall by one of the aggressive roots, curled up in a dark corner no different than an abyss. Trapped. In pain. *Overwhelming, unbearable* pain. No one outside could help or see you, so even if they wanted to help, there is no way to get in this box. Logically speaking, death was the only way

144

to have peace. To put an end to that thought: *'If I have no purpose for existing, why exist at all?'"*

I stopped talking, took in a deep breath and exhaled. Thaleia remained motionless and silent. I reached my conclusion.

"I felt that way before... her. With her. And after her."

"How about now?" Thaleia asked, softly.

I didn't answer her, but my silence spoke volumes. With nothing left to say, I looked down at Thaleia to gauge her expression. She lifted her head but struggled like her skull was full of bricks. I searched for her eyes and was surprised to find them drowning in tears. Reacting on pure instinct, I wiped the tears away but the act only served to open the flood gates. Thaleia shuddered and sobbed. I embraced her harder. She buried her face in my chest and wept silently with her entire body.

Another plane took off directly over us, the ground beneath us shook and trembled from its passing force, however Thaleia and I remained fixed, entangled in embrace.

"Did that make sense?" I asked.

Thaleia burst into laughter through a bout of sniffles.

* * *

We arrived at the laundromat just as the owner was calling it a day, preparing for someone else to take over for the night shift. The Guatemalan was generous enough to fold my clothes and set them aside neatly. Wracked with guilt, I repaid her kindness with a princely tip, while Thaleia loaded up my laundry in the trunk of my Monte Carlo.

We stopped at a burger joint on our way home. I watched as Thaleia scarfed down a double cheeseburger with all the fixings (including extra bacon), a large Coke, and two baskets of fries drowned in ketchup, all with the smile of an innocent child unsullied by the pitfalls of life.

She contemplated capping her binge off with a vanilla soft serve ice cream cone before she even finished wiping the grease and mayonnaise from the corners of her mouth; however, before she could make a firm decision, she received a call from the mechanic: her car was ready, but he was closing in fifteen minutes. We hopped in the Monte Carlo and peeled off.

I waited for Thaleia in the empty parking lot next to the mechanic shop, replaying the day's events. Thaleia emerged from the shop and marched over. She leaned over my open window.

"They're bringing it around," she said with the energy zapped from her voice.

"You let him have an ear full didn't you?" I asked.

Thaleia laughed.

"Let's just say he's probably wishing he had the balls of Van Gogh," she remarked. "He gave me a discount on the repair and on the next one, just to shut my mouth. He won't do that again."

I chuckled softly. We shared a silence.

"Listen," Thaleia began, "Thank you. Not just for coming through in the clutch for me these last couple of days. But also... you know, telling me about...," She was having trouble getting the words out, but I understood where she was going and tried to stop her from getting there.

"It's no big deal," I said.

"It is!" She said sternly. "See... my dad-"

Just as she was going to get to her point, the mechanic came around with the car. He was dirty and sweaty, his belly protruded below his tight shirt stained with oil and other liquids. His fingers were filthy with grime. His curly hair was sweaty, parts of it stuck to his forehead. He came over to hand the keys to Thaleia and saw her eyes were red and glossy like she was getting ready to cry. His eyes looked from hers to mine searching for a reason. He came to his own conclusion.

"Fine. Fifty-five percent discount," he conceded.

* * *

It was late in the evening when we got back to our apartment. Thaleia helped me carry my load of laundry up the four flights of stairs to our floor. I unlocked my door and Thaleia dropped the laundry on my futon. I walked her to the door.

"Welp," Thaleia began, "I'm going to go clean the dirt out of all my hair and my creases. Thank you for your help again. I know I messed up your plans today..."

"You did, but it's okay," I said, jokingly.

"I bet," Thaleia giggled warmly.

We shared another silence. I began to say something when Thaleia jumped on me and hugged me tight. I hugged her back. We could've stayed like that forever, clutching to one another in the doorway. It felt like we did. Thaleia unlocked her grasp and smiled at me.

"I release thee from servitude," she said, placing her hand on my right shoulder and then my left like a king knighting a warrior.

"You are too gracious, my Queen," I said.

She smiled from ear to ear and rolled her eyes.

"You're so dumb," she laughed.

She slid away from the entrance but stopped and turned to me. She wanted to ask me another question, but I can see she was trying to piece together the right words before she spoke them.

"Why didn't you go through with... you know," she finally asked.

I thought about my answer, my arms folded across my chest.

"Days like this, I suppose...," I answered.

Again, she smiled.

"You know, you say you have no purpose for existing, but I disagree. Even if you don't believe it to be, some people feel like they're born with their purpose already instilled within them by God, and because he gave us free will supposedly, the choices we make either lead us to our purpose or deters us from it. Others think our life experiences push us to *choose* a purpose. Either way, whatever your purpose is, it's out there, somewhere. It might not be what you expect it to be, but it's out there, waiting for you. You just have to be willing to look. In essence, you're choosing to deny yourself a purpose."

I drank in what she said but didn't say anything in response.

"Alright. I'll mind my own business," she quipped with a smile. "Goodnight, Perv."

"Goodnight, Tally," I said.

I watched as she unlocked her door and retreated into her apartment for the night. I closed my door and listened as Thaleia settled into her apartment and turned on her TV. I poured myself a glass of water, made my way around the counter to the living room, turned the TV on, and began putting my clean clothes away, my mind occasionally drifting away and replaying the day's events on a loop.

Chapter Nine

I spent the next morning cleaning my apartment. The rancid smell had returned, and this time I knew it wasn't the trash; I had made sure to throw the garbage away the night before to avoid this very issue. Still, the foul stench hung in the air. I tried locating the source, the kitchen, the bathroom, my bed, but I couldn't figure out where it was coming from, so I just decided to clean the entire apartment from top to bottom.

By the time I was done and satisfied that the odor was gone (or at least suppressed), it was already the mid-afternoon. I showered, got dressed and decided I should go over to my mother's house to get that package that was sent for me as promised. No use procrastinating.

It was a long drive out to my mother's estate from my apartment, the journey made more arduous by the afternoon traffic. I call my mother's house an estate because that's exactly what it is. She sits on nearly fourteen acres of land (13.95 acres as she likes to humbly brag), her house is made of brick and mortar like a Scottish castle, it has two stories, a veranda on the west end of the castle, an attic/artist loft, and a balcony overlooking the entire backyard on the south end. There is an indoor pool, an outdoor Jacuzzi, a tennis court, a green house, a garden, a chicken coup, a vegetable patch, a small maze, a gazebo, an observation post, three fountains (one in the roundabout in the driveway, one in the center of the maze, and one in the garden), a guest house, and a detached garage that her husband, Richard, uses as his private carpentry shop. All of this, surrounded by ten-foot-high brick walls and tall trees that rise up triple that size. In short: *a fortress.*

I pulled up to the black iron gate, pressed the call button on the intercom, and waited. Two stone lion statues were perched on the main columns of the gate. Their mouths were open like they were in mid roar.

"Hello?" came a gruff voice from the intercom. Richard's I gathered. I announced myself.

"Oh, hey. Your mom ain't here yet. She's out visitin' one of her quiltin' buddies," Richard informed me.

"Oh, no problem. I'll come back later," I said, ready to throw my car in reverse.

"What? Naw. Save ya gas; she'll be back soon. Come in," he said.

I began to protest but the gate was already straining open slowly. Every time they did this, I always felt like I was entering Jurassic Park; I could hear John Williams's theme song swelling in my head.

My Monte Carlo puttered up the cobblestone driveway. When I arrived at the roundabout, I caught a glimpse of Richard by the garage tending to his riding mower. A straw hat shaded him from the brutal sun, and his long-sleeve, dri-fit shirt was soaked with his sweat. He wore goggles and an American flag bandana that covered the bottom half of his face from nose to chin.

I cut my engine off and got out of the car in no particular hurry. Richard threw a quick glance my way and waved me over before disappearing behind the garage. I could hear birds chirping all around, and crickets calling somewhere out in the newly clipped grass and shaved shrubbery. I inhaled the scent of fresh cut grass before trudging over to the garage.

The lawn was evenly trimmed, not a weed or rebellious blade of grass in sight. The flowers around the house were so vivid the purple, orange, and yellow colors looked like they were slathered with a fresh coat of paint. When I made it to the garage, Richard was using a broom to clean the dead clippings from the riding mower and hosing the sand and dirt from the body. He turned the nozzle until the water stopped flowing and took off his soiled gardening gloves.

"Hey, kid," he called out affectionately. He took my hand into his and shook it. His hands were so strong and worked, it felt like I was shaking hands with a boulder.

"Grass looks great," I felt compelled to comment.

"It better. Been workin' out here since this mornin'," he joked, in his Hispanic-Redneck drawl. "Can ya do me a favor? On the back porch I have a cooler fullah beer. Can ya bring it here?"

He didn't wait for me to answer. He turned around and began drying off the wet mower with a green microfiber towel.

I found the cooler exactly where he said it would be and hauled it over to the garage. He exclaimed joyfully, opened the cooler, removed two beers, and tossed one over to me. I barely caught it with my fingertips.

"Oh, I can't," I politely refused.

"Yes ya can," he stated, cracking the lip of his beer and downing the can thirstily.

"I'm driving," I reminded him.

"It's *beer*," he stated as a matter of fact.

There was no sense arguing, his stubbornness was much more resolute than mine. Truth be told, I could use a beer, I convinced myself. The can felt nice and cool in my hands. I cracked it open and took a few generous swallows. It hit the spot. Richard basked in his victory as he finished his beer and fished another one out of the yeti.

Richard is the type of man Hemingway wrote about. Salt of the Earth men. The type of men that took pride in work that required sweat, spit, and blood. He came from a generation where dreams and aspirations did not put food on your plate or kept a roof over your head, clothes on your back, nor did it keep the heat on during harsh unrelenting winters. Long haul trucking did, construction work did, carpentry did, drilling for oil... you get it.

Richard was that man. Mexican born. Came to America at 10. Joined the Army at 17. Went to Vietnam. Came back and became a cop. Retired honorably. Started his own tile company as an installer, worked his way up to General Contractor. Then, when his back and knees gave out, he switched to distributor, took his business national, then international, sold it for millions and now spends his time tending to his garden, his chickens, and expanding his property.

My mother and he have built a lovely life and a lovely family together. He and I have never had a conversation that didn't go past the weather, but he always treated me warmly. That I could appreciate.

He took long pulls of the beer and set it down in the cup holder on the riding mower.

"I heard about ya dad," he said. "Man, sorry for ya loss."

"Ah, no, thank you. I didn't really know him very well, but thank you," I stammered.

"He's still ya father, though," he said. He took his beer and spilled a little on the lawn. "For ya dad," he said, holding up his beer to me, making a toast. I mimicked his ritual and touched his can with mine. We took another long pull of beer, finishing his second and reaching for a third.

"You'll never forget the day ya found out," he continued. "I remember the day my Papi died like it was yesterday, down to the last detail. The smells, the colors. I was on my way home from picking up my daughter from school when I got that 911 page from my mother. Everything to her was a 911 page; out of milk, the neighbors are making too much noise, someone is stealing her avocados, you name it," he laughed and took another sip of beer. "But when I got to their street and saw the ambulance, police, fire trucks... I knew right away he was gone."

"What did he die of?" I asked. The beer spread a refreshing warmth through my body. I didn't drink often so even half a can of beer was enough to get me buzzed.

"Oh, it was natural. He was ninety-three. My mother said he was watching TV, some novela he and my mother watched together, and having an early dinner. He was sitting in his chair, some ugly tan thing with sunflowers printed all over it, so weird," he chuckled. "He asked for a glass of water, and my mother got up to pour him a glass and when she came back to give it to him, he was dead. Just like that. My mother freaked out of course, you know, she thought he choked on her fish, but nope. He just died. On his favorite chair, during a commercial break. Ain't that crazy?" He chortled and drank some more.

He continued, "What amazed me is that my father, for being ninety-three, was still as sharp as a tack, and as strong as an Ox on cocaine. His memory was better than mine and he was in really good shape for his age. But, it just goes to show you when your string gets cut, the lights go out. That's it. It was his time."

"Wow, I'm sorry," I said.

"Don't be. My father led an interesting and fulfilling life. He wuddn't perfect, but he wuddn't a complete asshole either. He never explained how, but he was in World War I, survived the Great Depression, went to World War II, literally built a business from the ground up with his bare hands. He taught me to be strong, that education don't end when school does. That a well-rounded man is one who is disciplined enough to continue learnin' and applyin' the knowledge he gains to his everyday life. That it's okay to be a Jack of all trades as long as you're a master being one. So, when he died, I ain't cry or nothin'.' He prepared me and my sisters for this. His last lesson: *The life of man is not infinite, but rather finite.* Can you help me with this?"

He was trying to push the lawn mower back into the garage but was having trouble getting it over the threshold. I set my beer down on the concrete and helped him roll it over the curb and into the garage.

"What was I saying?" He asked me.

"Man's mortality," I said.

"Right!" He smiled, putting a thick nylon cover over the lawnmower. "We are mortal beings. All of this," he motioned to his property and what lay beyond it, the sky above. "This is what we have right now. Don't tell your mother this, I respect her devotion to Christianity, but for me, this is all there is. This is the time we have right here, right now. There ain't nothin' waitin' for us after that final sleep but eternal darkness. Bettin' on a Heaven makes fools out of people suffering now, waitin' for it to end thinkin' paradise is on the other side. Ain't nothin' there. But that don't mean you stop givin' a shit. It just means we gotta make the most out of the time we're given. Grab that."

Richard grabbed the end of a heavy piece of lumber. I grabbed the other side and helped him carry it to a partially built shed. We walked back to the garage for more.

"So, your father fulfilled his purpose?" I said.

Richard thought this over.

"If his purpose was to make sure his kids didn't struggle in life. Then, yeah."

We picked up another piece of lumber.Richard noticed I was struggling to keep the lumber above my waist.

"Western Red Cedar," he said. "The best wood for building outdoor sheds."

We dropped the lumber next to the others. Richard grabbed a shovel that was on the grass next to the lumber and began to dig a small hole. He stopped, wiped his brow, and chuckled to himself.

"I just remembered a story my father used to tell me when I was a boy," he grabbed his beer and cleared it. He handed the empty can to me. "Can you grab me another?"

I went to the cooler, retrieved another can and brought it to him. He cracked it open and the fizz came spilling out over his hands. He saved what he could and let the rest spill.

"For decades, a timber tree has grown in its forest surrounded by other timber trees, enjoying the sun, the rain, and the animals and insects that made its branches home," He took another sip of his beer, put it down and continued digging a small hole. "One gray foggy day, a group of men come into the forest, cut down the timber tree and all the other trees around it. They trim off all their leaves and branches, turn them into mulch, toss the timber's body on the back of a flatbed, and tightly tie them down, securing the timber to the truck. Then they're all hauled off to the lumber mill. The timber watches as the men set fire to the rest of the forest," He takes a moment to take a sip of beer.

"On the way to the lumber mill," he continued. "The timber began to speak excitedly to one another about what they wish to become. One said, 'I wish to become the paper on which the next great American novel will be written.' Another said, 'I wish to become a grand piano on which a beautiful sonata will be played.' Another said, 'I wish to become the planks on a great ship that will sail the seven seas on a grand voyage.' Another said, 'I wish to become the barrels that hold fine wine and liquor that will be consumed during celebrations.' Another said, 'I wish to be the baseball bat that will go on to break all records.'"

Richard poured cement in the hole and placed the timber into it, securing it with rope and other wood so it would stand upright.

"This goes on for a while until finally, they reach the last piece of timber. They asked the last piece of timber what it hoped they would all be made into. The piece of timber thought it over. It never knew it could be anything else than what it was. The timber continued to goad it. 'Come on, what do you think? Pencils that will sketch the tallest buildings? Brushes that will paint the most magnificent painting?' The timber couldn't think of anything. The timber arrives at the lumber mill, they're taken off the truck and sent to the mill. You know what

155

they all ended up becoming?"

I shook my head. Richard leaned in close to me like he was getting ready to tell me the secret of the universe through a dirty limerick. His lips curled into a small, amused smile.

"Toilet paper."

* * *

My mother came driving up the driveway in her matte silver-colored Mercedes Benz just as Richard and I finished polishing off our respective beers. She parked near the entrance of the house and emerged from the driver's side, retrieving her purse and suitcase. She was dressed in her typical work attire, a navy-blue blazer over a white silk blouse, black dress pants and black flats. Last time I saw my mother, her hair was shoulder length, so I was surprised when she came out of her car with her hair done extremely short and mostly gray.

My mother smiled at me and waved me over. I excused myself with Richard and walked over to her. She gave me a strong hug and a kiss on the cheek. I'm thirty years old, and somehow this act always made me feel like a child.

"Bendición, hijo," she greeted.

"Hello, mother," I responded in kind.

She let me go. "Sorry, to keep you waiting. Was Richard talking your ear off?"

"Not really," I said. Always the obedient son, I helped her with her bags, all full of quilting tools, a hobby she took way too serious. That was my mother, no matter what she decided to do, she did it to the extreme.

"I thought when he retired he'd finally take it easy, but he's as active as ever. The man practically lives outside. I swear, he only comes in to eat, sleep, and watch La Liga," she said. "I'm surprised the sun hasn't hard boiled his brain."

I followed her to the house. She pushed through the front door and walked through the courtyard where another water feature proudly put on its choreographed show, complete with lights and soft music, the kind you'd hear in a spa retreat. There was no traditional front door; once you entered through the main door and spilled into the courtyard, the actual entrance to the house was through large sliding glass doors. She slid the door open and walked in directing me to put her things down on the bench next to the sliding door. If the outside looked like a Scottish castle, the interior of the house looked more like a museum. Every decorative piece looked exotic, ancient, and expensive.

"Are you hungry? Do you want me to make you something to eat?" she asked, already pulling things out of the fridge and rummaging through the cupboards.

"I'm good," I said. I didn't want to impose.

"You're hungry. I'll make you something. It'll be quick. Sit down," she commanded.

I sat down at their nook and watched as she continued to remove leftovers and fresh produce from the fridge. She took out some pots and pans and set them on the spider burners on the gas stove. She poured a cap full of vegetable oil in the pan and turned the stove-top to medium-high heat. As the blue flames tickled the bottom of the pan, she quickly chopped up onions, green peppers, garlic, cilantro and tomato, and tossed them into the pan. The moment they hit the hot oil, they began to sizzle, sending a gentle plume of smoke stretching into the air and into the cooking vent. The smell assaulted my senses, triggering my stomach into a strong grumble. She was right, I *was* hungry.

Once the vegetables were fragrant and translucent, she added some leftover chicken drumsticks, let them sauté for a few minutes until they had regained their golden brown sheen, added a little tomato paste and poured some water over everything until it covered half the chicken, and covered the pan. Next she proceeded to wash a cup of dry white rice, draining the excess starch each time until the final time, the water was clear. My mother moved from one task to another gracefully and ritualistically, as if one wrong step could defile the meal. She put the rice in a rice cooker and let the machine do the rest of the work. I bought the rice cooker for her for Christmas since she would constantly complain that it took more time to clean the concón (burnt rice) from the bottom of the steel pans than it was to cook it. Yet, every time she uses the rice cooker, she feels the need to lecture me about how there are no shortcuts when it comes to preparing meals.

"This is not the way your abuela taught me, and her mother taught her. You have to put in the work," she would repeat ad nauseam.

While everything was cooking, she cut up some lettuce, tomato, cucumber, and radishes, tossed in some sweet corn and avocado, mixed everything into a large bowl, drizzled olive oil and balsamic vinegar over it, and sprinkled some salt and pepper. She tossed the salad once more before finally serving some to me on a small plate, handing me a tiny fork. I tried not to eat too quickly, but every bite I took only served to stoke my appetite until my stomach fully awoke with hunger.

Finally, the food was ready. She prepared two plates, put one in the microwave (presumably for Richard), and served me the other. She poured herself a glass of red wine and sat across from me.

"How is it?" she asked, as I took my first fork full.

"Disgusting," I quipped, shoveling the food in my mouth in heaps.

She lovingly smacked me upside the back of my head. She took a sip of her wine and watched me eat.

"You remind me so much of him," she said.

"Who?"

"You're father," she confirmed.

I grunted and continued to eat.

She got up, went to the fridge, and pulled out two bottles of water. She put one next to me. I shoveled so much food into my mouth, I was beginning to choke. I opened my bottle of water and swallowed its refreshing contents in two gulps. I took a few deep breaths, as if I was coming up for air after doing laps in an Olympic pool before diving back into my plate.

"You look just like him. Same slender nose, same dark eyes, same pouty lips," she grabbed my lips and squeezed them playfully. "I met him my first semester of college. He was a sophomore working on a degree in Communications. He was so handsome. Tall, dark, fit. He played basketball for our school, too. Shooting Guard. Off the bench, but whenever he came in, he injected life into the game. But what he really loved was DJ-ing."

She took a sip of her wine. Her eyes glossed over, floating in a happy memory. I didn't know it then, but she was grieving.

"He was the campus DJ. He agreed to do the evening shift that went from ten at night until two in the morning as long as they gave him free reign to play whatever he wanted, and they agreed. The first hour he played Hip-Hop: Salt-N-Pepa, Whodini, Kool Moe Dee. The second hour he played R&B: New Edition, The Isley Brothers, Sade. The third hour he played Jazz: Miles Davis, Dizzy Gillespie, Duke Ellington, Charlie Parker, Thelonious Monk. Then the last hour was special requests. My girlfriends used to gather around the radio and swoon over his silkie voice transmitting over the airwaves. I did, too."

Another sip of her wine.

"He was also so intelligent. He used to talk to me about philosophy and theology, I could barely keep up. There was one point he loved to make: *'the Benevolent God that we are all familiar with, was actually a concept constructed by St. Thomas Aquinas and St. Augustine. God can be all powerful. He can be ever-present. He can be all loving. But with all the pain and suffering in the world, why doesn't he come down and put an end to it? If he can't, then he is not all powerful. If he can but chooses not to, then he is not a loving God.'* I can't explain it the same way he did, but that really floored me. He had the world in the palm of his hand," she paused for a beat and heaved a short sigh that made her shoulders slump slightly. "He could've done anything."

"So, why didn't he?" I asked, still shoveling food into my mouth.

She shrugged her shoulders and gave her head a short shake.

"I don't know," she said. "When he returned from summer break for his final semester, he wasn't the same. The light in his eye didn't shine anymore. He was a husk. He didn't want to do anything. He gave up basketball. He stopped showing up to classes. He even quit DJ-ing. I'd be busting my ass working to pay bills and studying for tests, drafting reports, burning the candles on both ends, and he'd just be floating around like a ghost from room to room with no rhyme or reason."

I stopped eating and listened intently.

"Did you ever find out why?" I asked.

"No. I asked his sisters, his brothers if anything had happened while he was visiting them in DeFuniak for the summer and they said that he'd actually been the same way while he was there. I thought maybe he just got overwhelmed with the workload of school and the extracurricular activities, so I tried to help him get back on track, talked to teachers, his friends, but no one could get through to him. Whatever hole he was in, he just sank deeper and deeper and refused any type of help. Then I got pregnant with you," she finished her wine and poured herself another cup. "I don't know, I really thought that maybe if he saw you, held you in his arms, that it would rekindle his desire and passion, his *fight* but...," tears started to form around the corners of her eyes and trickle down her cheeks. She quickly wiped them away.

"For a little while, it looked that way. I put school on hold so I could take care of you and with his associate's degree he was able to find

Administration work that paid well enough for us to survive check to check. It wasn't easy but we made it work. After a year he got promoted and made a little more money. We were able to throw you a nice party for your first birthday. My family was there, kids from the apartment building, it was just such a happy moment. We gathered around your cake and sang you happy birthday. I took a picture of him holding you, fixing your shirt. When the party was long over, we put you to bed, and he and I just listened to music as we cleaned up and talked about people who were at the party. He was in good spirits. Laughing. Felt like he was back," she took another sip of wine. "Then we fell asleep. The next morning, I woke up and he was gone."

Her voice broke. More tears streamed down her face, those she couldn't get rid of them fast enough. They flooded over her fingers and down her hands. I sat in silence, not sure how or if I should console her. She cleared her throat and regained her composure.

"He was gone. All of him. His clothes, his vinyl records, his food, even his goddamn soap and toothbrush. He left nothing of himself behind, not even a note. It was like he ceased existing in the world all together. I cried for an entire month. Thank God my sister lived a block from me. She helped take care of you while I finished college, but it was hard. What I don't understand is how he could look at you in your crib, sleeping so soundly, and just walk out of your life. You didn't deserve that. Til this day, I never learned why he left that way. Now I guess I'll never know."

She downed what remained of the wine in one gulp, wiped all her tears away, and composed herself.

"I shouldn't be talking about him like this. It's in bad taste to speak ill of the dead. I don't want to remember him that way, anyway. If it weren't for him, I wouldn't've survived college the way I did. Most importantly, I wouldn't have you. I guess some wounds don't fully heal. We just carry them with us as scars on our heart. I just wish you would've gotten a chance to know the man I knew."

We both shared a moment of silence. I could see her thoughts traveling a private path in her eyes. She returned to the present and smiled at me tenderly.

"You know, when his brother called me to tell me your dad died, we ended up talking for a while. Your dad has so many siblings but he was always closest to his younger brother. I can tell it hit him the hardest," my mother twisted the cap off of her water and began to drink. "He actually told me that your father saved his life."

"How?" I asked, my attention fully on her, the fork in my hand

She hesitated for a moment. "Well, his younger brother was a drug addict. It was ravaging him, he said. One night, he was in a really bad way and your dad suddenly showed up. The drugs really messed him up. He said it was so bad, he pulled a shotgun on your dad with the full intent to kill him."

I gulped. I knew the story before she even finished it.

"He said he gave your dad no choice, and your dad ended up shooting him, right in the shoulder. He said, the pain from the bullet paled in comparison with the look of hurt and disappointment in your dad's eyes. When your dad left, he was ready to just die. But then your dad came back and got him help. Took him to the hospital, got him checked in to a facility. Was by his side for the withdrawals, the meeting, he even got him a job. His brother is doing so well now, and it was all because your dad gave him purpose."

I remained silent, replaying that memory in my head. I never had the entire picture of that night. I felt a weight lift off my shoulders.

Suddenly, a question welled up from deep within me and burst up and forth like a geyser before I recognized what it was.

"Are you happy?" I asked.

My mother's eyes widened, surprised by this sudden inquiry. Her brow furrowed.

"How do you mean?"

Clearly my mother was happy. She was a respected professional in her field. Toiled until she grasped success and built an incredible life for herself. She's been to all corners of the known globe, tasted the wine and authentic pasta in Italy, visited the Roman Colosseum, bathed in the famed springs of Japan, fish and chips in London. She's seen Messi play in Camp Nou, caught a Chopin symphony at the Sydney Opera House, drank Colombian coffee in Medellín, and has taken a cat nap on the beaches of Hawaii.

"I guess," I said slowly, "what I'm asking is," I searched for the right words but they had trouble forming, "have you found happiness?"

All I could do was reframe my initial question, but my mother stared into her empty wine glass and turned the thought over.

"Generally speaking, yes," she answered after a few minutes of silent contemplation.

"Are you fulfilling your purpose?" Again, the question sprung out of me without warning. My mother looked at me with a look of bewilderment.

"Well, that's a different question, isn't it," she said. "It depends, I suppose, on what I think my purpose is. If, for example, I felt my purpose for existing was to be a mother, then I would be fulfilling my purpose."

"Is that your purpose?" I asked.

She smiled warmly.

"I don't think so. No. I love being a mother - your mother - and I've certainly always wanted to be a mother, but that's not all I wanted out of my life. I've always found solace in helping souls in need." My mother uncapped her water and took a generous sip. "I grew up in Puerto Rico with your abuela. My sister was already in Chicago with my brother so it was just my mother and me. She was always working, whatever jobs she could get her hands on. I was home making sure the house was clean, dinner was cooked, and my schoolwork was done, before she got home in the late evening. One night she came home with an armful of books. Apparently, one of the clients she cleaned for was getting rid of some stuff because her husband had passed and she was giving away all the books he would no longer be reading. The books were in English but that was okay because my English at the time was really good, though I was still learning. There was a mix of decent books in the pile, some science fiction by Ursula K. Le Guin and Isaac Asimov, romance novels, books on finance and investing, but the book that caught my eye was *The Brothers Karamazov* by Fyodor Dostoyevsky. It was such a thick book, thicker than most of my school textbooks even, but I didn't feel intimidated. I sat down, opened the book, and read it end to end. Took me some time, but whenever I had free time, my nose was in that book. I was enthralled by the theology and humanity. Typically, everyone who reads this book relates to the idealism of Alyosha, but I was more touched by the section about Father Zosima's life. I won't go into it, but he started off as a young brash man, and consciously decided to devote his life to asceticism, to helping others on their journey through life. That stirred something in the core of my being. A burning desire to help others. Any time I found myself wandering in the dark, that desire was the beacon that pulled me back. It's why I am a dedicated member and active participant in the Catholic Church, why I decided to become a Lawyer specializing in Immigration Law. My purpose and my faith, those are the compasses that help me navigate my life. I don't know where I would be - or for that matter who I am - without them."

I nodded my head and absorbed her words. I took a sip of water and straightened out the fork next to the plate so it was perfectly perpendicular to the edge of the counter.

"Do you think it's possible to live a happy, fulfilling life, without a purpose?" I asked, staring at my empty plate.

The corners of my mother's lips curled into a sympathetic smile. She placed her hand on my back and rubbed it gently.

"I'm sorry, I wish I had a concrete answer for you, but I don't know for certain. I can only give you my opinion. And my opinion is this: God instills everyone with their purpose. It's all part of his design. His plan. It could be something as big as figuring out quantum mechanics, or simply loving someone. If we're not put on this Earth for a reason, then what is the point of existing?" she answered.

She stood up, kissed the top of my head, picked up my empty plate and took it to the sink. I sat and silently sipped my water watching her roll up her sleeves, soap up the sponge and proceed to clean the dishes, ruminating on her words.

* * *

The sun descended past oblivion. A half- moon occupied its position in the night sky, accompanied by a smattering of twinkling stars. I always forget how clearly you can see the stars out here on my mother's land. I stood next to my car breathing in the cool night air, the smell of fresh lawn clippings still clinging to it. Richard had long retired for the day; he was inside, clean, fed, and fast asleep in front of the soothing blue glow of the TV.

My mother emerged from the house with a large package. I rushed over to her and took it out of her hands. She wasn't lying, it was heavy.

"This is what came for you," she announced, a little winded.

"What is it?" I asked, adjusting my grip to distribute the weight in a way that was easy on my back.

"I don't know, I didn't open it," she said. "All I know is that it came from someone named Sofia. Do you know anyone by that name?"

"No," I said. "I've never met anyone by that name."

"I didn't think so. Who would you know from Montana?" my mother remarked.

My heart skipped a beat. *Montana?*

I secured the package in the passenger seat of the Monte Carlo and closed the door. I hugged my mother and kissed her cheek.

"Let me know what it is," she said, letting me go.

"I will."

I got in my car and turned the engine over. I rolled the window down to let the lingering afternoon heat out of the car and the evening coolness in. My mother stood on the steps of the house.

"Bendición, mama," I called out to her.

A proud smile etched on her face.

"Que dios te bendiga, hijo," she said.

I pulled out of her round-about and made my way down the cobbled pathway back to the front gate, and onto the main road.

Compared to the ride out to my mother's estate, the commute back was nice and smooth. There was barely any traffic, and I hit mostly green lights on my way home.

The moon was high in the sky by the time I got home, and was so bright, it made the need for streetlights virtually obsolete. I parked and took a quick scan around, looking to see if Thaleia's jeep was parked somewhere nearby. Either she was out on the town, or she parked somewhere else.

I lugged the package up to my floor and managed to get the door open without having to put it down and pick it back up again. When I pushed the door open, I was slapped in the face by that putrid smell again. I made my way into the apartment, closed the door quickly with my foot, afraid someone may walk by and smell that horrible smell and forever associate it with me, and set the package down on my kitchen counter. I read the package.

Sure enough, it came from Montana. West Glacier, Montana. And the name on the package was indeed from a Sofia. Sofia Guerrier.

I grabbed a small knife from the utensil drawer and carefully scalped the packing tape. Once all the seams were open, I opened the box. Inside was a large weathered, brown leather satchel. It looked like a treasure chest that had been recovered after being submerged for centuries.

I carefully removed it from the box and set it back down on the counter, tossing the empty box by the door for disposal later. I unlatched the satchel and opened it. My heart sank into the pit of my stomach. The satchel was neatly stacked to the brim with cassette tapes. Cassette tapes that no doubt, all belonged to my father.

Chapter Ten

I was dragged out of sleep by the sound of my phone ringing and vibrating on the windowsill. The morning sun was already piercing through the curtains and into my room. I found it odd that I didn't remember falling asleep the night before. Odder still that I slept through my alarm. I sat up quickly, grabbed the phone and rubbed the sleep from my eyes, swollen with weariness. I peered at the screen and my heart sank into my stomach: it was Evelyn.

I took several deep breaths to calm my beating heart and settle my trembling nerves. On the final breath, I answered.

"Hello?" I said, trying to inject as much calmness into my voice as I could. I only managed to sound confused.

"Good morning, Corazón," Evelyn said, her voice a near whisper. Her voice was sweet and soothing, like warm milk mixed with a touch of sugar. It traveled through the phone, into my ear and through my body. "Did I wake you? I'm sorry."

I cleared my throat, desperate to shake the sleep from my voice.

"Not at all. Not at all," that's all I could say; it was as if my auditory systems were overloaded by the sudden influx of emotion and thoughts, and in order to operate it had to be reduced to its most basic function.

"Good," she remarked.

"How are you?" my system asked.

"I'm okay," she whispered. "Listen. You're off today right? Do you have any plans?"

"No. Nothing at all," I said. My palms were starting to clam up, causing the phone to slip in my grip. I switched hands and held the phone to my other ear, wiping the palm of my other hand on my comforter.

"Can we meet?" She asked.

My heart pounced up from my stomach and into my throat.

"Just say when and where?" I said, coolly.

"How about our park? In about forty-five minutes? Is that enough time?"

Our park?

"More than enough," I confirmed.

"Great. I'll see you there. Bye."

She hung up and all my thoughts rushed to the forefront of my mind. Only one question loomed large over the rest: *why does she want to meet?*

I didn't dwell on the question, or at least I tried not to. I eagerly leapt out of bed, shaved, showered, picked, and dressed in the cleanest, wrinkle-free clothes I could find, comfortable cotton shorts, a light tee-shirt and running shoes, had a banana and a glass of water, brushed my teeth, gargled with mouthwash, and left my apartment.

I arrived at the park with fifteen minutes left to spare. I didn't mind waiting. Not for her. I preferred it that way. Better if I wait for her than if she waits for me. I parked near the soccer pitch and cut the engine off. My windows were rolled all the way down, allowing the morning air to waft through the car, a sense of rejuvenation riding on the back of the wind.

Our park. She called it *our park.* It hadn't been our park in so long. When we were together, we would come to this park to exercise. I'd be putting up shots on the basketball court, and she would use the soccer pitch to do her workout routine. Lunges, burpees, leg raises, stretches, all types of calisthenics.

Once she finished her exercises, she would then proceed to run laps around the soccer pitch. I'd join her every once and a while but, not being much of a long-distance runner, I was no match for her stamina. The most I could manage to jog was two laps before I felt my lungs burn and my sides cramp. Not Evelyn. She just ran. Ran as if the longer and further she ran, the lighter she became. She literally ran circles around me, and every time she lapped me, she'd laugh. She never seemed to tire out. Even by the end of her run, it never felt like she stopped because she was tired, but rather because she had fulfilled a need.

My phone vibrated in my pocket. I pulled it out, saw it was Evelyn and answered immediately.

"Hey."

"Are you at the park yet?" She asked. I could hear the sound of children laughing and yelling in the background.

"Yeah," I replied, "I'm parked by the soccer fields. Are you close?"

"I'm by the playground," she said. "Come over, here. I'm in the white Rover."

"Okay, I'm on my way," I said.

I hung up, cranked the car to life and cruised over to the parking lot near the playground.

I weaved through the lot scanning the area for a white Range Rover. It was parked right in front of the playground. She was standing by the open trunk, waving me over, and signaling to me an open space behind her. She was wearing slim pink leggings and an oversized plain white t- shirt she tied into a bun at her waist. Her hair was twisted into a ponytail, and she sported pink and white running shoes.

I parked my car, rolled up the windows and got out. She watched and smiled at me as I ambled over to her, acting as casual as I could with my hands in my pockets. When I reached her, she wrapped her arms around my neck and hugged me tight. Unconsciously, my arms wrapped around her waist and my face buried into her neck. I was assaulted by her Heavenly perfume. We held each other in this warm embrace.

"Thanks for meeting me," she said. We let each other go and our eyes drank each other up.

I shrugged my shoulders, and a sound akin to a scoff stumbled out of my mouth.

"Don't... no thanks necessary," I said.

"I haven't been to this park in so long," she said, looking around the area. "I don't even remember this playground being here. Do you still come here?" she asked.

"On my off days. Just to, you know, put up shots," I said.

She removed a large bag from the trunk of her car and a large something with wheels.

"Do you mind?" she said, passing me the bag.

I took the bag into my hands and noticed immediately how heavy it was. My focus was solely on Evelyn, so much so that my mind wrote the large something with wheels off as a make-shift wagon of some type. She pressed a button and the trunk closed on its own.

"Did this place always have a public pool?" she asked, lugging the large something with wheels with her as she made her way to the back passenger side of the car.

"No," I said. "It was under construction when we... a few years ago. It's only been open a few weeks. I haven't been, but I've walked past it a few times. It looks nice at least."

"In that case, we'll have to check it out one of these days?"

We?

"Sure," I stammered.

She unfurled the large something with wheels and clicked everything into place. She opened the back door and unbuckled the seatbelt of a little girl, who was busy entertaining herself with a doll.

"Yeah, she loves to swim," Evelyn said. "I don't know where she gets it from, not from mommy that's for sure."

All the words vanished from my mind. I was not even sure I fully comprehended the scene playing out before me. My mouth remained agape stuck between speech and gasp. Evelyn looked at me.

"Are you okay?" she asked.

"Yeah," I said, aware of how dry my throat had suddenly become. I tried to force a smile but the signal from my brain to the muscles around my mouth died en route, so instead, the corners of my mouth twitched and malfunctioned. "W-who's this?" I asked.

Evelyn's brow furrowed with amused bemusement.

"My daughter," she said in a tone that seemed to intimate that I should've had prior knowledge. Like a man coming out of a coma who didn't recognize his own family.

"Your... you have a daughter?"

She took her daughter out of her car seat and placed her in the large something with wheels which I finally realized was a baby stroller.

"Yeah, Esmeralda. You knew that right?"

"No," I said. "I didn't."

"Oh my god!" she exclaimed. "I forget you're not on social media. You basically don't exist," she chuckled. "In that case let me properly introduce you. This is my princess. My daughter, Esmeralda. Say hi, Esmeralda."

Her daughter was precious. The same large hazel eyes as Evelyn. Pink chubby cheeks, curly golden-brown locks of hair, and a smile that turns anyone who sees her into liquid mush. I stuck my finger out and she grabbed it tight.

"She's beautiful," I said. "How old is she?"

"She'll be two in a few months. I haven't had a good day off until today. Normally when we go out, it's to run errands and do groceries and stuff. So today I wanted to get out of the house and spend a real chill day with her. I figured she'd love the park."

I helped Evelyn lift the stroller onto the sidewalk. She pushed the stroller toward the park and I followed next to her. I felt strangely out of my body, as if my soul had been squeezed out of it and forced to hover above me.

We found an empty little pavilion and settled in. She took her daughter out of the stroller, put small pink socks on her chubby feet and little sneakers with unicorns whose horns lit up. This made little Esmeralda giggle, her eyes sparkling with glee.

"Do you want to swing?" Evelyn asked her daughter. "Let's go to the swing."

Evelyn picked up Esmeralda and began to head for the children's swing. She stopped and looked back at me.

"Are you coming?" she asked.

"I'll watch your stuff," I said, shaken out of a daze.

"It's not going anywhere. Come on," she insisted.

I followed her but kept my distance somewhat, watching as she carefully placed her daughter in the swing. She had trouble getting her legs in the holes. I came over and helped Esmeralda guide her legs through until finally Evelyn was able to settle her in completely.

"Are you ready, Princesa?" Evelyn asked her daughter. Esmeralda simply exclaimed with joy. "Okay here we go!"

Evelyn pushed her daughter gently and the swing rocked back and forth. Esmeralda clapped her hands and laughed loudly. A smile curled on my lips. I knew Evelyn for a long time. I've imagined her life going several ways. The one scenario I never considered was life as a mother. As an observer of this moment, it became immediately apparent to me that the role suited her beautifully.

Evelyn looked at me and smiled.

"Want to give her a push?" she asked.

"No, I can't," I began to stammer, unable to think of a passable excuse not to.

"All you require is - at minimum - one working arm, and *hey* you've got two of 'em. Get over here and push her. Just don't send her out of earth's orbit and she'll be fine, come on. You're really going to disappoint a child?" she teased.

I conceded to Evelyn's incessant prodding and traded places with her. Evelyn took position in front of her daughter and spoke with her while I gently pushed the swing back and forth. Every time I gave the swing a slight shove, Esmeralda would laugh loudly. The sound of her laughter was so warm that it washed the numbness from my body and allowed my soul to return. Evelyn took her phone and began snapping pictures of her daughter. For the first time in as long as I could remember, I was filled with a feeling that resembled pure happiness.

The morning sun continued to rise into the sky, bringing with it a clean wave of heat. Esmeralda played in a sandbox where children could dig for dinosaur bones. Evelyn and I sat on a nearby bench watching over her.

"You're daughter really is beautiful, all you," I observed.

"Right?!" Evelyn exclaimed with a cocky laugh. "I'm thinking about putting her up for those Gerber baby commercials. Do they still do that?"

"Probably," I remarked, "If they do, she'd be the face of the corporation for sure."

We laughed then shared a silence.

"This," Evelyn began to say but wavered. "She isn't why I...," I could see her thoughts pivoting, "I mean, I wasn't pregnant with her when you and I, you know... when we ended."

"The thought never crossed my mind," I said. It truly hadn't.

"Oh good," she said, genuine relief in her voice. "She was a complete surprise. I didn't know what to expect. I don't know how to be a mother. I mean, you know mine isn't really a great example to mold myself after. But honestly, I've never loved anything as much as her. That really makes all the hard stuff tolerable."

"Hard stuff?"

"Oh, you've clearly never had to deal with the soul piercing sound of a shrieking baby in the middle of the night robbing you of proper sleep, your nipples dripping milk, or a massive shit explosion that somehow goes all the way up their back," she explained. "It's enough to make you want to puke, which I have done. Several times."

"Well, the tits dripping milk thing doesn't sound so bad," I said.

"During an important presentation at work?" she elaborated.

I laughed out loud. "Okay, yeah, you're right."

"But," she smiled, "The sagging breasts, the raw nipples, the bags under my eyes, even my graying hair, it's all worth it. She's the best thing I've ever done," she said, looking at her daughter, swelling with pride.

The sky was a vibrant cyan blue. The morning sun continued to lift itself over the land while two ospreys chased each other high in the cloudless sky. It was a warm spring morning, yet the air felt rich with oxygen.

"So, have you given any thought to my proposal," Evelyn said, breaking the peace of the moment, in a tone that was all business.

And there it was. The real reason she brought me out there. I shifted uncomfortably on the bench.

"Honestly, no I haven't," I admitted. What was the point of lying?

"Why not? Ever since I got to Babylon things have been so great, financially. We got a house on the Island with boat access. We've traveled. I got to go to Europe last year. It was amazing. We're trying to plan a cruise to the Cayman Islands soon. If you take this promotion, you'd be well on your way," she pitched. "Not to mention I get a generous sign-up bonus for referring you."

I didn't answer. I just shook my head; I had nothing more to add.

Evelyn turned her head away from me and heaved a slight sigh of frustration. She was visibly annoyed but suppressed her disappointment the best she could. After a moment, she turned her eyes back to me.

"Is there some concern you have? Maybe I can talk you through it," she said, calmly.

"There's no concern," I said, plainly. "I'm just not interested. I'm fine where I am," the last bit came out rather abruptly.

Evelyn's eyes flashed, her corporate facade falling away, her nose flaring, she scoffed.

"So, your plan is to just stay in the clean room until you retire?!"

"Plan?" I repeated as if the word was foreign to me.

"Yes. A Plan. You know, for this reality we call life? What you wish to accomplish before you die? That kind of plan," she explained sardonically.

"I don't have a plan," I answered. "That *is* why you left me, isn't it?"

I could tell by the expression on her face she was not expecting me to respond in that manner. Neither was I. Not that I responded with any hint of resentment or the sense I had held a grudge. Quite the contrary, it came out bluntly and factually. It's just the fact that I had said it that caught us both off guard. I thought of reiterating my statement in a softer tone, but I let my words hang in the air, feeling ultimately that they were perfectly combined.

Evelyn's eyes misted over, like a slight film was spread thinly over her doe eyes. Her nostrils flared and her upper lip trembled. She turned away from me, got up and went to go sit next to Esmeralda in the sand, leaving me stranded on the bench that, at that moment, felt as large as an uninhabited island.

I closed my eyes and leaned back against the bench, head tilted upward toward the sun, allowing myself to feel its warmth caressing my cold cheeks.

You are an idiot.

She returned moments later and sat down next to me. I must've dozed off because when I opened my eyes, I was surprised by the amount of sunlight reflecting off the surface of the playground equipment. I closed my eyes and opened them slowly to allow them to adjust to the new intensity of light.

Evelyn cleared her throat. Esmeralda sat on her lap drinking water from a powder blue sippy cup with a pink top. Evelyn kept her gaze on her daughter but it was like she was looking through her and into another world. A sad world.

I opened my mouth, the words of an apology beginning to take shape on my tongue, but before they could fully form, Evelyn spoke in a low, almost imperceivable volume, as if the words travelled upward from the depth of a dark lifeless pit.

"You really think I left you because you didn't have a plan?" she said.

I didn't respond immediately. I let her question burrow into my body. She finally tilted her head toward me and looked at me with a single tear streaming down the bridge of her nose. She wiped it away quickly and awaited my answer. I didn't have one.

"I loved you," she began. That sentence made my body crackle with electricity. Seeing that I was not going to respond, she continued. "Even today, right now, sitting next to you, I feel I am where I should be. *Complete.* I look back at our time as the happiest of my life. I had never been with a man who loved me unconditionally, who not only believed in my dream just as firmly as I did, but supported me wholeheartedly, going as far as to help me try to realize it. I wanted to be a successful artist and travel the world. You... you just wanted my happiness."

She stopped to wipe the water from Esmeralda's chin. She then held her in her arms and patted her back, both in an attempt to burp her and put her to sleep.

"But, as time went by, my dream started to fade into obscurity. So much so, that any attempt to capture it and hold it firmly in my hand was like trying to pull the shirt off of a ghost. I felt it was time to let it go and move in another direction. When I looked around, all I found was that the only place in which I could elevate myself was within The Company. I had already put so much time into it, cultivated good relationships, and separated myself from those Plantation hens in the Clean Room as a serious worker. When the opportunity to make more money came about, to get great benefits, the whole nine, I jumped at it. I realize now, I jumped at it out of fear. But I couldn't expect you to support me on this. No. That's not right. I knew you would've supported me no matter what I decided to do. I just didn't want you to. What scared me most is the thought that you might think of me differently, and I couldn't stomach it. I couldn't stomach disappointing you. So slowly but surely, I pulled away from you. You didn't deserve that."

I couldn't speak or move. Her words were like a slow working venom sending my body into paralysis. She sniffled, wiped tears from her eyes, and continued.

"Maybe you're right. What use *is* a plan? I never expected to be a mother. I look at her..." Evelyn cradled Esmeralda in her arms. She was wide awake and babbling gleefully, oblivious to her mother's inner turmoil, "and I'm filled with so much love. Love I didn't know I was capable of feeling. I love her so much, and yet, every day, when I have a moment to myself, I can't escape the feeling that something, a piece of me, is missing."

Evelyn looked at me as if she wanted to say something more but decided against it. Unable to put her restless daughter to sleep, Evelyn took Esmeralda back to the sandbox and let her continue shoveling and throwing sand around. She returned to the bench.

"You've been walking around, thinking that you're the reason I ended things between us, when the truth is the complete opposite. I'm sorry. I'm so sorry."

The tears began to stream down her cheeks now. No matter how many times she wiped them away, they remained. She lowered her head in her hands and openly sobbed. I found myself unable to find the words to comfort her. Since our relationship ended, I no longer knew how to act around her. But she was being candid in a way I never knew her to be. The least I could do is return the favor. What exactly did I have to lose?

I took her hands into both of mine and kissed them softly.

"Look at me," I said melodiously.

Her eyes lifted to meet mine. I looked over at Esmeralda, happily tossing sand into the sky and marveling as the wind scattered it about.

"What do you think your daughter is thinking about right now?" I asked her.

Evelyn looked over at her daughter, then back at me.

"Sand? Playing, I guess, I don't-," she answered.

"You think she plans to play?"

Evelyn stayed silent.

"I don't know when we're supposed to develop a plan. I've never had a plan. I didn't plan to lose you, but I did. I didn't plan to love you. But I do. I can't think of the word *love* without seeing your face. I recall every moment with you as vividly as if it happened mere moments ago. You are etched into every molecule of my being. There is no doubt in my mind I will love you even after I'm reduced to ash. My soul is tethered to you, and maybe, if there is an afterlife, it will lead me to you. I didn't plan to feel this way, but I do."

I lowered my head and kissed her hands. She pressed her moist lips against my forehead.

"All that being said," I continued, "you made the right choice."

She searched my eyes for an explanation.

"I don't mean that I would look at you differently. You're right in saying that whatever you would've decided to do, I would've supported you. Even though you did say the day you gave up your art for the benefit of someone else, is the day you die."

"I said that?" she asked.

"It took me some time to realize this, but I am empty. Hollow. I have no purpose. So naturally I'm drawn to people who do. People with, and driven by, magnificent gifts. People who so wholeheartedly believe in something passionately, that they will die in its pursuit. Like you. Being surrounded by someone who is filled with this undeniable sense of purpose, gave me hope that maybe one day I would fulfill my own. I - albeit unknowingly - put that pressure on you, and that was wrong. If anyone should be apologizing, it's me."

I hugged her tightly and she quietly sobbed into my shirt. I could feel her tears soaking through the cotton and into my skin. We held each other like this for a few minutes until she finally calmed down. We broke apart and continued to hold hands.

* * *

The afternoon sun hovered in the sea of the ocean blue sky. A few mischievous clouds crept across the skyline. Esmeralda, finally tuckered out, was fast asleep in her carseat. While Evelyn secured her daughter, I loaded her baby bag and the folded stroller into the trunk and closed it. Anyone who would've seen us would've thought we were a normal couple taking their daughter to the park for a fun family day, I thought. I liked that thought.

I shut the trunk and made sure it was completely closed. Evelyn came around to the back of her car and stood next to me. She took my hand in hers and held it.

"There is no way I can convince you to take this job, can I?" she said with a smile on her face. I didn't respond, I simply smirked. Her phone vibrated in her hand and she looked at it. Her face contorted with conflict. She looked at me, then back at the phone. She let my hand go and stepped away from me to answer.

"Hello?... Hey!... No, we're at the park. The one off of Santa Barbara... Yeah that one... what do you mean? It's beautiful... No. No. You don't... we're already on our way home. She's asleep. Or recharging her batteries (she laughed)... Okay. Yeah that sounds great. Yeah order it, and I'll pick it up on the way. Okay see you at home. Bye." She ended the call and stood with her back to me, hands akimbo. She turned suddenly with a warm smile. I smiled back at her, but it was bittersweet: we both knew our time was ending.

She walked over to me and grabbed my hand again. She put my hand over her chest and sighed, looking into my eyes. My free hand found her cheek and caressed it. I was overwhelmed with the urge to press her against my body and kiss her voluptuous pink lips. I could feel she wanted the same; her heart was pulsating quickly in her chest.

But it couldn't happen. We each had our own paths to trek. Once we walked hand in hand, but our paths have since diverged. A tear formed in her eye and trickled down her cheek and over my fingers. I wiped them away with my thumb. I kissed her forehead gently, then her rosy cheek and her neck as I dove into her for a hug. Our final embrace.

"Okay," she said, breaking our hold and wiping away another tear. "I should get going."

"Okay, yeah," I said.

I escorted her to her driver side door.

"Thank you for coming out to meet me and Esmeralda," Evelyn said, opening her door. "She likes you."

"Really?"

"Yeah. She's normally shy around people she doesn't know but she instantly gravitated to you."

"Well," I started. I didn't know what to say to that. "I hope, if I'm ever lucky enough to have kids, I have a daughter like her."

"You'd be a great father," she said as she climbed into her car.

I scoffed at the remark.

"The only way a kid would survive having a father like me is with a mother like you." I quipped.

She laughed. "You sure you don't want to come to Babylon? We can have moments like this all the time," she said with a half- smile.

I shook my head. "I don't think my heart could handle more moments like this," I said.

She nodded her head sullenly. "Yeah, you're probably right."

She turned over the engine, closed the door, and rolled her window down. She put her seatbelt on and looked at me with a wry smile.

"Every time I think of you, I want to watch Punch Drunk Love," she said.

"Why that movie?" I asked.

"Don't you remember?" she asked, a little taken aback. "That was the first movie you took me to. Made me see Adam Sandler in a whole new light."

"You should thank Paul Thomas Anderson for that," I quipped.

She laughed and put her hand on mine as I held on to her car window, as if I had the power to hold the car in place.

"Siempre tendrás mi corazón," she said.

She knew she already had dominion over mine.

"You know that piece you say is missing?" I said.

"Yeah?"

"When was the last time you drew or painted anything?" I asked.

She thought about it.

"A very long time," she admitted.

"Do me a favor," I said.

"Anything."

"Whenever you have a free chance, pour yourself a glass of Pinot, put on some Chopin, light a cigarette, pick up a pencil and open a sketchbook," I suggested.

She pursed her lips and nodded her head.

"Okay, I will. I promise."

She put her car in reverse.

"Bye, Evie," I said.

"Bye, Corazón," she said.

I watched as she backed out of the parking lot and drove off. I tried to fight the feelings that came at me like a tsunami, but the further she got away the more it bore down on me. Being with her, playing with her daughter, imagining her rushing home, stopping to pick up food and have dinner, her, Esmeralda, and her man, laughing together, huddled on the couch watching a movie, falling asleep in each other's arms. These images washed over me, wave after wave crashing against my body. It wasn't until she was out of sight that I allowed myself one thought:

... It should've been you.

* * *

I spent the rest of the day in a fog. Somehow I ended up in the movie theater. Even now I can't recall what movie I watched. All I know is that by the time I emerged from this fog, the film score was blaring over the end credits. I spilled out of the theater and into the parking lot. The day had gone from bright and sunny to nearly pitch black. I checked the time on my phone. It was a few minutes past 11 p.m. I felt a malaise grab hold of my body. A chill ran through the air as I found my lonely car, got in and drove into the black night. I just wanted to get in bed and forget the day. Forget Evelyn and Esmeralda.

No. I didn't want to forget them.

I wanted to forget me. I wanted so badly to fall into a deep sleep and awaken as someone else entirely, with a new name, new memories. I wanted to look in the mirror and not loathe the person staring back at me.

My hands began to tremble and my vision blurred, my breathing had grown sharp and jagged, and my cheeks were hot and wet. I looked at myself in the rearview mirror; my eyes were bloodshot red.

I was crying.

I took a few deep breaths, wiped my cheeks until they were dry, and forced my hands to stop trembling by gripping the steering wheel so tight my knuckles turned purple.

I finally arrived home. I lumbered up the stairs. My body didn't want to do this. It didn't want to put one foot in front of the other. My mind didn't give it much choice. It sent the simple commands down to the legs: raise left leg, drop left leg. Raise right leg, drop right leg, until finally I reached my apartment..

I opened the door. The light from the hallway penetrated the room but it was so dark inside it felt like the light was swallowed by the blackhole. The smell was still lingering in the air, heavy now, but I couldn't care any less at that moment. I was desperate to fall face first into bed and disappear into my dreams. I closed the door behind me, tossed my things on the counter, crossed the room, and fell onto my bed, burying my head under he pillow. The silence of the night enveloped me, the only thing I could hear was this faint piercing ringing in my ears. I could feel my body dissolving into nonexistence, and I didn't fight it. However, just before I vanished into nothingness, someone began banging on my door.

Thaleia. There was no doubt in my mind it was her. There was no one else it could be. I stayed silent and still, hoping she would assume I wasn't home and go away. She pounded on the door again; it felt like the thumping was in my head. The sound was shaking my cranium so violently it felt like I could feel it cracking.

I climbed out of bed quickly and went to the door. I wasn't in the mood for whatever this was, and as I got closer to my door I was hell bent on telling her just that. I opened the door aggressively and was stunned mute.

Thaleia stood in my doorway wearing a loose fitting, turquoise colored midi dress with a large leather belt buckled around her waist which gave her curvy body an even more pronounced shape. Her legs looked as smooth as silk. Her feet were tucked into black strappy heels that made her calves and thigh muscles pop.

Thaleia was already beautiful in just her casual clothing. Seeing her in this attire, she was absolutely staggering. She grinned.

"Get dressed. We're going out."

Chapter Eleven

"Don't give me that look," Thaleia said, her hands on her hips. "This is not up for debate, we're going out. Right now."

"Thaleia," I began, rubbing my eyes both from frustration and exhaustion; I could feel a migraine hatching between my eyes. "I'm really, *really* tired," I stressed. So tired I didn't have the strength to sound remotely firm.

"It's not even midnight," she argued. "You've got dress clothes right? You won't be seen with me looking like *that*," she said, her eyes dressing me from head to toe.

"I'm not going out," I stated bluntly.

"Look, I was supposed to go out with my girlfriends tonight, but they've all abandoned me," she said. "I don't want to stay home wallowing in my loneliness, but I don't want to be that loser who goes to a bar and drinks alone, so please, let's have a night out together. Do not make me beg. Change and come out with me. I'll be waiting downstairs."

Before I could say anything she turned on her heels and walked toward the stairwell.

I closed my door, locked it, and stumbled back into bed. I closed my eyes and fought to get back to the edge of sleep but I couldn't cross the dividing line. My thoughts began firing off in so many directions, I kept seeing images of Evelyn and Esmeralda, their voices echoing in my mind. I tossed, turned, and tried to think of nothing, but I couldn't get comfortable. I lay on my back, my eyes open trying to focus on shadows and shapes in the dark. Moreover, the apartment felt like the air had been sucked out of the room. I began to feel like I was suffocating.

When I emerged from the apartment building, Thaleia was waiting for me, standing by her car. I was wearing a pair of navy blue dress pants I found buried in my dresser drawer and a collarless white button up dress shirt I had to iron to look somewhat respectable. The long sleeves were a bit too short - either I grew or the shirt shrank - so I rolled them up around my forearms. I dusted off some brown leather dress shoes and tied the ensemble together with a brown reversible belt and a cheap analog watch with brown straps. Thaleia grinned; she knew I wouldn't let her down.

"You clean up well," she remarked. She handed me her car keys. "You drive." She sprung up into the passenger seat.

"I don't know where we're going?" I said, making my way to the driver's side.

"Don't worry. I'll be your Nauplius ," she said as she closed the door.

There was no use fighting it. This was her rollercoaster, I was only along for the ride.

While I drove, she retouched her make-up until it was flawless and fixed her hair. The night sky was clear yet there were no visible stars. Just a lonely moon desperate for company.

With Thaleia's directions, we arrived at our destination in what felt like no time. It wasn't until the place came into view that I recognized it. It was an Italian Restaurant called *Tesoro*.

"We stopping for pasta?" I asked.

"No. This place is normally a restaurant, but on Sunday nights it becomes a nightclub. Tonight is 'Latin night.' You've lived here how long?"

"All my life," I reminded her.

"And you didn't know this?" She checked her hair once more before flipping the sun visor back up. "What else don't you know, I wonder."

The parking lot was jammed packed with sleek, souped up trucks and classic cars, all shined and polished to look their best for the night. People were scattered around the parking lot, some talking excitedly, some flirting. It took a while, but I finally found a spot to park far off in a remote corner of the shopping plaza by a Jujitsu studio.

I helped Thaleia out of the car and we walked arm in arm to the entrance. The closer we got to the entrance, the louder the music became, the better view I had of how truly full of people the club was. When we got to the entrance, a big security guard with an upper body so bulky his security jacket barely fit over his body, asked for ID and the entrance fee. I looked at Thaleia and she smiled with all of her teeth. The security guard handed us back our ID's and I paid for our entrance.

The room was electric. Men, women, all dressed to the nines, laughing, dancing, drinking. Strobe lights illuminated the packed dance floor with distinct colors, in sync with the rhythm of the music. Couples hand in hand dancing to the quick rhythm of the merengue blasting from all angles of the room. Trumpets blaring, drums and bongos pounding, all bound together with the pulsating percussive rhythm of the merengue guiro. The societal woes of the world did not exist in this room. Only joy. Only euphoric elation.

I followed Thaleia as she slithered through the packed room toward the bar. Except for the dance floor, the fringes of the room were mostly dark, seldom dim, bathed in a soft red and orange hue, but the bar was the beacon in the fog.

Behind the bar were three bartenders, two males in each corner and one female in the center. They all wore black dress slacks, white dress shirts and purple vests with black bow ties. Under the spotlights they looked like magicians wowing a crowd with their knowledge and showmanship of mixology.

Thaleia pushed her way to the far right of the bar and managed to get the attention of the male bartender. He was Caucasian, had a swimmers build, was clean shaven with a glorious mane of blonde hair, slicked and swooped neatly to one side with a slight part on the other. The diamond earring in his left ear sparkled in the spotlight.

"What can I get you?" he asked in his boyish yet firm voice.

"What do you recommend?" Thaleia said with a smile on her face as she bent over the bar counter.

"Depends," said the Bartender.

"On?" Thaleia asked.

"How you feel about gin and vermouth," he replied with a smirk.

Thaleia searched her vocabulary for a fitting word. She looked at me for a moment, then smiled, turning back to the bartender.

"Agnostic," she said.

The bartender looked at me as if trying to put a puzzle together without moving any pieces. He half smiled.

"Ever had a Negroni?"

"Are you allowed to say that?" Thaleia joked.

"Ask and answered," quipped the bartender. "Tell you what, you love it, you pay me. You don't, drinks are free all night."

Thaleia's jaw nearly dropped. "Are you serious?" she asked quietly, as if this transaction that was about to transpire was illegal.

The bartender didn't answer, he simply got the liquids and began to combine them all in the metal mixer. He did it all smoothly, with the illusion of not exerting any energy whatsoever. In no time, two full short glasses of Negroni's were waiting for us with a coaster and garnished with a thick orange peel and a singular maraschino cherry.

"Buen provecho," he said in flawless Spanish.

Thaleia took it in her hand and looked at him.

"I love it, I pay. I don't, I drink free all night?" she recited the terms of the agreement.

"That's right. And you have to love it. Anything short of love is not worth it," the Bartender said.

Thaleia raised the glass, tilted the drink past her lips and let it spill on her tongue. The Bartender did not look worried in the slightest. Thaleia looked at me, wide eyed.

"Pay the man," she said.

The bartender smiled proudly.

I slapped the cash on the counter and took a quick sip of my Negroni. Thaleia was right, it was delicious, a very bitter after taste but the orange peel and the cherry help soften the blow.

We thanked the Bartender and found a small high table to rest our drinks on and take in the sights.

"You could've lied, you know. We'd be drinking free all night," I said to Thaleia.

"What did I tell you when we first met?" she asked.

"It's all a blur," I joked.

"I don't like liars. Why would I - someone who doesn't like liars - then turn around and lie? That goes against my personal philosophy. Besides, that guy would've known if I did. He's a master of his craft," she took a sip and danced in place as the music switched over to salsa.

"I've got to know, where does this philosophy come from?" I asked.

"The Bhagavad Gita," Thaleia quipped.

"I'm serious," I said.

"So am I," she took another sip of her Negroni. "Truthfulness, according to the Bhagavad Gita, is one of the *five moral imperatives*. It's a fundamental virtue. Lying or hiding the truth is harmful to both the individual and society. Hence: I don't like liars."

"Everyone lies."

"Well, isn't that sad," she remarked.

"We lie. Whether it be to each other or to ourselves. Unintentionally, but still...," I said. I motioned to the crowd in the room. "All of this is a lie. They all think this is happiness. It isn't. This is intermission. Catharsis. A release from the maddening monotony of mediocre life. It won't last, but we lie to ourselves. We fool ourselves into hoping it will. You know what happens?"

"Enlighten me," she said.

"The sun comes up, and we wake up right where we left off."

"Shouldn't that be reason enough not to," she said, sipping her drink. "You think that's what I'm doing here? Lying to myself?"

"No, of course not," I said, feeling flushed. Perhaps the negroni was hitting me harder than I anticipated.

"Isn't that what all your proselytizing just now was all about?"

"No, just curious about where your aversion to liars originates from. While pointing out that everyone you meet, in some shape or form, is a liar," I said, my nose flaring.

"Not you," she said.

"Not yet," I volleyed.

We shared another silence while the Salsa changed to Bachata. *Dos Locos* by Mochi and Alexandra blared out of the hidden speakers. Thaleia studied my crestfallen face.

"You had a bad day today," she said.

"How could you tell?"

She smiled and took another sip. "What happened?"

"Got a glimpse into an alternate life," I downed the rest of the Negroni and examined the empty glass, making sure I didn't leave a drop, "then had my heart ripped from my chest," I said softly.

I turned around with the intention to go to the bar and get another. She placed her hand on my arm and gently pulled me back.

"My dad killed himself," she said, flatly.

She finished her drink and handed it to me, then turned her attention

191

back to the dance floor, swaying in place. I went to the bar and got us both a Negroni re-up.

* * *

"I was fourteen," Thaleia began.

We found a private little corner to sit and talk in. A particular section where the music didn't fully intrude. She fidgeted with the club napkin, tearing small pieces of it and rolling them up into tiny balls.

"My mom...," her voice hitched in her throat. She took a sip of liquid courage. "I was in school. Got pulled into the principal's office. It was early. I had only been to two classes but the day already felt like it was being dragged through mud. I sat in the principal's office, looking out the window, watching these crows playing tag on the power lines. No one would tell me why I was there. I thought I was in trouble for something, but for the life of me I couldn't think of anything I might've done. Hard to imagine now but I was a pretty good kid back then," she laughed to herself.

"I remember how strange I found it that my father was pulling into the parking lot. He was always so busy, he hardly had time to come to any of my school events. In hindsight, I should've known something was wrong. He came into the office, said something to the principal and walked in to see me. His eyes were bloodshot and he looked pale white."

Thaleia took a strong sip of her Negroni. Someone screeched out on the floor and people applauded and cheered.

"My mother... he told me... was killed in a training accident on the base. A stray bullet caught her in the temple. A mere half centimeter under her helmet. She died instantly. At first I didn't believe him. But looking into his grave face, that disbelief evaporated almost immediately, and I knew, I *felt*, that my mother was gone. I don't know how to explain it, it's like I felt a limb missing. I was shattered. I screamed. I balled my eyes out. I thrashed and raged like a wounded wild tiger, but my father, he was so strong, he held me so tight until my rage turned into sorrow and the energy left my body. I had to be carried out of school. But he kept telling me, everything was going to be alright. *'Everything is going to be alright. I'm here. I'm here. I'm not going anywhere. Everything is going to be okay.'*

"Everything after that moment happened so quickly, or at least that's how I remember it. There was no viewing. I never got to see her body. She was in the casket, an American flag draped over it. I just imagined her in her favorite light blue summer dress with the white daisy's - those were her favorite flowers - her hair straightened, but curled at the tips, a bouquet of white roses in her hands... and a bullet hole in her head. Soon after that, she was in the ground and my dad and I were home. Alone. But we had each other. My dad was still *dad.*"

She shifted in her seat and a glimmer came to her eye.

"You know. Thinking about it now. I don't remember him crying. Not at the funeral or the burial. He was so *strong.* On the days I couldn't get out of bed, the days I nearly succumbed to my own grief, he stayed with me, and guided me out, kept me from drowning. Little by little, we found something that worked. Some semblances of what we could salvage of happiness."

She ran out of napkins to rip up and began to drink.

"Two years went by. I was on the verge of my seventeenth birthday. I was supposed to be at a track meet, but I had gotten my period unexpectedly and didn't have any tampons so I had to bow out. I came home early and found that my dad was home before me. I didn't think much of it. He was a literature professor, and sometimes he came home early if he didn't have a class. I opened the door and walked in. The lights were all off and there was a chill in the air. Absolutely no warmth. You know when you walk into a room and you have the feeling that someone has been there? I ...had the... exact... opposite... feeling."

She began to hyperventilate. *A panic attack.* Her eyes shut tight, and she curled her hands into tight fists. I held her hands; it was the only thing I could think of to help ease her discomfort. She finally regained her composure. She rubbed my hands, grabbed her Negroni and finished it off. Then she grabbed mine and began to drink it. Tears began to form in her eyes. She took another napkin and dapped her eyes.

"I knew he was dead. I didn't have to check. He was sitting in his study, in his chair. From behind, you would've thought he just fell asleep while reading. But I knew better. For him it was a sign of disrespect to fall asleep reading an author's work, especially someone he revered in Vonnegut. *'It's the equivalent of reading the Bible on the toilet'* he'd say. No. He was dead. Pills. He left me a note. I burned it. I didn't even go to his funeral. *Fuck* him."

"Because he lied to you," I said, finally understanding.

She drank more.

"He said everything was going to be okay. That he wasn't going anywhere. I believed him. With all of my heart. I believed him," she drank a little more.

"I loved my father, but I couldn't forgive him. I couldn't forgive him because I couldn't understand why he did it. We had each other. Why didn't he want to share his pain with me? He could've. We could've healed *together*."

The tears began streaming down her cheek, slowly. She let it run its course until the single tear drop fell from her chin.

"Then you helped me realize why," she slid her fingers into the palm of my hands and squeezed them. "I still have trouble forgiving him but at least now I understand. At least now, I *want* to forgive him."

She polished off the rest of the drink and wiped what was left of the tear away. I didn't know what to say. I stood up and extended my hand to her. The music continued to fill the room.

"What?" she said, her shimmering eyes staring up at me.

"This was supposed to be a fun time out. I owe you that," I said.

"No," she said flatly, removing her hand from mine.

"You don't dance?" I asked.

"I do, but I'm not ready. When I am, all I need to do is make sure I recognize the next opportunity and make the decision to seize it," she handed me the empty glasses.

"I *will* take one more Negroni, though," she said with a soft smile.

I got to the bar and asked for two more drinks. As I waited for the bartender to mix them, someone tapped me on the shoulder. When I turned, I was surprised to find Martin standing behind me. He looked different out of the clean room gown. He was wearing black jeans, a tan cashmere sweater, and all black Air Force One's. Two gold chains hung from his neck, and his hair was gelled and slicked back into a bun. He scanned me from head to toe and smiled.

"I'm seeing you and still don't believe my eyes!" he exclaimed. He shook my hand vigorously and gave me a strong embrace. "What are you doing here?"

"Just having a night out with a friend," I said, breaking our embrace and growing anxious for my drinks.

"That's good, man. That's really good," he said. "I'm really glad to see you, you know, out in the real world. I was worried about you."

The bartender put the drinks on the counter and I paid him.

"Worried about me?" I repeated. "Why?"

"Ever since Evelyn, you've been... different," he said, in a careful tone.

"Different, how?"

He shifted his body weight. I could tell by the regrettable look on his face he had not intended to venture into this topic. He cleared his throat.

"You've always been a little quiet, you know. But when you were with her, you were happy. We all saw it. Everybody in the Clean Room. When you and her were together, it is the most I ever saw you laugh. There was light in your eyes. After Evelyn, that light went away."

It was both interesting and annoying to hear how people saw me from the outside looking in. Why it was any of their business was beyond me.

"If you think this is the real world, then I'm worried for you," I grabbed the drinks, turned, and smiled at Martin. "Enjoy your night. See you Tuesday."

I left Martin at the bar and maneuvered through the crowd, back to Thaleia.

The rest of the night went better. Thaleia and I kept our conversations light and laughed and drank and munched on house nachos while the music continued to boom. I attempted a few more times to get her to dance but each time she politely declined. We simply sat across from each other in our little booth, drinking and talking until finally, the house lights came up, the DJ thanked everyone for coming out, and reality set in: it was time to go.

Everyone slowly marched out of the venue. Thaleia and I finished up the last of our drinks and headed for the door. She was tipsy, stumbling slightly as we joined the herd. She clutched my arm and did her best not to look drunk, walking with her spine straight and her chin held high. As we got nearer to the exit, she tugged on my shirt sleeve.

"My god. Look at her," she said in hushed tones.

She pointed at a woman who was walking in front of us. She was wearing a plain black top, very tight-fitting jeans, and pink heels. Her hair was jet black, shiny, and straight. It came down to the middle of her back.

Thaleia let go of my arm, got closer to the woman, and grabbed her ass with both hands. The woman jumped up with surprise but when she turned around Thaleia was clutching my arm and pretending nothing happened. I averted my eyes, trying not to meet the woman's leering gaze as she scanned around to see who had the audacity to violate her body. Seeing that Thaleia and I looked too pathetic, she let it go and turned back around. Thaleia dug her face in my arm and started to laugh quietly.

We finally emerged into the late-night air and headed for Thaleia's car. Some people hung around in the parking lot talking. A car blasted music, doing its best to keep the spirit of the night alive. I escorted Thaleia to her car and helped her get in the passenger seat.

"What do you want to do now?" she asked me.

"You're kidding, right?" I scoffed.

"We're not going home. It's too early," she said. She never looked more serious.

I looked at my watch. It was nearly three in the morning.

"I don't know what you're expecting. It's officially a weekday. Everything is closed unless you want to walk around Wal-Mart until the sun comes up," I said.

"Let's go to the casino!" she said.

"Thaleia," I began, shaking my head. In her condition, the only place she should've been going to was to bed. "I'm not going to the casino. We're going home."

"Forget you then. I'll go," she began to climb over to the driver's side of the jeep. Her dress began to ride up and expose her bottom. I averted my eyes.

"They got food there?" I asked.

"The best burgers and fries you'll ever have," she said with a smile.

"I'll drive," I said.

She plopped back in the passenger seat as I rounded the jeep and got in the driver seat. I turned the engine over, pulled out of the parking spot and got out of the packed lot with little resistance.

* * *

The casino was quite a drive from the club. Thaleia barely spoke. She lowered her window and let the fresh night air rush over her face. Her full lips curled into a steady smile, the kind of smile drunks wear, somewhat satisfied. I even put on a little bit of music and that did little if nothing at all to disturb her inebriated state of nirvana.

I didn't expect the casino to be so full. Droves of cars poured into the parking lot. Flood lights beamed into the night sky. People crossed the road to get to the entrance, while others hung around outside smoking and talking.

I parked and helped Thaleia out of the car. The liquor was starting to wear off; she looked a tad bit pale and a thin layer of sweat covered her forehead. I could smell the vermouth coming out of her pores. We walked to the entrance of the casino arm in arm. As soon as we went from the humid night air into the sudden rush of artificial frigid air, Thaleia let go of me and rushed to the woman's bathroom. Before I could ask if she was okay, she was already through the bathroom door and out of sight.

I stood by the bathroom holding her purse, watching as people walked in and out of the bathrooms until Thaleia finally emerged. The color returned to her face, and she tied her hair up into a ponytail. She took a quick sip of water at the fountain and reached for her purse.

"Too many Negroni's?" I asked.

She shook her head.

"Nah, I'm just a lightweight," she said. "Ready to have the best burger and fries you've ever had in your life?"

We sat at the counter of a small restaurant and ordered. Thaleia ordered for both of us, assuring me that it's best to get a cheeseburger with all the fixings. Shortly thereafter, the burgers came out on heavy white plates with a nice amount of seasoned fries. The waiter brought us two glass bottles of coke and a bottle opener. Thaleia took the bottle opener and opened our drinks. She took a sip and savored it.

"Is it me or does a coke taste better out of a glass bottle?" she remarked, before grabbing her burger and sinking her teeth into it, ketchup, mustard, onions, tomatoes all falling out despite her attempts to keep it all in the bun. Her eyes rolled to the back of her head and she moaned with pleasure. I grabbed the burger and bit into it. To no surprise, Thaleia was absolutely right, it was the best burger I'd ever had. She looked at my expression and smiled.

"You can find joy in the most obscure of places," she said.

After the burger and fries, we shared a banana split, and then each had a soothing espresso. Once we finished replenishing our bodies, the color completely returned to her face, and I myself felt reinvigorated. We turned in our stools and looked at the casino.

It was nothing like I'd seen in movies. There were machines lined up in all directions, a few blackjack tables, some poker tables, but for the most part there were all machines, populated not by patrons in their best suits and sparkling dresses, but by average joes in trucker hats, cotton sweater vests, hoodies and jeans.

Waitresses glided through the isles with free drinks for the gamblers. There was a bar in the center of the casino where there was also live music being played and a large screen that projected a random channel where there was a mix of news and sports being played. It was all mello and underwhelming.

"You gamble?" Thaleia asked me.

I looked at her and smiled.

"Right, what was I thinking? Care to?" She asked.

"Not really. I don't see the point. You're basically throwing away money, and for what?"

Thaleia sighed. She grabbed her purse from the counter and began to sift through it. She pulled out a few dollars in cash and tossed it on the counter next to our empty plates.

"Do you know who Prometheus is?" she asked.

"Isn't he the Greek God who stole fire and gave it to humans?" I replied.

Thaleia almost fell out of her chair stunned.

"Yeah, that's right! Zeus was pissed about that. He hated the humans Prometheus created so when he learned Prometheus stole fire from Hephaustus, the God of Fire on Mount Olympus, and gifted it to mankind, Zeus had Prometheus punished, chaining him to a rock for eternity where, every day, an eagle would come and eat his liver," she explained. "Well, Prometheus had a brother, Epimetheus. Whereas Prometheus was tasked with the creation of humans, Epimetheus was tasked with creating the animals. Determined to ruin mankind, Zeus told Hephaestus to create Pandora, a beautiful woman, and with the help of the other gods, they made Pandora irresistible. Zeus then presented her to Epimetheus, who took her as his bride, despite Prometheus' warnings. Zeus gave Pandora a jar to give it to Epimetheus as a wedding gift but unbeknownst to her the pithos contained all of mankind's ills in it. What do you think she did? She became curious, opened the jar, and let out all of the woes suffered by mankind - sickness, plagues, sorrow, all the evils of the world. Pandora, was finally able to get the jar closed, but in doing so she trapped the one thing that all human beings want most...," She motioned to the casino. "Hope."

Somewhere out on the casino floor, the bells and whistles of a machine rang out.

"Everyone here is playing for the hope of another life. They may never get it, sure, but for a little while, they get to hope."

"What about you?" I asked.

"You risk nothing, you gain nothing," she said. She wiped the grease from her mouth with a napkin, grabbed her purse and waltzed to the machines. I followed after her.

We went to an ATM and withdrew some money, then had the cash transferred to a card at the players desk. No chips. No quarters. We sat at a machine that was Australian themed, inserted our cards and pressed the only button on the dashboard. The numbered columns spun until random symbols lined up on the monitor, some of which apparently had more value than others. What that meant was beyond my comprehension. It was like being in an arcade. Lights flashed and the monitor made sounds.

My attention, however, was on the money left. Sometimes it went up, but most of the time the amount just dwindled. Each machine we sat at basically performed the same function. I found none of this fun or exciting. Just mindless.

We drifted from machine to machine. Thaleia had her own ritual she swears was good luck. She would sit at a machine, slowly insert her card, press the button, and run her fingers over the screen to get a good combination of rows. Sometimes it worked, but mostly it didn't. The only benefit to gambling is that the drinks are free. We had a few to sip on as we floated from machine to machine. I found a machine I liked, mainly because it was Indiana Jones themed and played that one until I ran out of money. When I did, I took my last free drink and hung out by the bar and the live band, watching a replay of a basketball game, enjoying my drink and the soft jazz.

An hour later, Thaleia came over to the bar and sat next to me. She ordered a drink from one of the attractive waitresses that was patrolling the room and laid back against the soft couch, exhausted.

"How much?" I asked.

"All of it," she said. "You?"

"Same," I confirmed.

She smiled and closed her eyes, resting the back of her head on the cushion, crossing her legs. The waitress returned with her drink and placed it on the table in front of us. I gave her a generous tip and Thaleia watched her amble off.

There were no windows or clocks in the casino so I had no idea what time it was, but I knew it was late. I should've been tired, but strangely enough, my body was wired.

"Want to go home?" Thaleia asked me, leaning forward, grabbing her drink, and taking a sip.

"I'm in no hurry," I said.

She smiled slightly and took another sip from the tiny black straw. The band began to play a lively tune. She put her glass on the table, stood up, and extended her hand to me.

I grabbed her hand and she helped me to my feet, escorting me to the dance floor which was just a small space between the large screen and the band. Everyone at the bar watched us as we held hands and danced what remained of the night away.

* * *

We were still drenched in sweat from the dancing when we arrived back at the apartment. Somehow we managed to get our heavy legs up the stairs. We entered my apartment, chatting about the night. As I set off to retrieve some towels so we could dry off, Thaleia found the futon and made herself comfortable, but feeling restless, got up and walked around my apartment. She noticed the satchel full of my father's cassette tapes in the corner. She picked it up, placed it on the coffee table, and began sifting through them, amused.

"What are these?" she asked.

"Mixtapes," I said, handing her a towel.

"What?! These are authentic mixtapes?" she said, amused. "Do they still work?"

"Probably," I said, shrugging my shoulders, drying off my neck.

202

"Do you have something to play them with?" she asked.

"We'd have to go downstairs and get in my car," I said. "But to be honest with you I don't even know if my cassette tape actually works," I went to the kitchen and poured us a couple of glasses of ice water.

"Well, let's try it tomorrow!" She sounded so excited.

"Sure."

"Wow!" she said, pulling cassettes out and admiring them. "Look at this! Redman's *Whut? Thee Album*! Snoop's *Doggystyle*. No way a square like you collects this?"

I placed the cups on the coffee table and sat next to her on the futon. I leaned back away from the satchel. My body was exhausted.

"They belonged to my father," I said.

Thaleia looked up at me and back at the cassette collection.

"He left this to you? He must've really loved you."

"I wouldn't know. He and I didn't really have anything that resembled a relationship."

"Yeah, but look at these. They're so well cared for, it's like holding his essence in your hands," she said, thumbing through the tapes.

She stopped rummaging as her eyes fell on a tape. "I think I know which tape I want to listen to tomorrow."

She gently pulled out a tape and showed it to me. It was a mixtape with white packaging.

Written in what I can only assume was my father's handwriting, were three words: *To My Hijo*.

She flipped it around but that's all that was written on it.

"What do you think is on it?" Thaleia asked me.

"Music, if I had to guess," I joked. I took the tape out of her hand and placed it back in the satchel.

We sat for a while in silence, drinking water to hydrate.

"You really don't think highly of yourself do you?" she asked, suddenly.

203

"We've gone over this," I responded.

"Yeah that you have no purpose, blah, blah, blah," she sounded like she was getting upset. "You claim to be purposeless but I don't think *you* even buy that. You've convinced yourself of it, numbed yourself from feeling anything, so you don't have to feel pain. That's not the same as not having a purpose."

I continued to sip my water.

"No answer, huh? That's fine. You don't have to respond," she took a final sip of her water, set the cup down and stood up, straightening her dress.

"Thanks for the nightcap," she said. She turned and walked toward the door.

"You're leaving?" I asked.

"Give me a reason to stay," she said. She grabbed the door handle and turned it opened.

I didn't want her to leave, but I was having trouble admitting the truth.

"Good night," she said.

"Have you ever seen *Breathless*?" I asked her.

She stopped and stood at the door, waiting for me to speak.

"It's a French film from the early sixties, *À Bout de Souffle* by Jean-Luc Godard. There is a scene in the movie where the female protagonist, Patricia, played by Jean Seberg, where she and a bunch of newspaper columnists are interviewing a popular author, Mr. Pavulesco, played by Jean Pierre Melville of all people," I began.

Thaleia closed the door, walked over, and plopped on the futon next to me.

"All the columnists are shouting questions at him: Can one still believe in love in our time? Does the soul exist in modern society? Is there a difference between eroticism and love? So on and so on. He answers each question with wit and intellect as photographers snap pictures of him. Patricia asks him, *'what is your greatest ambition in life?'* Mr. Pavulesco hears the question but doesn't answer right away. He goes on answering other questions. Patricia asks again. Finally, he looks at her, takes off his glasses and answers."

"What did he say?" Thaleia asked.

"*Devenir immortel, du puis mourir,*" I said.

"What does that mean?" She asked.

"*To become immortal, and then die,*" I translated.

Thaleia let the words sink in.

"I've seen that movie hundreds of times. It's one of my favorite quotes. I think about it every single day. How does one reach immortality before dying? It's a universal goal. Everyone alive is working toward it."

Thaleia grabbed my hand and squeezed it.

"I saw Evelyn today," I told her.

"The woman on your phone?" Thaleia asked.

"Yeah. We met this morning. At our park. Or what used to be our park," I took a sip of my water but lost the taste for it and set it down for good. "I don't know what I was expecting. That's not true, I guess I was expecting her to tell me she still loves me, that she made a mistake leaving me, that she wants me back, wants to spend her life with me, raise a family with me. She already has all of that. She moved up in the company, has *the most* beautiful daughter, really, if you saw her, she'd melt your heart. I saw the life I could've had... had I been someone of worth."

I stood up and paced around the room. I went to the kitchen, and dumped my water out in the sink, just to have something to do. Thaleia remained on the futon, her eyes fixated on me, listening. I propped myself up against the counter.

"Every day, the second I wake up, I reach for my phone and teeter on the edge of sending her a message. I look at the screen and wrestle with the urge to say something, anything, but everything I truly want to say, how much I love her, how much she means to me, how this life I live means even less without her. Even if she told me she wanted me back, what do I have to offer her? Her daughter? A life in a box? She doesn't deserve that. I don't deserve her. So, everything I want to say, everything I want to do, remains there, at the precipice of my fingertips, simmering below the surface of 'hello'."

I wanted to stop talking but it all came pouring out of me, like a dam that was no longer able to retain a wall of water.

"I have nothing profound to add. I have nothing to be proud of. Not that I'm even capable of having pride. I'm just existing. When my time is over, it's over."

I suddenly felt tired. I wanted to crawl in bed and sleep, but I was too tired to move from the kitchen. Thaleia came over to me and stood close to me. I could feel her gentle breath on my chin. She put her hands on my chest and looked up at me.

"You're so full of shit," she said, a smile curled on her lips. She helped me to bed and sat me down, then she sat down next to me and held my hand, our fingers intertwined.

"You don't really think you don't have a purpose. You're just afraid of having one and failing to fulfill it. You left school before you graduated because you said you had no idea why you were even there, fine, but it could also be that you were afraid to fail. And when your relationship with her ended, it only confirmed for you that the pain of failure was too much to bear. So here you are, convincing yourself that you have no purpose for being alive. You don't deserve success. You don't deserve to be loved."

She grabbed my chin and moved it so my face faced hers.

"You do," she kissed my forehead. "You should desire to live," she kissed my cheek. "You should desire success," she kissed the other cheek. "It's okay to want to be loved.

"Fear is a double-edged sword. A little bit of it could be enough to propel you forward, force you to never get complacent. There is nothing wrong with failure. You can fail. You *will* fail. *Repeatedly.* On the other end, too much fear can push you into making desperate choices, or worse stop you from choosing anything at all. You *cannot* allow fear to cripple you," she said.

Our lips nearly grazed each other. She put her hands on my cheeks and caressed them. Our eyes met and locked. The sound from the room muted. I could feel my heart pulsing in my ears. I leaned in and kissed her softly. She was surprised by my sudden forwardness. I began to pull away from her, immediately regretting my action. She touched my lips with her fingertips and finally, we fell into each other. The moment our lips touched the ground gave way beneath us and the walls, the ceiling, the bed, the futon, the kitchen, everything, piece by piece, item by item, the entire room fell away into nothingness. We were no longer matter; we became balls of energy floating in the vastness of space. We streaked across the galaxy, zigging and zagging around planets, blue and red stars, dwarf stars, twisting and winding through star clouds and asteroid fields, reaching the end of the universe, looking over the ring of fire, and then crossing over into the white void beyond.

Chapter Twelve

Thaleia was gone. I knew it the moment I opened my eyes.

The sun spilled into my room. My bed sheets were covered in my sweat. I was naked. My head was pounding, and my mouth was extremely dry. I shuffled out of bed and walked around the apartment, looked into the bathroom, and found no one. There was no doubt about it: I was alone.

I found some cotton shorts and stepped into them. Every move required so much of my energy that just pulling them up and tying the strings left me dangerously fatigued. I crawled onto the futon and lay face down trying to catch my breath and slow down my heart rate. I desperately needed water, but to get up and go to the kitchen at that moment felt like getting up and walking through the thick marsh of the everglades.

My phone. I needed my phone. I needed to send a message to Thaleia, see if maybe she sent me a message, or tried to call. Where the hell was my phone? I could barely lift my head to turn and look. My eyes scanned the room but I couldn't spot it outright. The morning light around me dimmed, and before I understood what was happening, I had fallen asleep again.

A muffled boom woke me up. My body was sticky with sweat. I didn't know where I was, and I'm embarrassed to say how long it took me before I finally realized. I summoned what little strength I had regained from my little nap to sit up properly. When I was finally sitting upright, a terrible pain, like a vice squeezed tight around my cranium, struck me. Anytime I lifted my head high, the vice tightened.

Water. The urge rushed back to me. I stood up slowly and dragged myself to the kitchen, one step at a time. I poured myself a glass of water and guzzled it down. I was so dehydrated that I stood over the sink for five minutes drinking glass after glass until I became so full of water that I felt nauseous and threw up in the sink. Everything I had eaten and drank the night before came up.

My body purged, I washed my mouth out and once again drank water. This time it all stayed down.

I grabbed some aspirin from the cupboard and popped three, praying they will help dispel this headache, or at least weaken it. I flopped back down on the futon and nursed my head with the bottom of the cold glass, thinking of nothing, turning my back on any thought bold enough to pass before me.

After I finished my water, I could feel my strength returning to me, my hunger with it. I got up, went into the kitchen, and made myself a nice egg sandwich, microwaved a cup of instant coffee, and ate standing in the kitchen. The egg sandwich was perfect. Right amount of egg, mayo, salt, and pepper. Bread lightly toasted and coffee hot but not scalding.

When I was done, I stripped out of my shorts and jumped in the shower, scrubbing away all toxic remnants. When I emerged from the shower, I stripped the sweat-soaked sheets from my bed and replaced them with cleaner gray sheets, tossing the tainted ones in the corner by the laundry basket. My clothes from last night were scattered about the floor. I picked them up and walked them to the basket. Just as I went to throw in the pants, my wallet and phone fell out. I picked up my phone and checked the time: 1:13 p.m. It was later than I thought, but even more glaring to me: I had no missed calls or texts.

I swiped my phone screen, prepared to send a message to Thaleia, but when I scrolled through my contacts and couldn't find her name.

I threw on a clean shirt, left my apartment and walked over to hers. I knocked on her door. No answer.

"Thaleia, are you there?" I called out.

I started to reach for her doorknob but decided against it. I knocked again and waited. Again, no answer.

I returned back to my apartment and looked out the window down to the parking lot. I didn't see her car. I convinced myself she was out and about, but something felt off, and I couldn't shake the feeling.

Determined not to sit home and drown in anxiety, I got fully dressed and decided to salvage what remained of my last day off.

The first thing I did was take my car to a self-wash station and take my time to clean it. My car may not be worth much of anything but that doesn't mean it doesn't deserve to be well maintained. I always start inside, cleaning the console, the dashboard, vacuuming the rugs, under and between the nooks in the seats. When all of that is done, I spend a little more time and a few more quarters on cleaning the mold from the passenger side carpet where all the water spills onto.

After the inside is completely cleaned, I clean the outside, even the rusted spoked rims. Once soaped, scrubbed, and rinsed, I dry it all, and clean the mirrors. By the time I've finished wiping the last drop from the side mirror, the car is clean. It still looks practically the same, but cleaner. No one else can tell, but I can. I can feel it. Like it putters happily. I checked my phone. It was mid-afternoon, still no call or texts.

I stopped by the movie theater and caught a matinee at the Parthenon for a showing of Louis Malle's *Elevator to the Gallows*. I sat down with a small popcorn and a Sprite, and for an hour and thirty-one minutes, my eyes drank in Jeanne Moreau and the silver screen.

When the movie was over, I spilled into the lobby, tossed my trash, and checked my phone. Still nothing. I checked again to see if maybe Thaleia mischievously changed her name in my phone so I couldn't find it, but since I didn't have many people saved in my phone, that theory proved fruitless. My final stop for the day was to pick up some groceries and restock my fridge for the week.

When I returned home, I again was overcome with the urge to go next door and open it. Why hadn't she reached out to me? Was she really that busy that she couldn't even send a message? I'd take any sign from her, even a message to tell me that what happened last night was a mistake, I didn't care. Was she avoiding me? The questions grew louder and louder with each passing moment.

I put the groceries away, leaving some items out on the counter for me to cook with. That's when I heard some movement next door. She was home!

I quickly ran out of my apartment and was well on my way to give her a piece of my mind when, as I went to knock, the door suddenly opened and a man in plaster and paint spattered coveralls emerged from Thaleia's apartment. He gave me a queer look, clearly not expecting anyone to be standing in front of the door. He closed it behind him and locked it.

"Hey, if you're here to see the apartment, it won't be ready for a couple of weeks. Got a lot to clean up," he said.

"No, I live next door. The apartment is empty?" I asked, afraid of the answer.

"Yep," he confirmed. "You know anyone looking for a place?"

I shook my head slowly, confused. There was a ringing in my ears.

He shrugged his shoulders. "Too bad. It's a good space. Have a great night," he said and disappeared down the stairway.

I stumbled into my apartment and closed my door behind me. Thaleia was really gone. *Gone*. Without a word. Without saying goodbye.

211

She snuck into my life like a beautifully violent thunderstorm on a cloudless sunny day and left it just as suddenly... leaving me forever changed.

I completely lost my appetite. I put the food away in the fridge, turned off all the lights, crawled into my bed, and waited for my head to stop buzzing before I could close my eyes and be dragged down into the deep dark depths of sleep.

* * *

It didn't take long for me to fall back into my normal routine. I'd wake up, shower, get dressed, eat breakfast and go to work. After work, unless I stopped at the grocery store to pick up something for dinner, it was straight home. In between all that, laundry was done, bills were paid, and movies were watched. Three months passed like this.

Someone moved into Thaleia's apartment. A young man, I think, maybe early twenties. I've passed him in the hall a couple times. He always says, "what's up?" with a genuine smile. He seems friendly enough, as friendly as one can gauge from a passing greeting. On the rare nights that he's home I can hear him with a girl; not a singular girl, a different one every time. They are laughing and talking, watching TV, eating, and having sex. He wasn't shy about being loud, either. Almost as if he wanted everyone in the building to hear. Good for him.

I thought of Thaleia every day. When I got messages on my phone, my heart leapt, hoping this time it would be a message from her. It never was. When I heard footsteps coming up the hallway, I held my breath, waiting for a knock on my door. It never came.

So, I went about my day. Wake up, shower, eat, work, sleep. Before, the routine was comforting. It no longer was. Even going to the movie theater no longer provided me with much joy or peace of mind. I am fully aware of how tedious and monotonous my routine was, I always had been, but something was different now. Now it was... *painful.*

To make matters worse, the smell in the apartment was as strong and as putrid as ever. On my days off I'd open the window in my apartment and clean everything from top to bottom. This took several days to accomplish and yet, when I was done, the smell remained. And this wasn't a smell I could get used to over time, every time I inhaled, I could taste rotten garbage. No, worse than that. *Decomposing flesh.*

I could taste it in everything I ate, not just at home, but at work. No matter how edible it looked, when the food hit my tongue, it was rancid. I could barely keep anything down, and as a result, I lost several pounds. I went from 225 lbs to 165 lbs. My face was gaunt, my body emaciated, the fit of my clothes was noticeably looser. It's not that I didn't want to eat, I just couldn't keep anything down. To have enough energy to work, I had to resort to liquid protein shakes and even that proved difficult.

One day at work, either Yoel or Martin sat next to me and asked me if I was okay. He noticed I wasn't eating and my eyes looked sunken.

"I'm fine," I told him. "Just not getting enough sleep. I could tell by the look on his face he didn't buy it. I tried to smile but it was like trying to stretch burnt paper.

Later, while settling into my station after lunch, I felt cold. A chill ran up and down my body, and I could feel sweat forming around my forehead. I was nauseous. My heart was racing and my vision shrunk down to the size of a keyhole. I could feel my stomach heaving. I was going to throw up, and nothing I could do was going to stop it. I tried to get up quickly but my feet gave out underneath the weight of my body. The last thing I saw was Yoel or Martin running over to me and someone screaming, before the keyhole became a pin prick.

I woke up in the clinic. I was lying in a cot with an IV in the vein of my left forearm. My clothes were covered in my dry vomit. I'd been there for nearly three hours, I was told. I had an exceedingly high fever, 104 degrees; the nurse was getting ready to call an ambulance had I not woken up before the day's end. I'd been instructed to go home and not come back until I had seen a proper physician and was cleared to return. I went to my locker to retrieve my car keys; I could feel the eyes on me as I crossed the room through the large glass window into the clean room. Everyone was watching me, talking in hushed tones. I got my keys, my wallet, and my phone out of my locker, closed it and headed out.

On the drive home, I could feel the chill running through my body again. Whatever the clinic gave me in the IV was starting to wear off. I broke out into a cold sweat and the tunnel vision returned, as did the nausea. I lowered my car window to let in fresh air. It helped, but not much. Just enough for me to get home without crashing into a light post.

I somehow managed to get myself upstairs to my apartment. By the time I got in, my clothes were drenched in sweat. I immediately striped down and jumped in the shower. The chills and the nausea wouldn't go away and I ended up throwing up in the shower. When the water started to turn cold, I got out, got dressed in comfortable pajamas, heated up some ramen soup and forced it down, even though it tasted the way horse manure smells.

Desperation gripped me. I went on my phone and downloaded a social media app. I made an account and signed in. I immediately typed in Thaleia's name and nothing came up. I tried different variations, for nearly an hour, scrolling through random faces, faces that did not match *the* Thaleia. *My* Thaleia. My fingers gave up and began to type a name that had been ingrained in its tips: Evelyn.

Her profile came right up.

She had years of photographs: concerts, beaches, amusement parks, county fairs, dinners. Her finding out she was pregnant, baby showers, gender reveals, then the actual birth itself, her holding her Esmeralda for the first time in the hospital, Esmeralda using the potty, sleeping, playing, laughing, her first birthday.

I got lost going down the rabbit hole, a feeling of yearning and isolation overwhelming me. Then my heart fell into the pit of my stomach. A recent post of her holding her hand out and a large diamond ring on her finger. She was engaged. The pictures after that were pictures of her with her fiancé, the silver fox I'd seen before. Then a family picture of her, her daughter, and him, smiling, so happy together. I threw my phone across the room and heard it shatter and break to pieces.

After that I crawled into bed and lay under the covers shivering. Every so often, I kept falling asleep and waking up, and every time I did, I couldn't tell if minutes or hours or days had passed.

This is it, I thought. *I am dying. All of this, the vomiting, the smells, the terrible tasting food, all of it, are all symptoms of my body rejecting life and decaying into death.*

Suddenly, I felt the end of my bed sink as if someone had sat down. I peered over the covers. Sitting at the edge of my bed, at my feet, was my neighbor's headless corpse. He was holding a cup of tea, pinky out, his leg crossed over the other. His blue suit was tainted with dry blood. The corpse raised the cup to what remained of the bottom of his mouth and tipped it so that the liquid oozed down over his chin and spilled onto his shirt. It turned to me and spoke.

"No, you are not dying," the headless corpse said in The Voice. *"Not yet, anyway."*

Chapter Thirteen

"Did you hear me?"

I raised the covers over my eyes and waited for this obvious spell of delirium to ebb away. After a moment, I slowly peeled the covers back and peered over it. The headless corpse was still there, perched on the edge of my bed.

"I said you are not dying. Not yet. Everyone is dying. The minute a sperm penetrates the egg and nestles in the womb, the process of dying has begun. You did not ask to live, but you do, you are, and the burden of that realization has left you seized by constant crippling anxiety. I am sorry to be the one to have to shepherd you to this revelation. But alas...," the corpse stopped to take a sip of tea. *"... alas."*

I pushed the covers off of my body. I felt heavy with sweat. I could feel every pore on my skin perspiring. I struggled to sit up and, when I finally did, the room immediately spun. I closed my eyes but could still feel the room swaying, like a fisherman on the sea, my boat on the brink of capsizing, bashed and battered mercilessly by towering waves.

An ocean of nausea struck me, I could feel the color from my face drain away, taking the warm blood along for the ride, leaving me cold and pale. I scooted to the edge of my bed, carefully passing the headless corpse, simultaneously ignoring it while being aware of the very real possibility it may reach out and strangle me. It followed my movements and, as if it had eyes, watched as I escaped into the bathroom. I reached the sink and used it to hold myself up. I splashed chilly water on my face, trying to absorb it into my skin. It helped; the room slowed down to a gentle sway. I found my towel and dabbed my face softly.

I emerged from the bathroom and the corpse was still sitting on my bed, picking lint from its pants. I found my way to the kitchen and poured myself a glass of water. The corpse never took its "eyes" off of me.

This isn't real, I thought to myself, *it can't be.*

"**Can you be certain?**" it said.

A cold chill ran up and down my spine.

"Don't do that," I said, meekly.

As if raised by invisible strings, the body suddenly stood up and gracefully walked over to the kitchen, standing on the opposite side of the kitchenette.

"**Have you ever heard of Robert Nozick?**" The corpse asked. I knew the question was rhetorical, so I didn't even bother to respond. As expected, he went on. "**Robert Nozick was an American Philosopher. Perhaps one of the lesser known. I'm more partial to Du Bois and Thoreau myself but this is beside the point. Nozick is best known for his 'Experience Machine' thought experiment. Imagine, if you will, that your body is floating in a tank while your mind is hooked up to a machine. This machine can stimulate and manipulate your brain to conceive any experience you desire. Make a film, read, and understand Kant, be the world's most accomplished athlete, be a teacher capable of shaping future minds, or be moved by Millais' Ophelia. Whatever you could think of you could experience. Hedonists claim that the only thing worth pursuing in life for its own sake is pleasure. Nozick pushed against this belief. If people only want to experience things, then why not hook up to the Experience Machine to fulfill this? But people don't want to just experience things. According to Nozick, we** *want to do these things. No matter how thorough this experience machine makes the experience, it is still a fabrication of reality. You'd be experiencing all these things, but in the real world, you are a chunk of meat floating in a tank. In this way, connecting to this machine is a form of... suicide."* The corpse took another sip of this seemingly bottomless cup of tea. *"Whether I'm real or not, you are experiencing me."*

Another sip, then it continued.

"Though Nozick's thought experiment was an argument against ethical hedonism, I always viewed it as a question of purpose. The reason why people would even consider hooking up to an Experience Machine in the first place is because they are unable to fulfill a desire in the real world. A void that has left their lives hollow. So, it begs the question: Can one live a truly fulfilling life without a purpose? And if so, what does a purposeless life look like?"

I finished the last of the water and ambled over back to my bed. I crawled under the covers in an attempt to disappear, but again I could feel the corpse's weight descend upon the edge of my bed.

"Go away," I groaned.

"What do you think your purpose is?" The corpse pressed.

"To suffer, clearly," I quipped.

The corpse laughed with its body.

"Yes, I suppose that could be, but I'm inclined to disagree. Whether you believe God instills you with purpose before you are born, or you choose your purpose, suffering is a symptom of the pursuit of realizing it, or in most cases, the inability to pursue it. If you don't think you have a purpose, then what exactly do you suffer?"

My body temperature rose and I began to feel like I was suffocating. I tossed the covers off of me and looked at the corpse. It refused to leave my side.

"Please, go away!" I yelled.

"When you think about it," it went on ignoring me, *"the one thing everything alive has in common is death. Nothing comes from nothing. Everything is created. Everything that exists, dies. Nothing is everlasting. I think that's why the concept of Christianity or any religion that touts eternal life after death is so appealing. We can't think of what we consider to be 'us' as ceasing to be. We are but our memories, after all."* The corpse took another sip. *"What do you think your purpose is?"*

"I don't have one," I answered, exasperated. "Not everyone has a purpose. Some people live and die. They make no impact on the world."

"So, what is the point of living?"

"Does there have to be one? Like you said, I didn't ask to be born. In the same way that I didn't ask to be born, who is to say I have a purpose at all? I am perfectly happy just existing."

"Are you?"

"Yes," I affirmed.

"So, what does it mean to have a purpose?"

"Jesus Christ! Shut up!"

"Humor me," the corpse said, his voice even toned, unaffected by my increasing aggression.

I thought it over.

"Something you feel you want to accomplish," I answered.

"So, is it possible that being happy or experiencing all the beauty the world has to offer could be in itself considered a purpose?"

"I guess."

"What do you want?"

"Nothing! I just want to be left alone!" I said. The chill returned and I covered my body with the bed sheets, shivering under the covers.

The corpse sighed. It got up from the bed and walked around the apartment, deep in thought. It took another sip of the tea and placed the cup down on the coffee table, carefully, like the cup was both invaluable and fragile. It stood at the foot of the bed, hands on its hips.

"*You are a piece of shit,*" It said. The voice was so sharp and brutal, my heart leapt into my throat. I looked at the corpse, its cold shadow looming over me. "*You fat fuck. You are garbage. No, garbage is the carcass of something that was once useful. You are nothing. Insignificant. A worthless spec of aimless dust. You disgust me.*"

"Stop it," my voice was small.

"*The entire population of earth, mammal and otherwise, did not ask to exist, yet they seek - they choose - to make their time worth something. Yes, some fall short, but they at least attempted it. Even the people who think it isn't worth it, they at least try to make sense of it, so much so that the struggle of not being able to comprehend the incomprehensible drives them to madness. You think the answer is your pseudo nihilism, but the truth is this: you are a coward. You are afraid to want anything, afraid to choose a purpose because you are afraid to fail. It's so simple, it's pathetic!*"

"Please, stop," I whimpered.

I tried to hide back under the covers but the corpse tore them off of me and tossed them aside. It continued its tirade, seemingly growing larger with each breath.

"*That's why Evelyn left you. It's not because she was afraid to disappoint you, it's because she saw no future with someone who thought so little of life. A coward too scared to want. The only thing you've ever loved, what you've always wanted, gone, and you think this justifies your belief? You think this gives you permission to crawl into your box, drink warm milk and suck your thumb?!*"

The walls began to vibrate. I wanted to run but the corpse had grown so large I was unable to get past it.

"*Grant died before he could see the world, but at least he wanted to experience it. Your piece of shit father died unable to find happiness,*" *but at least he searched for it. Thaleia doesn't know what her purpose is, but guess where she is right now? Out there, looking for it, ready to embrace it when she does. And what are you doing? Waiting to die."*

I covered my ears but I could still hear the voice, louder still, filling my head.

"If you have no purpose, as you claim, if you don't want anything, as you claim, if you are living simply to exist, as you claim, then why wait? Do the world a favor and kill yourself."

The corpse grabbed my leg and dragged me off of the bed. Its cold lifeless hands on my flesh felt like fire. Its rotten nails dug into my skin. I howled in agony, but I didn't fight it. I didn't have the will to. The corpse took the satchel full of cassette tapes and knocked it off the counter. They spilled out and scattered on the carpet, and with it, my father's old .35. The corpse picked it up and checked the chamber. One bullet. It walked to me and kneeled down next to me. It grabbed my face, forced my mouth open, and shoved the cold nose of the gun in. He cocked the hammer back and pulled the trigger.

Click.

The tears began to stream down my face.

"What the hell are you crying about?" The Corpse hissed. Its body grew larger. Its shoulders, wider. It occupied so much space. *"What is your purpose?"*

"I... I don't have one," I said, with the steel taste on my tongue.

Click.

My body shivered and the corpse again, expanded exponentially. So much so, it had to kneel and crouch just to be able to fit in my apartment. It pushed the gun deeper into my mouth. The smell was making me sick.

"What do you want?"

"Nothing," I responded through tears and snot.

"If you want nothing!" the corpse roared, *"then return to nothing!"*

Click. Click.

I was trapped. There was nowhere for me to hide. Nowhere for me to run to, even if my legs would obey my commands to run for the door, the corpse had grown so large, there was no space for me to get by. Its crouched back was pressed against the ceiling and its shoulders began to bend and crack both walls. The lights in the apartment began to flicker as if possessed, before burning out completely. I was left in the dark with this monster.

"What is your purpose?" The voice came from the darkness.

I couldn't answer. I could only whimper.

"What do you want?"

An answer formed in my throat, but I choked on it.

Click.

"What do you want?"

My body shook. The answer was desperate to spring forth. But what if it's the wrong answer. I closed my eyes.

"What is your purpose? What do you want?"

"I *want!*" I shouted. Once the words were out of my mouth, I could not stop the rest that followed, mostly because I couldn't, but also because I was afraid that as soon as there was a period at the end of that thought, it meant a period at the end of my life.

"I *want* to be happy. I *want* to succeed. I *want* to fail. I *want* to feel pleasure. I *want* to feel pain. I *want* to see the world. I *want* to eat. I *want* to drink. I *want* to read all the books ever written. Watch all the movies ever made. I *want* to breathe in the morning air. I *want* to be warmed by the sun. I *want* to greet the night. I *want* to sleep under the full moon. I *want* to dream. I *want* to love. I *want* to be loved. I *want* to make love. I *want* to have children. I *want* to see them grow up. I *want* to pour whatever knowledge I have into them. I *want* to see them laugh, see them learn, see them live! I *want* to make my mother proud! I *want* to live as long as God will let me live. As long as God will allow me to experience the complexity of this life. I don't want to merely exist through it. I want, for once, to look in the mirror and not *hate* the man looking back at me. I want to *truly live!*"

BOOM!

The ground beneath my feet quaked violently. The plates and cups in the cupboard shivered against each other, the silverware and cooking utensils in the drawers trembled, and the metal sink rattled like a chain linked fence. The walls shuddered off of their studs and car alarms out in the distance screamed to life.

I opened my eyes and found darkness. The lights flickered on and off until finally they remained on. I was alone. The corpse was nowhere to be seen. I was on the floor of my apartment, on my knees, covered in sweat, face wet with tears. The gun was still in my mouth, but it was my own hand, the trigger half way pulled back by my shaky finger.

Night had fallen during my delirium, and outside, it was storming. Rain pelted my window panes, lighting webbed across the black sky, and thunder boomed maniacally, each strike threatening to crumble the foundation on which I stood with its supernatural power.

I slowly and carefully slid the gun out of my mouth and let it fall. It thudded on the carpet with heft. Trance-like, I stood up and slowly walked to the door of my apartment, opened it, and walked out. I descended down the steps and stood under the awning, watching the rain pummel everything on earth. Without a word, without a thought, I walked into the rain and whipping wind, walking until I was enveloped by the blackness of the beckoning storm.

Chapter Fourteen

The sun was dawning and the storm had finally ceased by the time I found my way back to Perdition Towers. I was soaked to the bone. The rain was in every fiber of my clothes; it felt like I would never be dry again. I stood in the hallway, in front of my door, rainwater pooling around my calloused and bruised bare feet. I grabbed the handle and pushed the door open.

My silhouette spilled into the darkness of the apartment as I stood at the threshold. The scene was exactly as I had left it: cassette tapes scattered about the floor, bed sheets bunched up in a corner soiled with dry sweat and tears, my father's pistol settled in the carpet, and a lone empty cup of tea on the coffee table.

The apartment felt smaller, the ceiling lower, the walls closer together, the doors narrower. I lowered my head and squeezed through the door, closing it when I was fully in the apartment. I stripped out of my wet clothes, discarding each article of clothing, reaching the bathroom nude before stepping into a hot shower.

I scrubbed every inch of my body, even the nooks and crannies some tend to overlook during daily washes; between the toes, belly button, the ridges of the inner ears, underneath fingernails, the underside of my feet, everything. Once I felt I'd succeeded in cleansing my body, I rinsed the soap off and watched as all the muck, all the filth, disappeared down into the drain.

I stepped out of the shower, dried myself with a clean white towel, brushed my teeth, shaved, and trimmed my fingernails, discarding all hair and nail clippings, and cleaning the sink of any excess foamy spittle with a warm cloth.

I hadn't done laundry in weeks. All I had left to wear besides underwear and socks was a pair of white cotton shorts, and a shirt; the shirt I bought from the mall of the indiscernible celebrity. I got dressed. Gathered the rest of my dirty laundry and tossed it all in the hamper.

I adorned the bed with fresh linen, and removed the dusty black curtain from the window, allowing sunlight to completely spill into the room. I picked up all the cassette tapes on the floor and reorganized them in the leather satchel, one by one. I was three quarters done when I came across the tape labeled *"to my hijo"* written in my father's handwriting. I put the tape in my pocket and finished putting away the rest, securing the lock.

After all of this was accomplished, I was struck with sudden hunger. Insatiable hunger. Hunger I had not felt in quite some time. I went into the kitchen, opened the fridge and took out all the eggs I had left, milk, butter, onions, tomatoes, mushrooms, green peppers, ham, and cheese. I beat all the eggs in a large bowl with a little milk and a few pinches of salt and ground black pepper, while the butter melted on the pan slowly. I diced all the vegetables and tossed them in the pan and sautéed them. Once they were nice and translucent, I poured in the beaten eggs and scrambled them with a rubber spatula. When everything was fully cooked, I put the eggs on a plate, fried the ham, put a couple of pieces of cheese over the hot eggs, toasted two pieces of bread, buttered them, poured myself a tall glass of orange juice, and sat down at the kitchenette. I forked a heaping portion of the meal onto the buttered toast and took a bite. *Bliss.* It was the first meal in a while that tasted good. I savored every bite.

My breakfast finished and my hunger fed, I cleaned all the dirty dishes, dried them, and put them away. I discarded all of the rubbish into the trash and removed the bag from the bin. Before I tied off the bag, I picked up the gun from the carpet. I opened the chamber and removed the lone bullet, placing it in my pocket. I disassembled the gun, tossed the parts into the trash bag, tied the bag closed and put it against the front door. I stood in the center of the apartment and looked around. Everything was clean and in its place. It felt whole again, cleansed.

I put the satchel of tapes on top of my laundry basket and carried it all to the door. I set it down and gave the apartment one last look. It indeed felt smaller.

On the coffee table remained the corpse's teacup, the notebook, and the pen. In my haze, I nearly forgot about them. I put the notebook in the laundry basket, and the pen in my pocket. I took the bullet out of my pocket and held it between my thumb and index finger. There was no reason for me to carry this with me. I dropped the bullet in the empty tea cup, turned the apartment lights off, grabbed the trash, stepped out into the hallway, and closed the door behind me.

The sun was finally reaching over the trees as I crossed the drenched parking lot to toss the trash into the dumpster. I loaded my things in the back seat of my car and got in, immediately putting the key in the ignition and turning it.

Nothing. The car wouldn't start. I smiled. I rolled the window down and waited.

As I waited my cracked phone began to ring. *The Company*. They were most likely calling looking for an update on my health. I sent the call to voicemail. The cracked screen cleared and showed me the picture of Evelyn and myself.

I admired the photo. It was certainly a perfect moment, of a time long past. I went into the phone, deleted the picture, and tossed the phone on the passenger seat. I turned the key in the ignition and the engine burst to life.

I drove through all the familiar traffic, by all the familiar landmarks. The same path I've travelled for well over a decade. All the same shopping centers, dealerships, restaurants, Wal-Mart's, Dunkin's, McDonald's, Target's, Chili's, and gas stations. I was fine with this for so long. I never thought there was a reason to see much else.

All of that gave way to the agricultural land, the signal I was getting closer to work; I could see the same building coming over the horizon, fast approaching. I slowed down and looked over. Everyone was gathered in the parking lot for the morning break, talking about the same things, enjoying each other's company. I could even see Martin and Yoel yucking it up on a bench, talking about their fantastic futures, I imagined. Slowly but surely the building fell away from view.

As I approached the towering loblolly pines, I pulled the cassette tape out of my pocket marked by my father for me. I opened it, stuck it in my tape player, and pressed play. I waited to see what songs my father had curated for me to listen to, what songs he thought would best fit me. I waited. I waited. I kept waiting. Nothing played. It finally dawned on me: the tape was blank. A smile crept across my lips.

The loblolly pines grew taller the closer I got to them. Right at the cusp of passing into a road I'd not yet traversed; a pang of fear gripped my chest. I eased up off the gas, causing my car to slow down. My chest tightened and I found retrieving air into my lungs difficult. I closed my eyes and took three deep breaths to regain my nerve. I expected to hear *The Voice*, laughing at me, telling me how much of a coward I am, telling me I'm not fooling anyone, telling me that it is not too late to turn back.

It never came.

I closed my eyes and took three deep breaths to regain my nerve. When I opened my eyes, I put the pedal to the floor forcing the car to accelerate forward as I finally ventured into the unknown, hurtling into the world beyond the loblolly pines.

The End?

Did you enjoy *Halcyon Suicide*?

Scan the **QR Code** below and leave a
(brutally) honest review.

Consider subscribing to our newsletter!

You can do so by visiting our website:

www.loblollypinespublishing.com

About the Author

K.J. Duff is the founder of Loblolly Pines Publishing and author of *Halcyon Suicide*. When he isn't writing or spending time with his family, he continues to cultivate his love of cinema and literature. K.J. Duff created Loblolly Pines Publishing as a way to publish his novels under his own banner, while also keeping his eye on the future in the hopes of publishing books for other authors who are in need of an outlet for their voice.